Also by An

The Fr

The

Homecoming

By

Anita Ward

This is a work of fiction, names, characters, businesses, organizations, places, events and incidents either are the product of the author's imagination or are used fictitiously. Any resemblance to actual persons, living or dead, events or locales is entirely coincidental

THE HOMECOMING

A SEQUEL TO THE FRENCH SECRET

PART 1

MY SISTERS

CHAPTER 1

Chantal Renaud had just finished work for the day. Rushing to the bus station afraid of missing the five forty-five bus home, little did she know as she quickly walked, that today would change the rest of her life.

Arriving at the station with time to spare, thinking to herself '*Thank goodness!*' as missing this bus would require a wait of another hour for the next one, she sat down on the bench in front of the stand to await the bus. Two minutes later, Francine sat down beside her.

"Hello, you! How come you're catching the bus home? Where is your car?" asked Francine.

"Hello, it's being fixed after that little accident I had - or what I should say – when that idiot smashed into the back of my car!" replied Chantal. "Anyhow how come you are catching the bus at this time?"

"I am exhausted. I've just spent all afternoon taking the second part of my midwifery examination. I just want to get home and sit in front of the television." Francine yawned.

"Oh sorry, Fran! I forgot it was your exam today. How did it go?"

"Fine I think, but you can never tell. But I answered all the questions. There was one that was a bit tricky but, fingers crossed, I got it right. I spoke with the other girls after, and I am feeling quite confident that I have passed, but I have to wait six weeks for the results," said Fran.

Francine was Chantal's younger sister by nineteen months. For as long as Fran could remember Chantal had shortened her sister's name firstly to Frannie, then as she got older to Fran.

Chantal had been born in France in August 1947, and she had just had her twenty-fourth birthday. She worked for the local police force in Jersey, an island in the English Channel between France and England. She currently worked in an administrative capacity, a job she had had since leaving school at sixteen. When she had first started, she had been the office junior - running errands, making tea and filing witness statements, caution statements and general reports covering any police incident from vagrancy to car theft and car collisions, from assaults to missing persons and general parochial affairs. Over the years she had slowly showed to her managers her expertise at handling important documents, liaising with volunteer parish officials and dealing with social problems in the community. This led to her being promoted to her current post as assistant manager of the administrative team. Now she worked more closely with shorthand typists, telephone operators, records officers, and secretaries. She certainly didn't miss making the tea!

The girls looked so much alike that instantly anyone could tell they were sisters. Both had inherited their father's dark looks and deep brown eyes. Chantal stood at five feet, five inches tall, and was slim with beautiful blemish-free olive skin and long wavy auburn hair, slightly lighter than her father's jet-black hair. Francine was an inch shorter than Chantal. Being a nurse, Fran mostly wore her hair tied back or pinned up, because she was required to keep it under her nurse's cap for work. When not at work, Francine wore it down in a similar style to her sister.

The bus arrived at its stand and they both stood up to join the queue of people waiting to get on. They found a seat together in the middle section of the bus and were soon on their way home. They chatted all the way, Chantal telling Fran all about her day and then discussing whose turn it was to cook dinner.

"It's your turn to cook, Chantal, as Papa did it yesterday and I did it the day before. So, it's definitely your turn!" said Fran.

"I know, I was only joking! I've got some pork chops. There were only four left at the butchers, so I bought them all as I know Papa will eat two!" said Chantal.

"Great, I will do some apple sauce to go with them. Auntie Angela gave me a load of cooking apples the other day. Perhaps, if I have time, I will make an apple pie for dessert," said Fran.

"Oooo and custard!" exclaimed Chantal, "I love apple pie and custard!"

With their stop in sight, the girls stood up from their seat so the driver could see them in plenty of time to stop and let them off the bus. It was a ten-minute walk from the bus stop to their home; they walked from the main road to the lane that led to their house. Walking arm in arm towards the farm where their Auntie Angela and Uncle Hedley lived, they passed the cottage where they had lived a lifetime ago. Both girls looked ahead down the road, they could see their father standing at the end of the track leading to the farm.

"Papa has come to meet us," joked Fran.

'That would be a first! Well, not since we were, like, five!" remarked Chantal.

They waved to their father, but they could see he was distracted by a taxi pulling up on the opposite side of the road. They watched as a girl got out of the taxi and as it drove away, Chantal stopped in her tracks.

Time appeared to stand still, Chantal could see her father mouthing words that she couldn't hear whilst staring at the girl.

"What's the matter?" asked a worried Fran.

But Chantal was looking at the girl. The face, the hair, and the person that she saw every day when she woke up – it was the one in the photo that stood on her nightstand – it was her mother!

Coming out of her trance, Chantal realized that the photo of her mother was over twenty years old. This girl approaching their father was similar to their age, so it couldn't possibly be their mother.

It was Liliane.

CHAPTER 2

Chantal's first memory was of when she was just over three and a half years old. The year was 1950 and they were living in France. Chantal was awakened by her father shouting at her mother, Clara, which was nothing new to Chantal's ears as her father would often come home and make so much noise that it would wake her up. However, on this particular night, she remembered her father arguing with her mother; there were lots of raised voices and banging about before she heard the front door to their cottage slam shut. She looked out of the window and saw her father walking, unsteady on his feet, down the path.

Chantal was just about to get back into bed with Francine, who was fast asleep with her thumb in her mouth and cuddling her teddy bear when she heard her mother scream. She quickly got out of bed and quietly opened the door of the bedroom. Chantal stood listening but all was quiet, then suddenly she heard her mother scream again. Gingerly making her way down the stairs and stopping halfway down to listen again, Chantal could hear her mother crying and moaning quietly. She went to the door of the living room and poked her head around, only to see her beloved Mama crying with blood seeping down the side of her face, whilst she held her large baby tummy.

"Mama! Mama!" cried Chantal, running over and hugging her mother. Her mother let out another scream, frightening Chantal.

"Chantal, I need your help lovey! Do you think you could find your way to Auntie Jeanne's house, all by yourself?" asked Clara.

Jeanne Pape was Clara's mother's sister-in-law. Jeanne was French and had married Clara's uncle, Clifford, shortly after the first world war had ended, in 1920. They had met when Clifford had been injured during the war and Jeanne, a nurse at the time, had nursed him back to health.

"Yes, Mama! I am a big girl now, Mama!" replied Chantal, feeling very proud that her mother had asked her to go by herself to Auntie Jeanne's.

"Go and get your coat and your shoes on, and then run as quick as you can! Don't speak to anyone on the way, just go straight there and ask Auntie Jeanne to come here!" asked Clara.

Chantal ran as fast as she could. It was beginning to get dark, so it was rather scary going along the lane on her own. The trees either side of the lane were casting shadows from the moon on to the road surface, which looked like witches to her young imaginative mind. Chantal ran straight into the bar owned by her aunt and uncle; she usually went around the back, but without thinking went through the open entrance to the bar. All the men in the bar seemed to stop and stare at her, she tried to speak but was so out of breath the words wouldn't come out of her mouth.

"Chantal! What's the matter?" asked a concerned Clifford, at the same time shouting his wife's name.

Jeanne came into the bar to see what Clifford wanted her for, and on seeing Chantal said: "What's wrong, Chantal?"

"It's Mama! She is hurt and crying, and she asked me to come and get you!" gasped Chantal.

Jeanne immediately picked up Chantal and quickly ran back to Clara's.

Clara was British and had moved from her home in Lancashire to live in Northern France in 1935, when she was fifteen years of age. Her mother had thought it would be a good idea for her rebellious young daughter to go and visit her brother, Clifford, his wife Jeanne and their daughter, Danielle.

Clara had quickly settled into the French way of life, and although she was initially meant to stay for only three months, those three months turned into fifteen years. The war years prevented her from returning home to England, and it was during this time that she met Didier, her very first boyfriend. Didier had been a member of the resistance movement known as 'the Maquis,' helping the English and Americans sabotage the occupying German forces in any way possible. The resistance group recruited Clara, and she took part in several missions alongside Didier. They both spoke perfect French and English, which was an asset to the movement.

Clara and Didier married a short time after World War II ended, having a double wedding with her cousin, Danielle. Clara was an accomplished pâtissiere and baker, and following her marriage she continued to work at the local bakery while also providing her own customers with bespoke cakes for all occasions. At the start of their marriage, Didier worked away from home helping the French government to rebuild the war-damaged towns and cities. They were happy together, or so Clara thought, but would often think to herself that due to the war, they hadn't spent enough time in each other's company. In some ways, they didn't know each other like other courting couples; it had been a whirlwind romance for Clara, having never had a proper boyfriend before meeting Didier.

The problems in their marriage started to materialize when the government job finished, and Didier had little or no work. Had he been a skilled tradesman, then his skills would have been required, but as a gardener he was no longer needed. With too much time on his hands and no permanent job, he would spend his days in the bar drinking. When drunk, Didier became a different person, - violent and nasty, and it was Clara that took the brunt of his anger. Although Clara would pretend to anyone that asked that the cuts and bruises were a result of her own clumsiness, everyone knew that Didier was beating her.

Chantal's next memory was waiting for a boat in France, the one that would be taking them across the channel to Jersey. She remembered her father tickling her so much that she would shout "Stop Papa! Stop!" and then when he did stop, she would say "More, more!". Chantal could remember being on the boat and her father holding her as they watched the boat crashing into the waves and nearly soaking them.

Following their journey to Jersey, the memories became a bit sketchy until that painful day; the last day she saw her beloved Mama. Chantal remembered her mother being in a strange mood that day; she and Francine were going to spend the day with Auntie Angela while Mama took Lilly, their baby sister, to the hospital. Liliane had been born in France in 1950 and since that day she had been known as Lilly, although Chantal had no memory beyond going to fetch her Auntie Jeanne that fateful night.

Lilly had been to the hospital several times because, Mama told her, Lilly's ears were poorly and needed to be looked at by a special doctor. With Lilly in the pushchair, her mother had walked her and Francine to Auntie Angela's house. Before opening the door, she had told Chantal that she loved her very much and that she should never forget that, and she had hugged her and Francine so tight that it hurt.

"I love you too, Mama," replied Chantal.

Mama appeared to have tears in her eyes when she kissed them goodbye, but Chantal thought that she was imagining it and didn't think twice as she turned to greet her auntie and granny.

Auntie Angela was her father's elder sister, and she was married to Uncle Hedley. They owned a big farm and Papa worked for them on the farm. Her granny, Marie Renard, was her father's mother. Chantal didn't always like her grandmother very much she was always grumpy and moaning that she had to look after Chantal and Francine. It always appeared too much trouble for her to look after them, and she would moan if they wanted a drink or something to eat.

Auntie Angela was a bit friendlier, and she would often tell her mother, their granny, to be quiet and to be a bit nicer to her granddaughters. Both mother and daughter were of similar stature, five feet two inches tall and not fat as such, but rotund. Her grandmother had short grey hair, her face had lots of wrinkles and she always wore a floral wrap-around apron tied at the back that more or less covered her entire body. Auntie Angela also wore a sort of apron, but it was more of the tabard variety with ties at each side and two pockets on the front, and she appeared to have these in an array of colours. Her dark brown hair with greying streaks was always neatly permed and she kept it cut to just below her ears. They always spoke French at Auntie's house, in fact, Chantal had very rarely heard her grandmother speak English. Chantal herself, was fluent in both languages but Francine being that bit younger, spoke her sentences in a mixture of English and French and would be perplexed when people laughed at her.

Auntie and Uncle had a son, John; he was just over a year older than Chantal, and he resented his two cousins coming to his house and playing with his toys. He was forever getting Chantal in trouble with their grandmother. When playing outside, he would push her into a puddle, getting her all dirty and wet. When inside, he liked nothing better than pinching her and making her cry, although he always denied any wrongdoing. Chantal and Francine were allowed to play with some of his toys, but he kept his best ones in his bedroom out the girls' reach.

Later that afternoon, her grandmother started to question as to where Chantal's mother was, saying to Auntie Angela, "Surely Clara should be here by now? It's almost two-thirty."

"Perhaps she missed the two o'clock bus and will be on the next one," said Angela coming to Clara's defence, "Or, she could have gone into town after the hospital appointment."

Angela felt sorry for Clara; the girl had been persuaded to come to Jersey, a small place where she didn't know anyone but them. Lately, she had looked so desperately unhappy, she felt nothing but sympathy for sister-in-law.

Four o'clock came and there was still no sign of Clara. Angela started making dinner; she fed not only the family but also the farmer workers, so she had a lot of cooking to do. By a quarter to five, Chantal was willing her mother to come home as they normally had their dinner at five o'clock and she knew that any minute now Frannie would be saying she was hungry. Sure enough, "I'm hungry, Auntie. Can I have something to eat?" piped up Francine.

Auntie Angela was not happy. "I will make you some beans on toast."

"I don't like beans," said an adamant Francine.

"I like beans, I'll have beans on toast," announced John.

"You are having scrambled egg," said his mother.

"But Frannie can have my eggs, and I will have the beans," said John.

Chantal could have kissed John at this point because she knew that Frannie hated beans and would kick up a fuss and refuse to eat or even touch the beans.

So, Auntie Angela made Chantal and John beans on toast and Frannie had scrambled egg on toast. They had almost finished their dinner when their father arrived and on seeing the girls sat at the table eating, he asked, "Where's Clara?"

"You tell us because she hasn't come back yet," said her, not very happy, grandmother.

Her father looked a bit worried "You don't suppose that they kept Lilly in hospital?" suggested her father.

"Surely, she would have phoned us?" said Auntie "I'll phone the hospital."

Auntie Angela left the room to make the call from the phone that was on the table in the front hallway. Nobody ever used the front door at Auntie's house. Instead, everyone used the side door that went directly into the scullery attached to the kitchen. It was the same with the front room, that was only for special occasions, Chantal had only been in it once and had been at Christmas.

The kitchen was the focal point of the house with a coal-fueled AGA taking up the most of one wall, a seven-foot long pine dresser stood against another wall which held a variety of display plates standing on the shelves and hooks from which dangled cups and mugs. At the bottom of the dresser, there were several cupboards storing crockery and an assortment of other items. The opposite wall had three large windows looking out on to the front driveway of the farmhouse. To one side of the AGA and next to one of the windows was granny's armchair, where she would sit and see anyone coming or going and at the same time, she was kept nice and warm from the heat emitting from the AGA. A large table dominated the centre of the room where all their meals were served.

Auntie Angela came back into the kitchen, "Well?" asked her father.

"There was no ear, nose and throat clinic today and there is no one with Lilly's name in the hospital," said a concerned Angela.

"What do you mean, no clinic? Where the hell is, she then?" shouted her father.

"I don't know," whispered Angela.

"I'll give her what for when she gets back! Come on girls, let's go home," said her father.

They walked home in silence, her father held her hand and carried Frannie. Chantal was fully expecting her mother to be at home, but thc house was in complete darkness, and you could feel the cold as soon as you entered. Mama usually had the range lit all the time, which kept the entire house lovely and warm, but not today. Their father told them to get to bed. It was too early for bed, but Chantal was too scared to tell her father this. Their Mama always gave them a mug of hot chocolate and a biscuit before bed, and then she always read them a story, but not tonight.

Chantal helped Frannie get into her nightdress, and then she put on her own. It was cold in their bedroom, so they quickly got under the bedcovers. Frannie normally had a nap in the afternoon but being at Auntie Angela's she hadn't had one today, so once she had her thumb in her mouth, she was asleep as soon as her head laid on her pillow. Chantal lay next to her; she wanted her Mama.

After lying in bed for about half an hour, Chantal heard the front door open and close. She sat up, '*It must be Mama!*' she thought excitedly to herself. She waited a few moments and then went to the top of the stairs, but everything was quiet she made her way downstairs where the kitchen was in darkness. Then she realized it wasn't her mother coming home, it had been her father going out. The girls had never been left alone in the house before; Chantal was frightened and quickly went back up the stairs to Frannie and she closed the bedroom door, scared that the bogeyman would come. Chantal got back into bed and held Frannie close. She must have eventually fallen asleep because she remembered waking up hearing her father call her mother's name, but there was no response. She then heard her father come upstairs and go to bed.

The next time she woke, she knew it was morning as she could hear the birds tweeting. She lay in bed keeping warm as it was still a bit dark outside. When it started to get lighter she made her way downstairs, but again it was silent downstairs so she climbed back upstairs. The door to her parent's room was open, and she saw that Papa was gone.

'*He must have gone to work,*' she thought to herself, and just at that moment, she heard Frannie calling for their Mama.

Chantal was frightened, cold, and hungry. She didn't know what to do and she tried to think what her Mama normally did. Get dressed - yes that was the first thing they must do, get changed out of their nightdresses and get their proper clothes on. She helped Frannie on with her clothes and then got herself dressed. Next breakfast, she held Frannie's hand and they made their way down to the kitchen, she couldn't make the fire as she didn't know how, plus her mother had always impressed on her that she mustn't touch the range or the matches.

She sat Frannie at the table and fetched the box of cornflakes and two bowls from the cupboard. Sometimes Mama made porridge, but today it would have to be cornflakes. She dragged a chair to the pantry and stood on it to reach the jug of milk, it was almost empty. Papa had forgotten to bring their daily jug of milk from the farm the night before. She carefully got the jug down from the shelf; luckily, it was almost empty, otherwise it would have been too heavy for her to lift. She poured the majority of the milk into Frannie's bowl, and she had the rest. Mama usually made them a cup of hot milk to go with their breakfast, but there was none left so they couldn't even have cold milk. Frannie was busy eating her cornflakes, whereas Chantal was having more of a problem with hers as there was hardly any milk, making the cornflakes very crunchy and hard to swallow.

After breakfast they played on the floor with their toys, soon Frannie was moaning that she was hungry. Her Mother would often say that she didn't need to look at the clock to see what time it was as she could tell the time by Frannie's stomach.

Chantal looked in the pantry to see what they could eat, she took the biscuit tin down from the shelf and wrestled to open it, nearly dropping the contents on the floor in the process. There were four biscuits left. They were ones that Mama had made, so they were nice big fat ones! She gave one to Frannie and then looked around for something to drink. The water jug was half full - it was a tall thin plastic jug kept on the floor in the pantry. Chantal struggled to tip it just enough to fill a smaller jug, although some did spill on the floor. The water was cold, and Frannie refused to drink it, "I want milk!" she demanded.

"Well, we haven't got any so just drink that," shouted a frustrated Chantal.

Chantal couldn't tell the time on the clock that stood on the mantlepiece, but when Frannie said she was hungry again, Chantal knew it must be near lunchtime. She looked in the pantry to see what they could eat. Mama usually cooked them an egg with toast soldiers or spaghetti on toast, or even sausages with beans. She looked in the bread bin, there was the end of a crusty loaf left, so she got this out and put it on the table. She was not allowed to use the bread knife, so she tore it in half with her hands, then got the jar of jam from the shelf, but she found it impossible to open no matter how hard she tried. There was butter in the dish on the table, so Chantal carefully buttered the bread and gave Frannie two pieces on a plate with another cup of water. She hoped this would satisfy her little sister.

After lunch, they both went upstairs, and after playing with their dolls on the bed for a short time, they both fell asleep.

CHAPTER 3

Didier was woken from his alcohol-induced sleep by the alarm clock; it was six o'clock and the realisation hit him as he felt the coldness coming from the other side of the bed - Clara was gone! He got out of bed and quickly dressed in his work clothes and without another thought made his way to work; the cows needed milking.

Attending to the cows was one of Didier's main jobs on the farm. The herd was fifty strong, and the cows required milking both morning and evening no matter what. The milking process was partially automated, and Hedley was always on hand to help. Directly after milking, it was Didier's job to herd the cows to the field where they would graze all day. Once the cows were secure in the field and their water trough replenished, he would make his way back to the farm to sweep and clean out the cowshed. Whilst he was gone, Hedley would pour the milk into the milk churns to be collected by the milk company.

Including Didier there were ten workers on the farm; three of them lived with their families in a row of cottages where Didier also lived, and the other six bunked together in two large cabins at the back of the farmhouse. Angela provided them all with breakfast, lunch and dinner. Breakfast always served after milking, in the scullery next to the farmhouse kitchen. Lunch was brought out to whichever field they were working in by Angela in big baskets. In the winter there would be flasks of hot soup with crusty bread followed by slices of apple pie and hot coffee. In the summer months, the soup would be replaced with pickles, cheese, and cold meats.

Today, some of the men - including Didier - were loading seed potatoes on to the tractors in readiness for planting the next day so Marie, Didier's mother, brought their lunch to the shed, while Angela took the other workers their lunch in the field.

"So, she's back then," Marie said to her son.

"No, and she isn't coming back either!" replied Didier in an angry voice.

"What do you mean, she's not back? Who is looking after the girls?" asked his concerned mother.

Didier looked at his mother as though it had just dawned on him what she had said.

"You stupid, stupid, selfish man!" she cried, storming off.

Maria returned to the kitchen, put on her coat, and grabbing a jug of milk she made her way to her son's house as quickly as she could.

CHAPTER 4

Didier was born to Marie and Jean-Luc Renard in 1917 in Northern France - his father had died fighting the Germans in the Great War in 1918, and his sister Angela was older than him by eight years. There had also been two boys born between Angela and Didier, but one had died at birth and the other when he was three years old, after a bout of pneumonia.

Life was tough for Marie after the Great War had ended with two young children and only a widow's pension to survive on. Work was virtually impossible for the men returning from the war - never mind a woman!

Maria lived in a grand chateau with approximately thirty other families; the chateau had been converted into apartments by the local government for families such as Marie's. The living conditions weren't ideal, with shared bathroom facilities on every floor in each wing. The small apartments varied in size but Marie was lucky enough to have two bedrooms, a living area, and a small kitchen. The children played in what used to be the vast front courtyard where once a French noble family had seen horses and carriages, bringing the aristocrats to the lavish parties that had one been held there.

At the rear of the property, there was lavandier, where all the women could be seen doing the weekly wash while gossiping the day away. When the women weren't doing their housework, they could be found sat on chairs outside, drinking coffee and knitting or sewing. There were some very talented lacemakers amongst the women, and they would make extra money selling their delicate completed pieces of lacework.

Marie's brother-in-law, Pierre Renaud, occupied a single apartment on the first floor above Marie's ground floor apartment. When Marie was out of earshot, the gossip would be about Marie and Pierre and their presumed relationship. Nothing was ever proven but when Pierre announced he was to be married Marie appeared desolate, so when in 1925 the chance of seasonal farm work in Jersey was on offer Marie took it. She arrived in Jersey with her two children along with fifty or so other French workers.

Didier went straight to school while Maria and Angela formed part of a gang that went from farm to farm doing whatever job was allocated to them. It was hard, backbreaking work, some weeks they would spend day after day picking potatoes, following a tractor that lifted the potatoes from the ground.

The accommodation provided was a two-roomed cabin on the grounds of a farm. They would come home from work filthy dirty and have to queue with the other farmworkers to have a bath or shower.

Didier learned English quite quickly at school, and he would try and teach his mother and sister. Whilst his sister was eager to learn, his mother was very reluctant to do so; as far as she was concerned, she didn't need to, everyone spoke French - even the farmers!

Angela made friends amongst the other workers her age, and she loved getting dressed up on a Saturday evening to attend the Young Farmers' dance nights, and it was at one of these events that she met Hedley. Hedley was the only son of Hedley Chevalier Senior, one of the farmers that they occasionally worked for. He was three years older than her and worked for his father. Their courtship flourished much to his disapproving father, who was not altogether happy that his son might marry a French girl. Hedley Junior inherited the farm from his father when he died unexpectedly in an accident with his tractor, leaving him free to marry Angela. The couple married in 1932; it was a simple registry office wedding attended by a small number of their family and friends.

Angela and her mother had spent the first few years in Jersey as farmworkers and it was by pure chance that Marie, while in town one Saturday morning, had seen a card in the French newsagent's window for hotel workers. She had gone directly to the hotel and got them both a job, Marie as a kitchen assistant and Angela as a chambermaid. The accommodation provided was luxurious compared with the farm, a bit cramped in that the three of them had to share one bedroom, but they had full use of the hotel's facilities, and all meals were provided.

Angela moved out of the hotel and resigned her job just before getting married and moved into the farmhouse with Hedley and his mother, Roselle. It was a battle with her mother-in-law over control of the kitchen, however, they became firm friends when a tractor accident similar to the one that had killed Hedley's father happened to Hedley Junior. Luckily enough, Hedley only suffered a broken leg, but it brought the two shaken and shocked women closer together.

Didier left school at the end of the school year following his fifteenth birthday in 1933; his mother has secured him a job in the hotel gardens as an apprentice to the head gardener, Eddie Page. The hotel had substantial grounds together with its own vegetable garden which was all looked after by five men. The head gardener had his own cottage in the grounds of the hotel and Didier was offered lodgings with Eddie and his wife, Thelma.

The work has hard but rewarding, and Didier learnt a great deal over the years from Eddie. Every day they had to provide the chef with boxes of seasonal vegetables of all varieties. There was one huge greenhouse where they grew tomatoes, cucumbers and even flower seedlings for replanting in the gardens. There was also a section in the garden for flowers that were cut to decorate areas inside the hotel.

By the time Didier was seventeen he was a strapping man of six feet tall. When working his jet-black hair would be kept under a flat cap but when not at work it would be slicked back with hair cream.

Each day he would deliver the vegetables and flowers to the kitchen and he soon learnt how to flirt with the young female kitchen staff and the chambermaids. He was a big hit with the women as he reminded them of Ronald Colman with his broad chest, swarthy looks and deep brown eyes.

The hotel grounds lead directly on to the beach, with its golden sands and blue sea. Didier could often be found mid-morning tidying the garden near to the steps leading down to the beach. He was waiting for the young female holidaymakers making their way down to the beach, he would shout out, "Hello, lovely day for sunbathing!" and they would often stop to chat to him.

The next couple of years were heaven for Didier. He had a different girl on his arm every week, each one falling in love with him. He always vowed to write to them, a promise that was very soon forgotten once the next intake of visitors arrived. Some parents had to drag their daughters to the airport or harbour to take them home, crying "I'll be back! Wait for me, Didier!" "I'll be here waiting," he would reassure them.

Occasionally, some of the girls did come back the following year and he would struggle to remember their name. But he always had a good excuse as to why he didn't reply to their letters.

Didier was a French national and in 1937, six months after his eighteenth birthday, he received his conscription papers from the French government. The first thing he did was visit the French Consulate where he was able to establish that although he was obliged to complete a two-year conscription, this could be delayed.

However, with talk of war in Europe during 1938 and visitor numbers at the hotel subsiding, Didier was aware that his job at the hotel was no longer secure so he made the decision to return to France and join the French army. His reasoning, as he explained to his mother, "Perhaps in two years, the entire 'war thing' will have blown over, and I can come back here to work."

Didier was enrolled into the French Infantry Division and sent, together with a large number of new recruits, on an extensive three-month training course. The newly trained troops were then sent to join various divisions; Didier was sent to Lille in the northeast of France where he joined a division preparing to defend the French border from any German advances.

During those first six months the troops did very little - they surveyed the borders with Belgium and carried out mock defence battles. War was declared in September 1939, but it wasn't until May 1940 that together with the British Forces, did the war come to Lille. They fought hard to defend the border. However, it was soon realized that the troops had been trained in defence, and with no offence strategy they were ordered to retreat. Although a number of the units were able to escape capture, the advancing German army was too strong and well prepared, enabling the enemy forces take Didier and his unit as prisoners of war.

The men were initially deported to Germany and incarcerated in prison camps, but the fitter, young men and women were transferred to work on farms and in factories. Over one-third of the French prisoners were released back into occupied France on various terms - Didier being among them.

Didier and several of his colleagues were making their way to the north of France when they were approached by the Maquis, and being fluent in English he soon became an asset of the resistance movement.

Under the code name of Henri, Didier assisted the British Forces and later the American Forces, sabotaging the German movements throughout France and assisting with the British Air Force parachute landings and maintaining escape routes for those trapped allied soldiers.

It was in early 1942 that he first set his eyes on Clara who was working under the code name of Vivienne. He had been instructed to exchange certain information with her in a café in St. Brieuc. Watching from behind a curtain that separated the café from the kitchen, he was surprised to see this attractive young woman arrive and ask for him. For some unknown reason he was expecting an older, plainer woman. Didier was astonished at the way she fell into a natural conversation with him, anyone watching would have been in no doubt that they were cousins and had known each other all of their lives. He wanted to continue their conversation, but knew that time was of the essence and she needed to leave to carry the information he had given her to her contact.

The next time Didier saw Clara was when he had been given the task of transporting two small Jewish girls from the Alsace region of France to Nantes. It had been suggested that Clara undertake the role of his wife. It was felt that a married couple traveling with their two daughters would not arouse any suspicion. Didier was charged with persuading Clara to help him. He remembered her embarrassment when he turned up unannounced at her home in the village of Plérin. Didier later found out that Clara was from England and lived with her aunt and uncle, who owned and ran a bar in the village. Clara had blushed from head to foot when she saw him being virtually interrogated by her friend, Claude.

Didier took her for a walk along a nearby beach, taking her hand in his. As they walked, he explained the task required and he didn't have to convince her as she agreed to help with no hesitation.

That first assignment together proved to be nerve-racking when by pure chance Clara was recognized by a German officer at one of the checkpoints on their way to Alsace to pick up the little girls. Didier was impressed by the way Clara talked her way through the situation, which could have resulted in a complete disaster. He was also in full admiration of the way she reassured the two girls, who spoke a language that neither of them could understand.

It was when Didier dropped Clara off at her home the next day that he realized he had fallen in love with her, and over the next couple of years he would visit her and take her out as often as he could. Clara knew these were dangerous times and that his work took him wherever he was needed, so understood when she didn't see or hear from him for months at a time.

When the end of the war was announced, Didier made his way to see Clara, arriving at Plérin just as a celebration party was taking place. He spotted her in the distance, and as she turned around towards him, the huge smile on her face enforced his feelings for her. Clara ran into his arms and kissed him, "It's so lovely to see you! Come and join the celebrations, I will get you a drink."

"It's good to see you too, Clara! But before you run off to get me a drink, there is something I want to ask you," he said seriously.

"And what is that?" she asked laughingly.

Going down on one knee and taking her hand, Didier asked, "Clara, will you marry me?"

It appeared that every person attending the party stopped whatever they were doing and looked at the two of them. Clara blushed with embarrassment as they all cheered when she answered, "Yes, I would love to marry you." Didier took her in his arms as everyone cheered and whispered in her ear, "I love you."

They were married a month later. It was a double wedding with Clara's cousin Danielle Pape. When Danielle announced she was to be married to her sweetheart Léo, Clara's aunt had suggested the double wedding, especially as food rationing was still in force and the guests would be practically the same.

Didier was so proud when he saw Clara in her wedding gown walking down the aisle on the arm of her uncle. He felt tears welling up in his eyes but soon blinked them away not wanting to appear too sentimental in front of the congregation, especially his mother and sister.

Marie and Angela had returned to France almost nine months after the war started when the German forces captured and occupied the Channel Islands. They had been advised, as non-Jersey born residents, to leave the island and the local government organized boats to take them to Cherbourg. They settled in a small cottage on the outskirts of Dinan. Angela was devastated to leave behind her husband, Hedley, but fear of being incarcerated in a German prison camp left them no option but to leave.

Although Didier would visit them from time to time, he couldn't tolerate his mother's criticism of him. She felt he should have been fighting the war not roaming around the countryside doing nothing, unaware of the useful work he was actually undertaking, but he could say nothing. Everyone in the country was potentially a German informer, he couldn't trust anyone - not even his own family!

Didier soon discovered that Clara was an avid organizer and homemaker. Clara, Jeanne, Simone, who was Clara's best friend, and Léo's mother organized the wedding reception. The two brides shared a cake made by Clara and Simone, with everyone contributing their rations. The entire village attended together with Léo's family, with everyone providing some food or drink for the reception.

Simone was Clara's closest friend. She owned the local bakery with her husband Gui, where Clara helped out. It was Gui who had first allowed Clara the opportunity to sell her own pastries at his shop. Gui had been taken prisoner by the Germans, like many young French men during the first years of the war. He had been sent to work in one of their many factories. Knowing that it was just a matter of time before the Germans caught up with him, he taught both Clara and Simone how to bake the bread so that they could keep the bakery going and so provide an income for his wife and three children.

The reception party was held in the church hall. The hall was decorated for the occasion, with flowers and greenery from the hedgerows. Paper chains and balloons hung from every possible space.

There was a centre table ladened with food ready for everyone to help themselves, in the middle of which stood a glorious three-tier wedding cake. Clara had decorated the cake with delicate handmade sugar paste flowers dyed in a variety of colours. Clara's Uncle Clifford had set up a side table serving beer from a barrel, wine, and soft drinks for the children.

After all the guests had eaten and a nervous Didier had given an informal speech, a band formed by some of the villagers stood on the makeshift stage ready to entertain the guests. There was a harmonica player, a piano accordionist plus a man with a tambourine. As the band started to play, the tables were moved out of the way to against the walls. Everyone joined in with the dancing and some guests even got up on the stage to sing.

Before the end of the evening, Didier and Clara sneaked off to their little cottage on the outskirts of the village. There was to be no honeymoon, just the two of them in their new home.

Didier didn't know what to expect of a home. Although he had gone with Clara to view the little cottage that she had found, to him it was just a roof over his head. He hadn't had a proper home since he was a boy. In Jersey it had been a cabin on the farm, then a room with Eddie and his wife. In the Army it had been a bunkhouse or a tent. During the war, if he wasn't able to get a bed for the night, then he slept in his car.

But Clara had created a cozy little home for them. She had spent a lot of time cleaning every corner and then begging from her friends around the village for any pieces of spare furniture. She had gone into town and bought new linen for the bed with her savings. They had also received an array of wedding presents, from mismatched crockery to homemade cushions.

It was only looking back that Didier realized how selfish he had been in not offering to help get the cottage habitable; he hadn't even offer to dig the garden. At the time he thought himself to be the provider, everything else was woman's work. The cottage was always lovely and warm when he arrived home, and he always looked forward to the smell of cooking. Clara cooked him beautiful, delectable meals.

Initially, Didier was employed by the government together with many other ex-servicemen to help get France functional again. He had no skills, so he helped clear bombed sites in readiness for the skilled workers to arrive and rebuild. He travelled wherever he was sent, coming home to Clara at regular intervals. The wages he received he kept to feed himself and buy petrol for his car. Occasionally, he would give Clara money towards the rent, but as she was also working and earning a wage, in his opinion, she didn't need any extra from him.

Didier also liked to gamble. He had learned to play poker in the Army and during that time, when there were long days and nights spent in the middle of nowhere with nothing to do, they would play cards. In the early days, they played for matchsticks as nobody had any money to spare, however, during his time with the resistance Didier would spend a lot of time in bars drinking and would play poker for money. He became a good player and often his winnings would buy him a room for the night, and of course, his next pint of beer. Didier didn't always win at cards, and there were times when he lost his entire weeks' wages, but he never told Clara this.

They had been married just over a year when Clara announced she was pregnant. Didier was over the moon. '*A son,*' he thought to himself. And so, in August 1947, Chantal came screaming into the world. Didier was besotted with this baby girl; she was so tiny, and he had made her. He would proudly walk around the village with her in her pram.

Didier's mother had recently moved into the village and taken up a post of housekeeper to the local priest. Thankfully, it was a live-in job, as Didier was sure that she had wanted to come and live with them. He would often take Chantal to visit his mother, allowing him to slip to the bar and get a drink.

The work with the government ended, and suddenly Didier found himself with no job and now a wife and child to support. He and a couple of friends decided to set themselves up as a team going from farm to farm in the region, offering their services. This arrangement worked well during the harvesting and planting months, but at other times, there was no work to be found.

Didier didn't worry too much as Clara was back at work and she would take Chantal along with her, so they had money and food on the table. The only problem was that as Didier didn't have a job, he didn't have a wage and so would have to ask Clara for money, which he found demeaning.

Difficulties started to arise in their marriage, not serious in his opinion. Clara expected him to help around the house when he wasn't working, which as far as he was concerned was her job, not his. The first occasion he lost his temper with her was when she came home from work with a meal from the bar kitchen; he was furious. He didn't think it was unreasonable to want his dinner on the table when he came home.

"I have been working all day, Didier. I am tired, and I still need to feed Chantal, bath her and get her ready for bed. So, either you eat this, or you see to Chantal while I cook you something else!" she said angrily.

"I am not eating this shit, and it's not my job to see to Chantal! I'm going for a beer while you do all of that," he said, thinking to himself that would put her in her place and went off to the bar.

Didier had started to avoid drinking at the bar run by Clara's uncle, Clifford. It appeared to him that every time he entered the bar, he would get disapproving looks and if he drank more than a couple of pints Clifford would suggest that he had drunk enough and should go home.

Didier soon made new friends at a bar nearer to St. Brieuc, which was the nearest town to the village where they lived. In this bar, there was no one to criticize his drinking habits or tell him what time to go home; he could drink himself into oblivion, and no one cared. He joined a group of poker players, and sometimes he would win and be able to pocket enough money to cover his next drinking session, but other times he would lose and stagger home empty-handed.

The men would discuss at length what their wives should or should not be doing around the house, and with these thoughts in his mind, he would go home and try to enforce these ideas with Clara. He didn't intend to hurt her, but she would insist on answering him back, and the words of his pals from the bar ringing around in his alcohol-fueled head did little to stop his anger. At first, he would just push her to try and coerce her into listening to his drunken ramblings. In the morning when reality hit, and he would see her with a bruised face, he was always sorry, promising never to touch her again. However, this was always short-lived.

Chantal was eleven months old when Clara she announced she was pregnant with their second child, and Didier was quite proud that he was to be a father again, thinking to himself that perhaps this time it would be a son. He didn't think about the implications of a second child on Clara, her work and their finances, only his prowess which he could brag about to his pals.

Didier was not happy when he came home from work one day when Clara was heavily pregnant, to find Jeanne talking about someone looking after Chantal.

"What this about?" he asked.

"I was just telling Clara that my friend Marielle would be willing to look after Chantal while she is at work," said Jeanne, not very happy at having to explain herself to Didier.

Didier wasn't pleased with this suggestion, "Why can't you take Chantal with you? It hasn't been a problem until now." Clara started to explain but could see that no amount of explanation would satisfy Didier.

"We will talk about it later," she said, and Jeanne quickly left, not wanting to get involved, "See you in the morning, bye-bye."

"I can see my dinner is not ready, again - I'm off for a beer!" said an angry Didier.

"It is ready!" shouted Clara as Didier went out of the door, slamming it behind him, but he wasn't in the mood to be listening.

All Didier could think about was the money he would have to pay out for someone to look after one little girl. Why couldn't Clara look after her? Where was the difficulty in that? 'For goodness sake!' he thought to himself, 'One of my pals has five children, and his wife didn't need any help!'.

Discussing the situation with his pals later that evening, they all agreed. "One baby is nothing. They sit in the pram all day or are asleep. Wait until she has five like my wife!" said his pal.

Didier staggered home later that evening and sat down at the table. Clara got his dinner out of the oven where it had been keeping warm.

"I told you as you were going out that dinner was ready, but you chose to ignore me; now it is a bit dry." Clara said as she laid out two plates on the table. Didier started to eat then overturned the plate on the table, complaining that the meal was inedible. Clara started to clear up the mess he had created, when he started shouting at her telling her how useless she was and that she couldn't even look after her own child. Clara tried to explain to him that it was difficult to work and take care of Chantal at the same time.

"Well, give up work then!" he shouted.

"Yes, that would be helpful wouldn't it? How would we pay the rent? Certainly not with the wages you give me, especially after you have spent half of it on beer and cigarettes!" she yelled back at him.

Didier grabbed hold of her. "Don't you shout at me!" he roared, and slapped her hard across the face, stunning her into silence.

When Didier woke in the morning, he realized that Clara had not come to bed and had slept downstairs. When he saw the red weal on her cheek, he felt guilty and shocked with himself, as he only vaguely remembered the argument.

"I am sorry, Clara, my love! Please forgive me." he begged, trying to hug her, but Clara was unresponsive. Knowing straight away that he was her bad books, he grabbed a quick cup of coffee and left for work saying "Bye, see you tonight." As he went out of the door, hoping that by the evening all would be forgiven and forgotten.

That evening when he returned from work, Didier didn't dare say anything about Chantal being looked after by Marielle, as the atmosphere in the house was still very hostile. Didier tried to apologize to Clara again, even offering to bath Chantal and put her to bed.

CHAPTER 5

Clara and Didier's second daughter was born on 28th March 1949, weighing seven pounds two ounces and looking exactly like Chantal but with more hair. They christened her Francine Olive Renard.

Chantal was the 'apple of her father's eye'. At nineteen months old she would chatter away in both English and French, mixing up the two languages on occasions in one sentence. She was a clever little girl, asking questions that at times were impossible to answer. Didier liked nothing better than taking her for walks around the lanes, collecting wildflowers from the hedgerows and presenting them to Clara to place in a vase. He would sit on the floor with her building towers of bricks ready for her to topple in readiness to start all over again. He loved his little girl, unconditionally.

Unfortunately, 1949 continued to be a difficult year for Didier as work was spasmodic. He maintained his seasonal work with the farmers in the area, however, he still did not have a permanent job.

During the first two months of Francine being born, Didier soon realized that Clara was relying on handouts of food which irritated him immensely, but he daren't challenge her as he found since Francine's birth she had been in a strange mood and he never knew how she would react, so he kept his distance. He felt no matter what he did, it was wrong - if he stayed home, she moaned that he did nothing to help and if he stayed away, he was accused of spending all his time in the bar.

Towards the end of the year, the villagers decided to throw a New Year's Eve party to welcome in the new decade and Clara was heavily involved in the preparations. Tables were set up in readiness for the evening; chairs were borrowed from all around the village, and even several marquees were erected. Didier was surprised on arrival at the party leading Chantal by the hand and carrying Francine, to see the entire square decorated with paper chains and fairy lights; the girls were enthralled. Both girls, especially Chantal liked dancing to the music, but soon tiredness took hold. Clara put them both to bed in Jeanne's spare room where she had agreed with Jeanne that they would stay until the following day, leaving Clara and Didier free to enjoy themselves. While Clara danced the night away, dancing with anyone and everyone and singing along to the music, Didier sat in a corner by one of the many of the wood-burning fires keeping warm and drinking himself into oblivion. As the church clock struck midnight, everyone cheered kissing and hugging the nearest person, Clara sought out Didier to wish him a Happy New Year only to find him slumped in his seat fast asleep.

Didier could remember very little of that night, only the feeling of anger as he watched his wife making a spectacle of herself. Three months later, he felt the full force of her fury when she announced she was pregnant with their third child. Didier was dumbfounded, how could that possibly be when she hadn't allowed him near her for months? He made the faux pas of saying, "Well, it can't possibly be mine!" which unleashed an anger he had never experienced from any woman! Clara then proceeded to tell him, holding back none of the details, how he had beaten her and raped her on New Year's Eve. Their relationship changed that day and not for the better.

It was his mother's idea to move to back to Jersey, Didier wasn't that sure, but Marie convinced him that it could be a new start with the promise of a job working on his brother-in-law's farm, with a small cottage where the family could live.

"Think, son. Clara won't be able to work with three young children, and you will be able to provide for them," said his Mother.

"Let me think about it," he replied.

The problem was his mother, interfering as usual, mentioned it to Clara before he even had time to digest the proposal. Clara was furious with him, firstly for going behind her back and secondly, for not even discussing it with her to establish if this was, she wanted. Perhaps at this point, he made the wrong response plus having had a few beers, but he was angry with his mother and angry at Clara's reaction. He realized as soon as he said, "I am going and if you don't want to come, then so be it. But the girls are coming with me!" He was absolutely furious, and he knew he shouldn't have kicked the chair she was sitting on making her fall against the wall, before storming out of the house. But who did she think she was screaming at him like a demented woman? Didier hadn't meant what he said; he would never take the children from Clara, but in his usual tactless way, he had said the first thing that came into his head.

Their third daughter, Liliane, was born that night. Didier arrived at the bar after taking a walk around the village to calm down, only to be sworn at by Clifford telling him in no uncertain terms to get home as quickly as possible. He arrived home to mayhem; Jeanne was there, and Clara was writhing in agony on the floor. Jeanne screamed at him to go and get the doctor.

Running as quickly as he could to the doctor, he tried to explain to him that he thought the baby was coming, but that he wasn't exactly sure - it was just a guess. The doctor gave him a disapproving look, and together they rushed back to Clara's side.

The baby was born before they arrived, so the doctor tenderly attended to both Clara and the baby. Didier was told, in no uncertain terms, to go to Jeanne's house for the night, while she stayed and looked after Clara and the baby. Didier didn't know what made Clara change her mind, but two months later after Liliane was born, they were on their way to Jersey.

The boat journey was awful, but the girls, especially Chantal, loved it. Didier tried to make the journey exciting for them, showing them around the boat and taking them outside to watch the waves splashing against the stern of the boat.

Hedley, his brother-in-law, met them at the boat, and Angela welcomed them with a cooked meal on their arrival at their farmhouse. Didier's mother was to live with Angela. Didier and his family had been allocated a small cottage down the lane from the farm. It was dark when they eventually arrived at the cottage, making it difficult to see it from the outside, but inside was lovely and warm as Angela had lite the range in the kitchen. It was a cold October night and the warmth in the kitchen didn't extend to the two upstairs bedrooms. Didier took their luggage upstairs while Clara put the kettle on the range so she could fill the hot water bottles that Angela had given her, and the girls were soon in bed and sound asleep.

Didier had vowed to himself that this would be a new start for them all, but this was short-lived as he was soon propping up the bar at the local pub with his neighbours and workmates. The arguments between him and Clara started again with her complaining that she didn't have enough money to feed them and pay the bills, even though he handed over his wages each week. Yes, Didier asked for some money back to buy a drink, but it was him earning it not her. Things got even worse when Clara asked Hedley to give her his wages each week - how dare she? They were his earnings! Clara was making him look small in front of his family.

It was only when looking back did Didier realize that Clara had become thin and looked terribly unhappy, but by that time it was too late as one day, less than six months after they arrived in Jersey, Clara left. Didier never knew how Clara managed to leave the island with Lilly, leaving behind Chantel and Francine, nevertheless she did, leaving him a note saying she had gone and hoped that one day she would be back for the girls.

At first, Didier was disorientated, not knowing quite what to do and much to his mother's dismay, he went to work as usual the morning after Clara left. Didier had forgotten about the girls, leaving them at home alone. And so, Didier's mother stepped in to help with the girls until that fateful Sunday - the day of the accident!

CHAPTER 6

Lilly had taken a taxi to the address her Aunt Jeanne had given her; it was the last address she had and was over 20 years old. She got out of the taxi across the road from the address and she immediately noticed the man standing in the road at the entrance to Rotherwood Farm. Lilly knew instantly it was her Papa - how, she didn't know - perhaps it was just instinct. The man was staring at her and Lilly was unsure whether she imagined it or whether was it was wishful thinking, but she was certain he mouthed her name. Lilly crossed the road thinking that she would merely ask the man if he knew the family she was looking for, but as she approached, she didn't need to say anything as he put his arms out and held her shoulders, looking directly at her.

"My Liliane! My baby is it really you?" he asked pleadingly, as though he couldn't quite believe his eyes.

"Yes, Papa," she cried, tears running down her cheeks. They hugged briefly before Didier held her away from him so he could take a good look at his youngest daughter. She had been just over six months old when he had last seen her and now, she was a young lady of twenty-one years.

Lilly had grown up on a tobacco farm with her mother and father in North Carolina. It was an idyllic childhood; she had two younger brothers, Jeffrey and Timothy, and life couldn't have been any better for her growing up in a loving family. Yes, there had been heartache when her grandparents had died - she had missed them terribly at first, but then life appeared to move forward.

Lilly had done well at school, first at the local primary before moving to the nearby high school followed by university. She had chosen the University of North Carolina (UNC) since it was the only one within Carolina that offered the course she wanted. Much to her parent's concerns, she had chosen to study archaeology and history; they were unsure of the prospects this degree would offer their ambitious daughter, but her enthusiasm was enough to convince them. Lilly had become interested in archaeology at high school, when one of the teachers set up an extracurricular activity that she and her best friend, Bella had been enticed to join when told they could miss their last lesson on a Friday. The girls immediately grabbed the chance as the last lesson was mathematics, which they both hated. Lilly fell in love with digging up all sorts of interesting artifacts almost immediately, whereas Bella was not so keen and found a new activity after a few months.

In May 1971, having completed her three-year university course and before commencing a teacher training course the following October, her tutor Professor Hatcher asked her if she would like to join him in making up a team to undertake a dig in Italy.

Lilly was ecstatic and said yes straight away; there were four of them going with the professor, and they would be joining a friend of the professor and his team in Italy. Lilly couldn't wait!

Lilly went home and told her mother, who didn't appear to be as enthusiastic, especially when Lilly said she would need her birth certificate for a passport. At first, Lilly thought it was because she was expected to help in her mother's café during the summer months before embarking on her teacher training course. But she was soon to discover that this was not the case.

Lilly's mother appeared a bit hesitant when she handed over the birth certificate. "Lilly..." she had stuttered. Lilly just looked at her mother questioningly; she couldn't understand her mother's reluctance it was only her birth certificate after all! Looking at her mother as she took hold of the folded document, Lilly suddenly felt a dread in the pit of her stomach. Something was definitely amiss. Lilly initially merely glanced at the certificate as she unfolded the piece of paper, however, one written word caught her attention, and it was then upon reading the contents more closely that Lilly's world fell apart!

According to the birth certificate, she was Lilly Renard not Lilly Kennion - her beloved dad, Carl, was not her father! Lilly ran to her dad in tears, Carl hugged her tightly and tried to explain, but she didn't want to listen. Shocked and shaken by the news Lilly left home as soon as she could and before long was on a plane to Italy.

Clara and Carl were left devastated at home. They understood but they were very hurt by the way Lilly had reacted. They were seriously worried about her and whether she would ever grow to forgive them for keeping the truth from her.

The dig in Italy was everything she had imagined and more, and when their time at the dig ended, the group decided to explore parts of Europe before returning home. Lilly, not looking forward to going home, willingly joined them. Their first stop was Paris. On their second day, the boys in the group wanted to go and see the Catacombs, but Lilly said she would give this a miss and go window shopping along the Champs de L'Élyseés instead. She stopped for a coffee and pastry at one of the many cafes along the street next door to a tourist information centre; there was a map of France on the wall that caught her eye, so when she had finished her coffee, she went into the centre.

"Bonjour Mademoiselle, puis-je vous aider?"

"Sorry, I don't speak French! Do you speak English?" asked Lilly.

"Yes, I do Mademoiselle, how can I help you?" queried the assistant in perfect English.

"I was wondering if you could show me on the map where a place called Plérin is?" inquired Lilly.

"Well I have not actually heard of it, but I have a detailed book of maps here, so let me see if it is the index!" The assistant opened a large book and turned to the back page.

"Yes, here it is!" exclaimed the assistant, as she turned to another page and showed the location Lilly on one of the pages.

“Where exactly is that on the larger map?” asked Lilly.

The assistant went to the large map on the wall and showed Lilly where it was, then pointed to Paris so she could see how far away it was.

“How could I get there?” asked Lilly, “Is there a train, do you know?”

“I am sure there is a train, but you will need to go to the train station to find out,” the assistant suggested.

So, the very next day Lilly found herself on a train, travelling to the place where she had been born. To say she felt nervous was an understatement, she had no idea what to expect - would it be just a waste of time? Maybe, but at least she would be able to see where she was born! She thought to herself.

As Lilly sat on the train watching the countryside pass steadily by, her thoughts returned to her time in Italy; she had had an experience she had never expected. All member of the group, each had turns digging and then labeling the items that had been uncovered and she longed to go back as she had enjoyed every minute. Lilly wanted to discover more about all the items they had dug up and hoped that one day she would be able to return.

Lilly had shared a tent with her friend Jenny, and the entire team shared duties such as preparing meals in the common room. Professor Hatcher’s friend, Alan, from Boston and his group of students had joined them, and each evening they would all either go to the local village bar, or sing and tell stories around a campfire. All members of the group got on well and there were a few characters, one of which was Millie.

Towards the end of their time in Italy, the group went down to the bar as usual, stopping for a pizza on the way, and Lilly found herself sitting next to Millie. She wasn't too sure about Millie, who was obviously from a very posh family, as from the way Millie talked and how she expected other people to do things for her. Although none of them did the work for her, they just showed how to do it. "It amazes me," said Lilly to Jenny one day, "That she doesn't even know how to wash her clothes! I wonder how she managed at university?"

"She probably would have just gone out and bought some new ones!" laughed Jenny.

Millie got very drunk that evening and told Lilly how she hated her parents and that she didn't want to go home.

"My entire life has been a lie, and *they* have been lying to me all this time! I hate them - it will serve them right if I never go back!" she exclaimed, slurring her words.

Lilly tried to humour her and said that everyone hated their parents at one time or another, thinking how at this present time she hated her mother.

"Yes, but for me to find out I am adopted at the age of twenty-one and by accident is just not on! I bet if I hadn't come here and needed a passport, I would never have known and my parents don't appear to care how I feel!" sobbed Millie, who then stormed off back to the site.

Lilly empathized with Millie, having experienced a similar emotional upheaval upon reading her own birth certificate and seeing her true name, Liliane Renard. But Lilly didn't feel like opening up to Millie about their similarities.

In fact, the following morning Millie nursing a hangover apologized to Lilly, saying, "I am so sorry for burdening you with my problems last night. I have only ever been drunk once before, and the hangover I had that time matches the one I have now. My head feels as though someone is inside trying to get out with a hammer."

Millie went on to explain to Lilly how she had discovered, purely by accident, adoption papers with her name on. Lilly listened trying not to get too emotional herself. Millie reminded Lilly of someone, but she couldn't think of whom. The announcement '*Next stop Plerin!*' over the train tannoy brought Lilly out of her daydream, and she was now too anxious about her imminent arrival to think any further about Millie and her dilemmas.

Lilly finally arrived in the pretty village of Plérin. A large granite Church dominated a central square and it was here that she spoke to the local priest. He was about to close the church door as Lilly approached him. Lilly soon discovered that unfortunately the priest didn't speak English, and she certainly didn't speak French! However, the priest directed her towards a bar across from the church and appeared to indicate that someone there spoke English. Lilly felt embarrassed with everyone looking at her as she entered the bar; there was an elderly man behind the bar staring at her. He instantly called out "Jeanne, Jeanne!" and an old lady came out from the back and followed the man's stare, "Oh! My god, Clara!"

"No! No, I am Lilly!" exclaimed a surprised Lilly.

Lilly soon learned that Jeanne was her grandmother's sister-in-law, and it was Jeanne that told her about her mother's time in France as well as her father. But what shocked Lilly the most was a photo on Jeanne's mantelpiece. It was of two little girls clinging onto a tiny baby in a christening robe.

"That's you and your two sisters," said Jeanne, and Lilly froze. She looked at the photo and then at Jeanne. It was at this point that she discovered that she had two older sisters.

"And that's your mother. That's why I thought you were her! Look at how much you resemble her, dear Lilly!"

Lilly stood there taking it all in, but feeling absolutely in a state of shock.

"I need to meet them, Jeanne! Where are they? Are they here in France?"

"No, my dear girl, they left France with you shortly after this photo was taken. You all went to Jersey. I have an address here somewhere, but I can't guarantee that your father and sisters are still there," answered Jeanne.

Jeanne went to a draw and rummaged through a lot of papers and took out an old letter from Clara. "Here it is!" she announced. "I'll write down the address for you," said Jeanne, as she sat to write it down. Lilly tried to stay calm.

"I think this is where you will find them," stated Jeanne, handing Lilly the piece of paper.

Lilly would have loved to stay in France a longer than two days, but she was anxious to see her sisters. She was eternally grateful to Jeanne for helping her with the travel arrangements to Jersey and promised to write and let her know if she found her family.

Lilly arrived in Jersey the next day. She made her way to the address that Jeanne had given her with both eager anticipation and a sense of foreboding. When she alighted from the taxi and spotted the man standing at the entrance to the address, she had known instantly it was her father. How? She didn't know, and why she called him Papa as opposed to Dad or Father - again she didn't know, it was just instinctive!

Meeting her two sisters after greeting her father was all she could have asked for, hugging first Chantal then Francine. Their appearance was so different from her own; they were dark like their father, whereas she was blonde like their mother. She felt an instant warmth from Chantal but not from Francine, or Fran as they called her.

"Let's go home," said her father, ushering them towards the house.

CHAPTER 7

The first few weeks after Clara had left, their grandmother would come to the cottage each morning after their father had gone to work, getting them out of bed and giving them breakfast before taking them to Auntie Angela's house. At the end of the day, their Papa would come to take them home again.

Chantal always felt as though they were a burden, but their granny never moaned she just appeared to get on with looking after them. Chantal would try and talk to Auntie Angela about her Mama, but nobody seemed to want to talk about her. Francine didn't understand and only cried a few times for her Mama before appearing to forget all about her. Chantal would cry herself to sleep each night at first, praying that her Mama would come back, especially as most nights their Papa would leave them alone and as she found later, go to the pub and come back drunk.

Chantal couldn't remember exactly how long after her Mama left that the accident happened. Papa always went to the pub on Sunday mornings taking the girls with him; they would play with the other children left outside the pub, usually in the churchyard opposite, much to the Verger's annoyance. Their Papa would give them a bottle of Coca-Cola and a bag of crisps, and they would sit on the wall of the churchyard waiting for him to come out when the pub closed.

On this particular Sunday, the girls sat on the wall waiting, both feeling tired after running around the churchyard playing hide-and-seek amongst the gravestones with the other children. The year was 1951 and cars were a novelty and a rarity, so the road between the church and the pub was nearly always clear of vehicles. The church bells were ringing indicating the end of the final church service of the morning, and this also indicated that the pub was about to close. Frannie knew this and anticipating that her father would come out of the pub any minute, she jumped down from the wall.

With the churchgoers chatting away as they walked down the church path to the road and the bells ringing nobody heard the approaching car and unfortunately Frannie was only concentrating on the pub door. When her father appeared, she ran toward him and the car. There was a screech of brakes followed by a thud as the car tossed Frannie into the air. Didier, shocked sober, ran to his little girl's lifeless body lying in the road. Somebody shouted to the pub landlord to call for an ambulance, and one of the churchgoers covered Frannie with her coat to keep her warm.

Chantal was screaming as she ran towards to scene of the accident, Audrey de la Mare, their near neighbour, quickly caught her and held her in her arms, "Don't look, Chantal," she whispered in her ear.

Audrey quickly shouted to Didier over the mayhem, that she would take Chantal home which was met with an affirmative nod from Didier's traumatized face. Clara had met Audrey when she first arrived in Jersey becoming instant friends, and she had soon become known as Auntie Audrey to the girls. Audrey's son Michael was the same age as Francine, and the girls would often play with Michael, but Audrey hadn't seen the girls since Clara had left.

Audrey ran as fast as could carrying Chantal to her grandmother's house, she arrived out of breath and quickly told Marie and Angela what had happened. Chantal was still crying uncontrollably, between tears she stuttering "Frannie is dead, Granny! Frannie is dead!"

Marie arrived at the accident at the same time as the ambulance and Francine was carried gently into the ambulance. Marie cried with relief when the ambulance man said, "I am sure she will be okay, just a few broken bones and a bump on the head." Didier accompanied Francine to the hospital where the doctors confirmed that she had a broken arm and broken leg, but she would need to stay in hospital as she was suffering from concussion, and they also wanted to make sure that she had no other injuries. The hospital told Didier to go home and come back the following day at visiting time. With no form of transport and no money, Didier started the long walk home. The walk gave Didier time to think and realize his responsibilities; he had two young daughters that relied on him for love and guidance for their future upbringing.

Marie had been holding Chantal tightly in her arms, trying to comfort her. However, she became very concerned when Chantal started shaking so much that her teeth were chattering, so Marie decided to call the doctor. Chantal hadn't stopped sobbing since Audrey had bought her home and she was constantly asking for her Mama. The doctor arrived quite quickly, explaining that the little girl was in shock and gave her a sedative.

"This will calm her down and send her to sleep. Put her to bed and I will come around in the morning to see how she is," advised the doctor. The sedative worked almost immediately, and Marie laid a sleepy Chantal gently into bed.

By the time an exhausted Didier eventually arrived at Angela's house, his mother's temper had reached boiling point. Although she was relieved that Francine was going to recover, she was angry with Didier for his lack of thought.

She was fuming when she said, "Francine is only just two years old and Chantal not yet four! What were you thinking leaving those babies on their own? You are nothing but a selfish bastard, the only thing you think about is your next pint of beer! Well, that has got to stop! Those girls are going to stay here and perhaps one day you will realize that not everything revolves around you! Just get out of my sight and go home!"

So, feeling downhearted, Didier left and went home alone to his cold, empty cottage.

It was still dark when Chantal first woke up. For a moment, she didn't know where she was, but then everything came back to her and she let out a small cry, feeling an arm instantly go around her. It was her grandmother.

“Sssh, Frannie is fine,” Marie whispered and Chantal fell back into a natural sleep.

CHAPTER 8

Didier went to work as usual the next morning, where he was met with a wall of silence from his workmates. He could see the look of disgust and sympathy in their eyes. He desperately wanted to explain but knew that no words could describe his shame, however, he was thankful that Frannie would recover from her injuries fully.

Francine stayed in the hospital for two weeks, and Didier visited her every evening. Marie visited every afternoon, often with either Audrey or Angela. Chantal was disappointed that she couldn't go to the hospital, but her grandmother had explained to her that she was too young.

When Frannie eventually came home from hospital, it was to her grandmother's home. She was confined to a chair as she couldn't walk with her broken leg and was unable to use crutches with her broken arm. Chantal would bring her toys and play with her tirelessly; she only wished she could read a book to her but unfortunately, she hadn't yet learned to read.

Audrey would, on occasions, come and put Francine in Michael's pushchair and take her and Chantal to their house to give their grandmother some time to herself. Michael would jump in the pushchair with Francine taking care not to hurt her arm or leg. Michael and Chantal had covered her plaster casts with coloured pictures and anyone that visited wrote their names on the casts. Francine was so proud of her casts and was disappointed when they were eventually removed.

Within three months, all sign of Francine's injuries had disappeared, although she became very anxious when a car drove past her. The girls remained with their grandmother during this time, although Didier saw them every day after he had finished work. Unfortunately, Marie didn't even trust him to take them out at the weekend, so he resorted to spending his Sundays with the girls at the farm. He would either play ball games outside with his daughters when the weather allowed, or board and card games indoors.

What Didier hadn't told anyone was that he was going to night school. Whilst reading the local newspaper one evening, the idea came into his head. There was an advertisement for a new course aimed at the construction industry learning all manners of trades. The advert appeared to be for youngsters, but when Didier made enquiries, they informed him that it was open to anyone interested in learning. So, Didier enrolled and chose plumbing as his first course, quickly grasping the fundamentals.

It was his tutor, who was a plumber himself, who saw the potential in Didier and asked him if he would be interested in a bit of work on Saturdays. His tutor, whose name was Laurence Vautier, owned his own business and he explained to Didier that he needed extra help to complete a job quickly. Didier didn't hesitate and said 'yes' straight away. Initially, the work entailed mostly labouring for the tradesman and then gradually, as he was a quick learner, he began carrying out jobs on his own under supervision. The urgent job that Laurence had needed him for completed within a few weeks, but Laurence asked him to continue to help Saturdays, and even some evenings after he had finished at the farm.

The night school course continued, and Didier moved from plumbing to bricklaying and then plastering, finally finishing with an electrician's course. Didier became master of none of the trades, but learned all the basic rudiments.

After six months of working for Laurence on an adhoc basis, he was offered a full-time permanent job. Didier's first thought before accepting the offer was that he would lose his cottage as this was linked to his job with Hedley. Didier needed the cottage as it had always been his intention to earn his mother's trust and have his daughters back living with him.

Since the day of the accident Didier had not touched a drop of alcohol. At first, he had missed the camaraderie of his mates at the pub but he soon realized that it was a fickle relationship and not one of his 'so-called' mates got in touch to see why they hadn't seen him.

Didier soon made new friends with other students of his age on the course as well as the men he worked with at weekends and evenings. They didn't seem concerned on the few occasions they went to the pub that he drank orange juice; they didn't try to tempt him with a beer, they just accepted that was not what he wanted. These men were not hardened drinkers like his previous friends, they were nearly all family men working overtime to support their families.

Didier spoke to Hedley and informed him of the offer he had received from Laurence. He explained what an opportunity it was for him and the girls, but that he was concerned that he would lose the cottage.

"I understand, Didier," said Hedley. "This new job will give you a good trade and it has prospects, whereas farming is hard work for little pay. You are a good reliable worker and given your problems with booze, it hasn't affected your work so far. So, as you are family you can stay in the cottage, but I will have to charge you rent as this was part of your wage."

"We can work out an agreeable amount." continued Hedley hesitantly. "Or, perhaps we can work something else out - The cottages are desperately in need of updating, so maybe you could install plumbing into them for me? I could provide the sanitary ware, and you could do the rest. What do you think?" asked Hedley.

So, Didier started work with Laurence the following week and enjoyed every minute. Didier found it a pleasure watching a job develop, and he took pride in the finished project. He helped with the tiling of bathrooms, firstly just passing tiles to the tiler and mixing the cement, and gradually he soon learned to apply the tiles himself. The more jobs he learnt, the more he wanted to study, and so he continued with the night classes and even helped the tutor on occasions.

During the spring of 1952, Didier started installing plumbing into Hedley's properties. Initially he started on his own cottage. It was tough work digging trenches to get water from outside the property to the inside, but within a matter of weeks he was the proud owner of an inside bathroom, having converted the scullery next to the kitchen. With the help of one of his workmates, they were able to get hot water from a back boiler attached to the kitchen range and Didier was immensely proud of his work.

The only ‘fly in the ointment’ was his mother - he wanted his girls back living with him. Tentatively, in early summer of 1952, Didier invited her and the girls to his cottage the following Sunday. “I will cook lunch, Mème,” he pleaded, “Please say yes.”

Marie was a bit skeptical that her son could even cook never mind be sober on a Sunday lunchtime, but she had to admit to herself that she hadn’t smelt beer on him for some time, especially when he came to see the girls on a Sunday. So, she agreed.

The girls were excited to be going home even though it was only for the day, and the surprise they got when they walked through the door was overwhelming - gone was the dark dingy kitchen! Even Marie was in awe not only by the delicious smell of lunch cooking, but by the bright newly decorated room.

CHAPTER 9

Chantal didn't enjoy living at her Auntie Angela's house - she longed to go home. Lying in bed at night she would worry that her Mama would come home and not be able to find them.

John, their cousin, was always horrid to both of the girls, but a least he was at school during the day. He would leave early to catch the school bus, as his school was not the local primary but the private Catholic school in town. He had a smart uniform with a cap and a satchel to hold all his schoolbooks. The school bus would bring him back at four thirty each afternoon, so they didn't have to tolerate him for long before it was time to go to bed.

Each evening their Papa would eat his dinner with them. Sometimes he would read them a story before he left to go home, but other times he would rush off claiming he had something to do, although Chantal was not sure what.

The girls often visited Auntie Audrey during the winter of 1951 and the summer of 1952. They loved going to her house. Frannie and Michael were inseparable doing everything from colouring to playing in Michael's pretend house in the barn outside. Chantal liked nothing better than being in the kitchen with Audrey, especially on a baking day when Audrey would let her mix her own cake ingredients. She would make and decorate little fairy cakes, which she would take home.

It was Auntie Audrey who took her to school on her first day, dressed in her brand-new uniform of a grey pinafore dress with a white blouse underneath, and a blue and yellow striped tie neatly knotted around her collar. Granny had painstakingly sewn a label with her name on in each item of clothing. Papa had taken her to town to get her uniform which also included a navy-blue cardigan and black lace-up shoes. He also bought her a brown satchel, in which she placed the new pencil case that granny had given her containing lots of pencils and colours, plus a rubber and pencil sharpener.

Chantal was both excited and nervous walking down to road to the school that first day. She held tightly on to the pushchair into which Frannie and Michael had squeezed. They were getting too big for the pushchair, but Auntie Audrey said that they needed to get to school on time and that the youngsters were slow walkers hence the pushchair. Auntie Audrey walked her to the school entrance, where a teacher took charge of her.

"I will be here to pick you after school," said Auntie Audrey, giving her a hug and kiss goodbye.

Chantal had her own coat peg with her name above on which she hung her satchel, which also contained the lunch that Papa had made her that morning. The relationship between her Papa and granny had improved greatly over the last few months, and she and Frannie were now spending every weekend at home with Papa.

They had gone home that first day with Granny for Sunday lunch. It was a lovely surprise for her as Papa had decorated their home, and it was almost unrecognizable. However, it was their bedroom that had impressed them most. Papa had wallpapered the walls in a lovely pink wallpaper with fairies on it; there were pink curtains at the windows, and on their beds they each had a beautiful eiderdown cover. Frannie had a Fairy Godmother on her bed, and Chantal had Cinderella on hers.

"Granny, can we sleep in our new bedroom tonight?" the girls had begged.

Granny had looked at them both and slowly sat down on Chantal's bed, bringing the girls towards her. "I am sure you will get a chance to stay here very soon, but not tonight. No, not tonight. We haven't brought any of your things!" she declared, looking at Chantal.

The girls were so disappointed. But only a few weeks later they were allowed to stay one night, and now they stayed every weekend. Papa had bought them new toys. He told them that they weren't new, as he had got them at a jumble sale. The girls didn't mind where he had got the toys, as Frannie had a lovely dolls pram that she would put all her dolls and teddy bears in, and Chantel had a scooter on which she would zoom up and down their lane.

Chantal's teacher was Miss Neale. She was only twenty-three years old, petite and slim standing at five feet two inches tall. Her light brown hair was tied back in a ponytail. This was her first teaching job, so she was nervous as the children. There were 18 children in her infants' class, ten girls and eight boys, and the classroom had twelve double wooden desks with lids that opened up to store their books. Each desk had an inkwell but no ink, as they were only allowed pencils in the infants' class.

Miss Neale introduced herself to the children and told them to choose a desk to sit at. Chantal chose the very front row, and a girl by the name of Lucy Cornick sat down next to her. They shyly said hello to each other at exactly the same time and then giggled that they were in unison.

Lucy had bright red curly hair that was tied back in a vibrant blue ribbon which unfortunately by mid-morning, was so loose that most of her hair had escaped the ribbon. Chantal was envious of Lucy's curls as her hair was totally straight without even a single kink. Lucy also had a row of freckles that ran from the centre of her cheeks across her nose making her, in Chantal's opinion, the prettiest little girl she had ever seen.

Lucy eventually became her best friend, and together with Celia and Anne, they forged a firm friendship which was last all of their school days.

"Good morning, children," said Miss Neale.

"Now, I want you to reply, '*Good morning Miss Neale'*," instructed Miss Neale.

Almost altogether the class replied, "Good morning, Miss Neale." She was on to a good start, Miss Neale thought to herself.

"I will take the register every morning, so when I say your name, you must reply '*present*,' is that clear, class?" asked Miss Neale.

"Yes, Miss Neale," they all responded.

"Before I take the register today, can you each stand up and tell me and the rest of the class your name? We will start at the back and go across," she said pointing to a boy to the back left of the class. Chantal felt embarrassed having to stand up and say her name, but at least she wasn't the first, so by the time her turn came, she felt a bit more comfortable.

That first few months were a bit of a blur, but Chantal would have a small bottle of milk at break in the morning, before going out to play. There was a big playground split into two; one half for the boys and the other for the girls. The boys played football and marbles, however to Chantal's young eyes they always appeared to be fighting whereas the girls played skipping, whilst others were throwing two balls against the wall trying to throw one then catch the other, which seemed very complicated to Chantal. Some of the older girls played 'Jacks', a game where you bounced a small ball and you had to pick up little metal objects with six prongs then catch the ball before it fell to the ground. There was also a hopscotch grid drawn with chalk.

When Audrey picked her up that first day, she could see that Chantal was tired; it had been a long day for a five-year-old. Audrey asked her about her day. "Well, I made friends with Lucy, and I sit next to her, and we had a bottle of milk, and we played in the playground," replied Chantal. That's was all she managed to get out of Chantal, which made Audrey smile as she was sure that they must have done something else.

Chantal loved school and especially liked being able to bring the pictures she had drawn home. Sometimes she gave them to Papa, sometimes to Granny and other times to Auntie Audrey.

It was the beginning of 1953 when the girls went home for good. Their Papa had bought home all their clothes and some of their toys from Granny's, leaving some of the toys behind as they would continue to spend time at Granny's when Papa was at work.

By the time Frannie started school at the end of the summer of 1954, Chantal could read well above her age group and her writing was above average, as was her arithmetic. She was now seven years old and felt very grown-up when her little sister arrived for her first day at school. She showed Francine where her coat peg was and where her classroom was. Frannie was adamant that she was going to sit next to Michael even though Chantal tried to encourage her to sit next to a girl.

During the start of 1956 Chantal started to notice changes in her granny. She didn't know quite what to say at first, and it took her some time before she made a comment to her Papa.

CHAPTER 10

Audrey had first met Clara at the local shop run by Mrs. Lafolley. Mrs Lafolley was in her fifties with short greying hair mostly hidden by a scarf tied behind her ears. She appeared to wear the same wrap-around floral apron whenever she was in the shop and never had a good word to say about anyone, especially if they were French. Audrey could help but suppress a smile when Clara entered the shop that day and her children instantly asked for sweets in French. Mrs. Lafolley commented sarcastically to one of her customers, "Another Frenchy who can't speak English!" to which Clara, in perfect English, told her children to speak in English not French. When Audrey left the shop, a baby about the same age as her Michael was sat in a pram outside. So, she stopped to speak to the little girl and waited for Clara to finish her shopping.

When Clara came out of the shop, Audrey introduced herself. As they walked down the road, Audrey chatted away to Clara telling her all about the area and how the shopkeeper Mrs. Lafolley didn't like the French very much.

"The French men go to the pub next door on payday and get very drunk. On numerous occasions they have been sick in front of her shop! As you can imagine she is not happy having to clean up after them, so that is why she doesn't like the French. Unfortunately, she tars them all with the same brush," said Audrey. Audrey invited Clara back to her house, and over tea and biscuits Audrey told Clara where all the shops were and the best places to go.

They soon became friends and Clara would often bring her girls to play with Michael while they chatted over a cup of tea. Audrey watched Clara slowly get thinner and more haggard; she didn't like to comment on the bruises on her face that Clara had tried to disguise with makeup. Clara did comment about being clumsy and walking into the door, but Audrey didn't believe her.

Audrey was shocked when she heard the gossip that Clara had just up and left Didier with her youngest daughter Lilly, leaving behind Chantal and Francine. She couldn't quite understand why she would leave her toddlers behind as she adored those little girls. But on the other hand, she knew that Clara was desperately unhappy, so perhaps it was the last resort. If only Clara had come and spoken to her, she might have been able to help.

It was sometime after Clara had left that Audrey witnessed the accident.

Audrey was an only child and lived with her husband Gerald, in the annexe of her parents' farmhouse. Gerald worked side by side with her father, Helier Cabot, on the farm, and one day the couple would take over the farm.

Audrey's mother Shirley always looked after Michael on a Sunday morning giving Audrey the chance to go to church where quite often, she would help with the Sunday school. Shirley enjoyed taking charge of Sunday lunch for the family

That fateful Sunday, as she was leaving the church and was just about to cross the road, she saw the car and almost at the same time she saw Francine running into the road - it was like watching in slow motion as the car screeched to a halt hitting Francine and propelling her little body onto the road. Audrey heard a gut retching scream and looked around to see Chantal running towards her sister. Audrey ran and grabbed the little girl, holding her wriggling body close to her. She wouldn't forget the look on Didier's face as he knelt beside Francine, as she shouted to him, "I've got Chantal I will take her home," he merely nodded in acknowledgment.

The accident and the imagine of Francine little body lying in the road haunted Audrey for many years after the event. Francine was lucky escaping with only a few broken bones, cuts and bruises. Audrey went to visit Francine at the hospital on the days that Angela and Marie couldn't go, but she knew that Didier went every evening. Audrey would read her stories and comfort her, often taking her treats to eat and it wasn't long before she was back home asking Audrey if she would take Michael to play with her or bring her home to play.

Both girls became frequent visitors at Audrey's home. Chantal liked nothing more than learning to cook and Audrey took great joy in teaching her, whereas Michael and Frannie would spend hours playing games together.

Chantal loved to talk about her mother and she would ask Audrey all sorts of questions which Audrey found hard to answer, as she had only known Clara for a few months and would have to come up with some answer to satisfy Chantal curiosity.

Audrey felt sorry that Clara missed her little girl's first day at school and the day Frannie lost her first baby tooth. She wished she had a camera to record all these special moments for Clara, as Audrey felt sure that one day Clara would come back for her babies.

It was following these thoughts that Audrey started to keep a diary, she had never kept one before thinking it was just a waste of time. Her mother had bought her a diary the previous Christmas, so she dug it out of the cupboard and started recording memorable moments. Audrey even managed to obtain a camera and would take photos from time to time. She knew that Marie had taken a photo of Chantal in her new school uniform, so she got a copy of the photo from her and placed it in her diary. When her diary was finished at the end of that year, Audrey started keeping scrapbooks - one for Michael and one for girls. She would stick all sorts of things from photos to pictures they had drawn and birthday cards.

Chantal must have been about six years old when she mentioned that she had received a birthday card and present from her grandma. At first, Audrey thought Chantal meant from Marie, but then she realized it was from Clara's mother. Discreetly, Audrey asked Angela if she had an address for the grandma.

"No, there is never an address. She has been sending Christmas and birthday presents since they have been in Jersey. I presume she doesn't want Didier turning up on their doorstep, demanding Clara's return," said Angela. "Hopefully one day she will want to hear from the girls and send an address."

Audrey was so proud the day Michael and Francine started school, taking photos of them in their school uniform as they walked hand in hand to school with Chantal leading the way, telling them what to expect as any big sister would.

When Chantal told Francine that she should find another girl to sit next to in the classroom, Frannie was horrified "No, no, I am sitting next to Michael! He's my friend - I don't want another friend!" she cried adamantly.

Audrey laughed to herself, feeling sure that things would all change when Frannie started playing with the other girls. But she was wrong. Although Frannie did make other friends, those friends also became Michael's friends. The bond between Michael and Frannie was too strong to be broken.

Audrey's husband, although an understanding man, he would often worry that his wife was too fond of Chantal and Francine. He didn't mind the girls being at their house as they were no problem, always polite and well behaved; however, he was concerned when Francine would often call Audrey 'Mummy', copying Michael. Yet, Audrey always corrected her saying, "I am not your mummy, sweetie, I am Auntie." Audrey loved those girls as though they were her own, but she was sensible enough to know that she was not their mother.

As the years went by, it was Audrey who helped the girls cope with puberty, and when Chantal broke up with a boyfriend when she was fifteen, it was Audrey who helped her through the heartache.

CHAPTER 11

Chantal couldn't quite understand what was wrong with her granny, but she started doing strange things. For instance, one day Auntie Angela was looking everywhere for the sugar bowl and eventually found it in the fridge. Another day she found an open packet of butter in the drawer with the tea towels. Nobody owned up to these occurrences, but Angela suspected it was Marie.

On a different occasion, Marie put the kettle on the AGA and forgot to put any water in it, Angela was furious as it burnt a big hole in the bottom of the kettle and filled the kitchen with acrid smoke! Plus, she had to get an engineer to fix the hotplate on the AGA! That same day not only did Marie put the empty kettle on to boil, but she then left the house and went missing for hours before a neighbour eventually found her wandering in a nearby lane, totally confused.

At mealtimes, if there were a lot of people around the table, Marie became flustered as she tried to join in with the conversation and then appear to forget what she was going to say.

Chantal heard Auntie Angela say to her Papa, "If she asks me once more what day it is, I think I will throttle her!" Papa only laughed at this.

"She is almost seventy-two! Surely, she's entitled to forget a few things! It is seventy-two isn't it? Now I am forgetting!" joked Didier.

"Not only that but she keeps losing her handbag and then when I find it for her - for the umpteenth time - she accuses me of stealing money from her purse! The absurdity of it is that she only ever has a few pound notes in her purse and I've given her those! It's no joking matter, Didier," said his sister.

It was the innocent remark by Francine that made Didier take the matter of his mother more seriously.

"Do you know Papa, that Granny has forgotten my name? She keeps saying to me 'what's your name little girl?' and I have told her over and over that it is Frannie! Then she asks me again!" said Francine in all innocence.

This comment led to Angela and Didier deciding to call the doctor for advice; and he made them an appointment at the hospital for their mother to have a few tests. A week later, they received the distressing news that Marie had the onset of dementia. "There's not much we can do. Unfortunately, you will need to keep an eye on her, and if it becomes too much work for you then we would have to consider a care home. However, at this stage, she is best at home with her family," stated the doctor.

Over the next eighteen months, Marie's condition steadily deteriorated; she wouldn't eat and would gag on the food that Angela tried to spoon-feed her. This resulted in Angela having to give her only soup which she could drink through a straw. However, even this was difficult as sometime Marie would refuse to put the straw in her mouth!

Initially, two district nurses came to the house twice a day to help Angela. In the morning, they would get Marie out of bed, wash and dress her and then every evening they would put her to bed. Marie would spend her days sitting in her chair vacantly looking out of the window. Angela had purchased a commode for her mother to use, but even this was a chore trying getting Marie to use it. When Marie started wetting the bed at night, the nurses suggested incontinence pads for her and these were soon a permanent fixture with Marie eventually becoming totally incontinent. During this time, the nurses would visit three times a day to help change her Marie's pads.

It was sad for Angela and Didier to watch their once strong and hardworking mother reduced to a little old lady, in a world of her own. Marie gradually became weaker and weaker, and as the nurses put her to bed one evening, they told Angela that she should stay with her mother that night. "I am sorry to say, but I don't think she has long in this world," said the nurse.

The nurse was right as Marie died in her sleep that night, with Angela at her side, holding her hand as she took her last breath. Angela cried quietly; the entire family were deeply upset but felt that she was now at peace.

The funeral was held at the local church a week later. The family, including her three grandchildren, walked down the aisle behind the coffin, with friends and neighbours packed inside the church. The burial in the churchyard followed the church service, and Didier hugged his children close as they all watched the coffin lowered into the ground. Didier later wished he hadn't let the girls watch the burial as Francine suffered from nightmares for months after.

Two weeks after Maria's death, a letter arrived for both Angela and Didier requesting them to contact a firm of lawyers regarding their mother's will. To say they were both surprised was an understatement.

"When on earth did, she make a will?" asked Didier.

"I would have thought, why? What did she have to put in a will?" questioned Angela.

When the lawyer revealed the contents of Marie's will, they were both shell-shocked; Marie had a healthy amount of cash in the bank but most surprising of all was that she had purchased two pieces of land attached to Hedley's farm, some years previously.

Hedley hadn't realized that the field he had been renting for years had belonged to his mother-in-law and it now belonged to Angela.

"Will you be charging me rent now?" he jokingly asked his wife.

The second plot now belonged to Didier. It had once housed a small cottage that had been derelict for over three decades. The cash in the bank account was left to Angela and Didier, equally. This inheritance was to change Didier's life.

CHAPTER 12

Didier made arrangements to view the plot he had inherited with a gentleman from the local planning department. It was a large plot of approximately one acre and Didier was eager to know what he could do with the land.

The planning officer - a tall thin, balding man in a grey suit holding a clip board in his left hand and a pen in his right - introduced himself as Mr Le Gresley. He told Didier that according to their records the land had previously belonged to a farmer who had no family when he died. It had taken considerable time for the States of Jersey to discover that there were no heirs before taking possession of the land. Exactly how Marie had managed to buy the land, he was unsure, but she had.

"I want to know what I can do with it. Obviously, my sister will take that field," Didier said, pointing to the field where Hedley's cows were currently grazing. "They will just incorporate it into their farm - but I am no farmer! That's why I have asked you here to advise me on the best course of action," explained Didier.

"There are a few options available - subject to planning consent of course! You must understand that what I suggest would have to be approved by the planning department," said Mr Le Gresley, and he went on to explain to Didier that as there had previously been a dwelling on the plot it would not be classified as agricultural land, and therefore a house ,or houses, could be built.

"How many houses do you think would fit on this plot?" queried Didier.

"On one acre I would say about twelve, maybe a few more depending on the size of each house and how much garden is allocated. You would need to get an architect and discuss this with him." suggested Mr Le Gresley.

"Wow, twelve? Really? Twelve seems an awful lot!" exclaimed Didier.

So, following the advice given to him, Didier contacted an architect recommended by his boss, Laurence. It was several months before plans were drawn up and submitted to the planning department. And unfortunately, six months before permission was granted to build eleven houses, Didier's plans were a bit dashed when he approached the bank for a loan. Unfortunately, his request was refused.

However, Laurence stepped in, saying, "I will lend you the money to build the first two houses on the condition that once they are sold, I get 50% of the profit plus my money back. If you sell them at the price, we discussed you would then have enough profit to pay for the building of the next stage," offered Laurence.

Didier considered this offer and did all the calculations - even building in a contingency sum - the offer was too good to turn down! And four months after planning permission was granted, they had two completed houses and had obtained a buyer for each.

Didier had worked every weekend and evening helping the builders, he even took time off work to help cut costs. And his gamble worked, his 50% profit set him up to build the next eight houses. With money in the bank and seeing the success of the first two houses, the bank agreed to lend him money to go forward. His plan was for the eleventh house to be his own home; t was going to be on the biggest plot and would be a four bedroomed house with plenty of garden.

Didier soon realized that the builders had obviously made a profit working on his houses, and with this in mind, he made the decision to give up his job with Laurence and set up his own building company. This decision would again change his life, as two years later Didier and the girls moved into their brand-new home! It had been a hard two years, juggling both looking after the girls and working every hour he could.

Chantal was mature for her age and been a great help to Didier; since the age of nine, she had come home from school and prepared all the vegetables for their evening meal, and by the time she was eleven she was able to cook an entire meal.

However, Didier didn't want his young daughter to have the responsibility of cooking for the family. He didn't mind now and then but he wanted her to be able to go out to play with her friends and not be stuck in the kitchen cooking. So, one year after setting up his building firm, Didier employed a lady by the name of Ethel Brown.

Ethel was godsend; she came to their home three days a week and did all the cooking, washing and cleaning. Their cottage was spotless after she left at the end of the day, with a tasty meal awaiting the family on the stove and a further meal in the fridge for the following day.

Ethel moved with them to their new house and stayed with the family for ten years until she retired. No one could replace Ethel; the new generation of domestic help didn't want to cook, they were willing to clean and do the occasional ironing but that was about all. So, the ever-organized Chantal set up a rota and the three of them took turns with cooking and the laundry.

Didier's building firm was doing well and he now employed forty men with differing skills. After the success of the initial eleven houses he had built or helped to build, his work had become sort after with 'word of mouth' recommendations.

Didier was happy - after all, he had two beautiful daughters and a lovely big house - what more could he want? Unfortunately, since Clara had left, he had never found a partner with which to share his success. He had met a few women through friends but none that he wanted to become a permanent fixture in his life. He didn't miss female company, as he had his two daughters. He knew he had treated Clara badly, and the memories of those times were always in the back of his mind. He didn't want this situation to happen again, so subconsciously he kept away from relationships.

Chantal reminded Didier of Clara; she was ultra-organized and had superb cooking skills, he presumed she inherited from her mother. But then again, Chantal was a worrier and Didier was forever having to reassure her, especially when there were changes in her life. Didier hoped that, in time, she would grow out of this.

When they first moved home, Audrey had told Didier that Chantal had mentioned to her that she was worried that her mother wouldn't be able to find them if she came looking. I tried to reassure her that if her mother did come, she wouldn't have far to look to find her. After all, she knows where I live and where Angela lives", said Audrey.

Whereas, Francine had always been a shy little girl and although she became more confident as she got older, she was not as outgoing as Chantal. However, she did have a mind of her own and when she decided to do something, there was no stopping her!

Didier was thankful for Audrey who had been a constant presence in all of their lives, and he was especially grateful that the girls went to her for feminine advice, as he always felt a bit embarrassed if they mentioned such things to him. Didier lived in a man's world and his sister was a lot older than him, so other than his mother and his short marriage to Clara, his knowledge of women's affairs was limited.

Didier frequently thought of his youngest daughter, Liliane. She would be in her teens now. Who did she look like? Perhaps her mother or maybe her sisters - would he ever find out? On occasions, he would think about searching for her, but he had no idea where to start such a search.

CHAPTER 13

In 1958, five months before her eleventh birthday Chantal took her eleven-plus examinations at school. She had excelled at primary school. The entire family was in no doubt that she would pass which would enable her to go to the local grammar school. As predicted, she passed with top marks.

The family were so proud seeing her in her new grammar school uniform; head to toe in green with a white shirt and red tie, on her head a green beret with the school badge on the front and with her long dark wavy hair tied up in a ponytail that reached beyond her shoulders. She looked so grown up.

Audrey took a photo for her scrapbook. Her Papa had already gone to work but he had wished her good luck and given her money for the tuck shop. For the first time Chantal didn't have a packed lunch, as the school canteen would provide lunch. This was a first for her; she had visited the canteen when they had all visited the school but was worried that there would be nothing that she liked and would go hungry - not that she was a fussy eater!

Today would begin the next five years of catching the school bus to her new school in town. She was so nervous. There were only three other girls from her primary school that were going to the all-girls' grammar school. The others were going to the secondary modern school.

Chantal was so happy that Lucy, her best friend, was also going to the grammar school with her. The other girl Jackie, although a friend, didn't hang about with them. However, on that first day, they all stuck together. They knew that their teacher had asked for them to all go in the same class, and they did. Their class was 1a, and their teacher was Miss Andrews, a woman in her forties with greying hair. There were twenty-four girls in their class altogether. It was embarrassing to have to stand up that first day and tell the rest of the class their name, and which parish they lived in. Chantal felt herself go very red in the face.

The school was huge with over 400 pupils, and it took some weeks before Chantal was able to find her way around without getting lost. She soon got to know all the girls in her class and then a few more in her year, especially when she joined the netball team. For each subject they had a different teacher and either the teacher came to them, or they went to the teacher for subjects such as science and needlework. In the second year of school, domestic science was introduced as a subject, and for half a day every two weeks, they would go to a cookery school nearby. Chantal would be excited to take home the dish she had cooked for their dinner. Most of the time, Frannie pulled a face and held her nose saying, "I am not eating that!" But her father always ate her creation saying how delicious it was, even when it wasn't.

Chantal found it strange at first being in a school with no boys, but it was more sedate with no boys fighting in the playground. But then again, by the time they reached their third year all the girls appeared obsessed with boys. Some would even hang around outside the boys' school after school had finished for the day.

Chantal, Lucy, and Jackie, at fourteen, started going to the local youth club every Friday night which was run by a Mr and Mrs Geary. Their names were shortened by the children to Mr and Mrs G. It was part of the Young Farmers' Club, and when you reached sixteen you could move up to the older group that met up every Saturday evening. The girls enjoyed going on outings with the youth club such as camping out at weekends, or hiking trips to various parts of the island. They also loved going to the cinema. Initially they went almost every Saturday afternoon, then as they got older, if they didn't go to youth club on a Saturday night, they would go to the cinema and catch the last bus home.

Chantal got her first boyfriend when she was fifteen; his name was Robbie and he went to their youth club. The girls' small clique had now extended from three to ten, with Robbie being one of them. Her relationship with Robbie lasted nine months. They would hold hands everywhere they went and sit in the back row of the cinema, where more kissing took place than the actual watching of the film on show.

Robbie went to the same private school as her cousin John, and they were also in the same year at school. Although John went to their youth club, he was fond of saying he only went because there was nothing else to do, as though it was a bit beneath him. Other than seeing John at family gatherings, she rarely saw him, for which she was grateful as he never had anything nice to say to her or Frannie.

Chantal was heartbroken when Robbie broke off their relationship for no apparent reason other than saying that his mother didn't like him having a girlfriend from the grammar school.

Chantal cried her heart out to Auntie Audrey who tried to pacify her by saying 'There are plenty more fish in the sea!' and 'No boy is worth all these tears!'

Robbie didn't attend their youth club for some months after their break-up which pleased Chantel, as she didn't want to face him. By the time he did return, she had moved on with her life.

The last two years at school were extremely busy; their entire year would be taking their GCE's at sixteen and they were set at least two hours homework each night, and more at the weekend. Two evenings a week after school, Chantal and some of the other girls from her class would go to the boys' grammar school for tuition in physics, and it was here that she met Paul Cosgrove, who was just three months older than her. Paul soon became a permanent fixture in her life and they would often go to each other's houses at weekends to revise for their forthcoming examinations. If Chantal wasn't at Paul's house then she would be with Lucy, helping each other with their homework.

Their first examination was English, and Chantel was the most nervous she had ever been - she was shaking so much that she could barely write her name at the top of the sheet of paper! By the time she sat her last exam, she was much more relaxed - still terrified of the questions, but not so anxious.

Chantal has already decided that she would leave school after her examinations. There was the opportunity to stay a further two years and take GCE 'A' levels, but she felt it would serve no purpose. Not many girls in 1963 went to university. If she decided to go, it would mean that she would have to go to England and she didn't want to leave Papa and Frannie. Chantal wasn't too sure what she wanted to do for a job. Each morning after the examinations had finished and before the end of the term, the school secretary, Miss Long, would come to their classroom and read out the jobs on offer for school leavers. After reading each one out, she would comment 'This will suit Maureen, or Rosemary or Jackie,' then one morning she read one out, but Chantal was only half listening when she heard her name.

"Sorry Miss, can you repeat that one? I didn't hear properly," said an embarrassed Chantal, as she hadn't been listening at all.

"It was for a job at Police Headquarters. They are looking for a trainee administrator. Come and see me at break and I will give you the details and application form," said Miss Long.

Chantal took all the paperwork home for her father to look at. Before heading home, she stopped off at Audrey's and showed her the details and asked what she thought. Audrey had been the mother that her father could not be and ever since she could remember, it was Audrey's advice she had sought.

Chantal hardly remembered her mother, and it was only the photo on her bedside table that reminded her of what her mother looked like. When she was about eight, she told Audrey that she kept forgetting what her Mama looked like, the next day her father had given her a framed picture of her mother. The photo had stayed by her bed ever since, even when they moved into their new house.

"This could be a good job, Chantal; it even says that they will give you time off to go to a day-release class to learning typing and shorthand. See what your father says, but I would apply if I were you," suggested Audrey. Chantal stayed for a cup of tea with Audrey and waited for Frannie so they could walk home together. Frannie was now at secondary school with Chantal, but chose to take different bus home so she could be with Michael.

The interview for the administration job was an ordeal that Chantal hoped she would never have to experience again. It had poured down with rain two minutes before she arrived at the building where the interview was held, so she had looked like a drowned rat as she sat in front of the three men behind a desk. When Audrey later asked what questions they asked her, she couldn't say as she couldn't remember a word the men said, never mind her answers!

Nevertheless, a week later, a letter arrived offering Chantal the job. She was elated running down the road to tell Audrey the good news. Her father was also happy for her.

"I must work out...," said her Papa taking out a piece of paper and pen from the kitchen drawer.

"What? What must you work out, Papa?" queried a perplexed Chantal.

"How much board you are going to pay me!" joked her father.

"Very funny, Papa!" she replied, returning his smile.

It was sad leaving school. Chantal had purchased an autograph book and got all her classmates and teachers to sign; some merely signed their names whereas others drew little pictures. She kept the book as a remembrance of her school years.

So, at just sixteen years old she started work as an office junior, and spent two years making coffee for everyone in the office every morning and tea each afternoon. This minor job that gave her a good grounding, as she had to learn everyone's name in the office quickly and it taught her good communication skills. She was thankful that after two years, a new junior was recruited to take over her tea-making duty.

Once a week for the first six months Chantal had the afternoon off to go to secretarial school. She would start at lunchtime and finish at eight o'clock in the evening, and she was taught typing, shorthand, and office organization. During her lunchtimes at work, she would practice her typing proficiency, and whilst at home, she rounded up anybody that was available to practice her shorthand skills. At the end of the six months, she gained a distinction certificate.

Paul, her boyfriend since the age of fifteen, had left school and been articled by a firm of chartered accountants. They would meet any lunchtime they could as his weekends and evening, especially leading up to crucial examinations would be spent studying. Although they would meet every Saturday night when they would either go dancing or see the latest film at the cinema. They both had a passion for tennis and could often be found at the local tennis club at weekends, playing doubles with their friends. Neither of them was of a professional level, they just enjoyed the game.

By the summer of 1971, Paul was a fully qualified accountant, and Chantal been promoted to deputy manager of the administration office at Police Headquarters. The couple had been engaged for two years and were planning their wedding that was to take place the following Easter. They were looking forward to their own home and eventually children.

Chantal still frequently thought of her mother, but had come to terms with the fact that she may never see her again. She had attempted to find an address for her grandparents, but with so few facts to go on she had hit a brick wall. She wanted to ask her father for information but felt it disrespectful given the sacrifices he had made for both her and Francine. So, with wedding plans in full flow, she had put her search to one side, but her dream would be to have her mother at the ceremony.

CHAPTER 14

Didier's business had gone from strength to strength. He had lost count of the number of houses he had built and the renovations undertaken, there had been so many.

In 1969 when Chantal and Paul had announced their engagement, he was delighted. Paul was a fine young man and would make the perfect husband for his headstrong eldest daughter.

Over the years Chantal had become Didier's rock, from an early age she had ensured that Francine got out of bed and dressed ready to go to school on time, then from her early teens she had taken charge of the house and with the assistance of Ethel, their daily help, and she kept the house clean and tidy. When Ethel retired it was Chantal that vetted her replacement, with a little help from Audrey.

Didier was already planning Chantal and Paul's wedding present, which would be a new house. They had purchased the plot of land and he was going to build it; there had already been a lot of discussion on the layout, and now all they need was the money to build it! This was going to be Didier's present to them.

"No, Papa we will pay for it ourselves," declared Chantal. "We've got an appointment with the bank to get a mortgage. We do want you to build it, but we will pay for it ourselves," said Chantal.

However, Didier had other ideas! What did he work for if it wasn't to give his girls all that they wanted? He didn't need the money that was accumulating in the bank, he had everything he needed.

He was preparing himself for this time next year when he would be living by himself with his faithful Dollie, his 12-year-old cocker spaniel. He would miss the companionship of his daughters, even when their music was blasting out around the house. He never complained; he was just pleased that they were home. The two girls argued like mad at times but they were best of friends, and any argument soon forgotten. Yes, there had been times when he had to reprimand them, especially in their mid-teens when they arrived home later than expected or the times he couldn't quite come to terms with the shortness of their skirts!

Didier had been known to say, 'Surely you are not going out in that - I can almost see your underwear!' with the response '*Oh! Papa, you need to move with the times; all the girls wear miniskirts!*' What could he say? What would their mother say if she came back now and asked him why he had let them go out half-dressed? Sadly, that was something that wasn't going to happen.

Francine had announced shortly after Chantal's announcement, that she too was going to be getting married. Her planned wedding was to take place three months after Chantal, so it was going to be an expensive year for Didier!

CHAPTER 15

Francine's memories of her early childhood where virtually non-existent; she didn't remember her mother other whatsoever and therefore had no feelings for her. The nearest person she had to a mother was Auntie Audrey. All her life she had wanted Audrey to be her mother; she remembered one time when she had mistakenly called her mummy and Audrey had gently reminded her that she was not her mother. She remembered thinking in her young mind, that Michael called her mummy, so why couldn't she? Well now Audrey was going to be her mother-in-law, which was the next best thing in Fran's mind. Although she now called Audrey by her Christian name, having dropped the 'Auntie' some time ago, calling her mum didn't seem quite right! Everybody shortened her own name to Frannie, which she preferred to her full name, and it wasn't until she was about fifteen that she became Fran.

Fran didn't remember the accident - the only reminder she had was the scar on her forehead running from just above her eyebrow to her hairline. She vaguely remembered starting school with Michael and insisting that she next to him in class - she was the only girl in the class sitting next to a boy! Fran did eventually make some girlfriends; there was Lynne, Pamela and Sandra, but none of these girls were as close to her as Michael. She couldn't remember a time without Michael. Fran felt deflated when at eleven they moved to secondary school. Everyone else was excited to be moving to a new school, but Fran hated the idea of being separated from Michael even though it was only during school hours. However, Fran soon settled into her new school and enjoyed the sole company of girls, sitting next to Sandra who soon became her best friend.

Didier always came on his own to parents' evening or open days at school, and it was on these occasions that other girls would ask questions about her mother. Fran would always try and avoid the question or change the subject, as she didn't know what to say. She wanted to say she was dead, but that didn't feel right as Clara wasn't dead, they just didn't know where she was, or even who she was.

From the age of fourteen, Fran and Michael started attending youth club and by this time Michael was known to everyone, with the exception of his parents, as Mike. They both had a lot of friends and took part in all the sporting activities available. At weekends she would find herself cheering Mike on from the sidelines of the football pitch, or he would be trying to look interested as she played netball, saying to her jokingly 'It's just not football.' They both joined the St. John's Ambulance Brigade, as they could attend together, unlike some of the other organizations, which were purely for either boys or girls.

It was shortly after Fran's fifteenth birthday that their relationship changed. They were walking home from youth club one Friday night when it started to thunder. Fran was terrified of thunder and had grabbed hold of Michael in fright, and it was as he held her to him and she looked up at his face that he placed his lips on hers and they kissed for the very first time. Her heart was beating at what seemed like a million beats an hour and the butterflies in her stomach rapidly flapping their wings. Fran fell in love with him instantly, but then she had always loved him, just now in a different way.

The next day they independently told their families and were surprised by the responses.

"I thought you were going to tell me something new," responded Chantal.

"About time!" said her Papa.

Audrey laughed and said, "I thought you two would never get around to it!"

Mike attended the secondary modern school and was due to leave when he was fifteen, his career was already mapped out for him. He was born to be a farmer, just like his father and was to join his father on the farm, as he already helped his father as much as he could. He liked nothing more than being out in the fresh air attending to the crops and their animals.

Whereas Fran wanted to become a nurse. Audrey had been a nurse before Michael had been born, and it was perhaps her influence that had put the idea in Fran's head. Then once she had joined the St. John's Ambulance Brigade, it had re-affirmed her decision. Fran knew that she had to get good examination results, especially in science and biology, to enable her to commence training at the local hospital when she left school.

By the age of twenty, Fran was a State Registered Nurse working various shifts, and some weeks she hardly saw Mike. When she worked nights, she would have dinner at the farm with him and the family, before going off to work, and when she was on day shift, they would spend their evenings together. Fran moved around the hospital to work on different wards and it was while working on the maternity ward that she fell in love with the idea of being a midwife. The maternity unit was a specialist area, so as soon as she was able, she began studying for her midwifery qualification.

Both families were delighted when on Fran's twenty-first birthday, the couple announced their engagement; they were planning to marry in the summer of 1972.

Chantal plans were to marry the same year as Fran, following two years of engagement.

"We could make it a double wedding," suggested Chantal, before adding "Mama and Papa had a double wedding - we could do the same."

"I think that is a good reason not to have a double wedding, so thank you, but I want my own wedding! Sorry, I don't want to be mean but…you do understand, don't you?" asked Fran.

"Of course, it was a stupid idea anyway. I want to be the centre of attention on my wedding day, not share it with you!" joked Chantal. Fran never knew if Chantal was serious or not.

Over the years Chantal would frequently mention their mother, she had a photograph on her bedside table of their parents on their wedding day, which was yellowing with age. Fran knew that Chantal had tried to find an address for their grandparents in England; each birthday she would be disappointed when she received a card with no address on the back of the envelope. Fran had no such longing to see her mother! In her mind, her mother had abandoned them and not once bothered to contact them to find out if they were dead or alive. If she didn't care, why should she?

The day of her final midwifery exam when she met Chantal by chance at the bus station, was to change the dynamics of her family forever.

Fran hadn't initially noticed the girl getting out of the taxi. It was only when Chantal gasped, 'Mama!' that Fran followed Chantal's eyes to see where she was looking. She saw the girl in her father's arms, thinking to herself 'Who is that?' but within seconds Chantal was almost running towards her father. Fran couldn't quite grasp what was going on, as they were all hugging and crying - even her!

CHAPTER 16

Didier couldn't quite believe that he had all three daughters in his house. They were all sat around the dining table; Chantal was firing question after question at Lilly and Fran sitting quietly, hardly saying anything.

"We'll make some dinner. Come on Fran, come and help me," said Didier grabbing Fran's hand and leading her to the kitchen.

"What's the matter, lovey? You're quiet, are you not happy to see your sister?" questioned Didier.

"I'm not sure Papa. I don't know her Papa and it's hard to take it all in! To me she is just a name that you and Chantal have mentioned from time to time, whereas to you, she is a real person because you remember her but I don't!" cried Fran.

Didier took her in his arms and let her cry.

"Try to look at it from her point of view, she has two sisters that she has never seen and also me, her father, whom she has never seen. She has come searching for us Fran, all the way from America, judging by her accent! So, it's the same for her as it is for you," explained Papa.

"It's hard though, Papa. I feel like my life has suddenly changed," replied Fran.

Fran and Didier made the dinner and took it through to the dining room.

Chantal was crying and as soon as they sat down, Chantal said: "Tell Papa and Fran what you have just told me, Lilly."

Lilly explained that she had just told Chantal that she only found out three days ago that she had two sisters.

"What do you mean?" asked her father and Fran, almost simultaneously.

"Up until three months ago I thought I had been born in America - North Carolina in fact - and that my Mama, obviously was my mother but that Carl, my Dad was my father. Then I asked for my birth certificate to get a passport and to my astonishment, I find out that I am not who I thought I was! In fact, I found out that I am Liliane Renard - born in France! - and that my father was a man called Didier Jean Renard! Well, you can imagine my shock! I was so angry at my mother; I have hardly spoken to her since! But don't get me wrong, I do love Mama."

Lilly stopped speaking for a moment, suddenly realizing that all her life she had called her mother 'Mama' and not 'Mom' like her brothers. She had never thought about it before, but of course it was the French version that she must have learned before arriving in America.

"Sorry, I got lost in thought for a second," Lilly explained before continuing. " Anyway, I needed a passport to go to Italy - I went on an archeological dig with my university friends. When the dig finished, we thought we would all go to Paris before going home, to do a bit of sightseeing while we were in Europe.

"Then, in Paris, I found myself in front of a tourist bureau and I asked where this place was, the one where I had been born - just out of curiosity - and there it was just a train ride away! Anyway, I thought while I was so close I might as well have a look.

"I must admit on the train to Plérin I started to regret my decision, suddenly finding myself in the middle of France on my own. I arrived in this little village a bit lost and not sure what to do, when I saw the church and thought that there must surely be someone there that would speak English, and I could ask about you - Papa that is! At this point, I didn't know about you two," said Lilly, looking at her sisters.

"As I approached the church a priest came out and I asked him if he spoke English, but he just pointed to a bar indicating they spoke English. So, I went across to the bar and as I entered the old man behind the bar stared at me and shouted out a name. Then a few seconds later, an old lady appeared."

"Auntie Jeanne! Oh, I missed Auntie Jeanne so much when we left France!" interrupted Chantal, "How is she? But she is not old?"

"It was over twenty years ago since you saw her Chantal, she is bound to be older - she must be over seventy!" explained Didier.

"Oh yes, I was forgetting! I suppose you remember people as they were the last time you saw them. Sorry Lilly, carry on," said Chantal.

"Jeanne was well, and they are just about to retire and move to live with their daughter. I have taken some photos. My brother gave me a camera before I left, so I have loads of photos."

"Whoa! Whoa, stop!" shouted Chantal. "Brother? You have a brother? An older brother?"

"No, younger - two in fact! Jeffrey, and Timothy who is the youngest," replied Lilly innocently.

"You mean to say we have two brothers? Two brothers? I can't take this in," said Chantal, turning to her father. "Papa…!"

Didier stood up and hugged his crying daughter.

"She abandoned us Papa and had a new family! Did she even think of us for one second? All the years I've wasted longing for her to come back," sobbed Chantal.

"I'm sorry Chantal, I didn't mean to upset you. I can't answer for our mother, but it is hard for me to take all this in as well. The thing is, we have all lost out and what I can't understand is that Mama is a good loving mother, and it's difficult for me to equate that your mother and my mother are the same person," said Lilly. "Shall I carry on?"

"Yes, carry on. I want to hear more," replied Fran.

"Well, Jeanne explained who she was and took me into the back room. She really is a lovely lady and insisted I stay with them for the night, and it was while she was out of the room that I noticed the photos on the mantelpiece. There was one of three little girls, so when she came back in the room I asked if they were her grandchildren and to my astonishment, she told me that the photo was of me and my sisters! Sisters I didn't know I had - to say I was surprised was an understatement! Like you just now Chantal, when I mentioned brothers, you can now understand how I felt when she said sisters!" declared Lilly.

"Oh! My goodness," said Fran, "Now I understand! I am so sorry I was so cold with you Lilly! This is such an awful situation for us all," said Fran standing up and taking Lilly in arms and hugging her, repeating, "Now I understand!"

CHAPTER 17

Lilly had only planned on staying a few days, not realizing the impact of meeting her other family would have on them all. Her Papa had insisted that she stay with them, so the following day she went to the hotel where she had left her luggage and explained her change of plans.

Chantal had taken Lilly's several rolls of film to get developed, as they all wanted to see her photos and luckily enough there were photos of her mother from her graduation on the first roll.

Over the next few days, they all exchanged their life stories, crying and laughing over the stories they each had to tell.

Lilly told them about the time she played the narrator in the Wizard of Oz at primary school and being a substitute for Dorothy. How she so longed for the girl set to play Dorothy to suffer some sort of accident, and how everyone had to endure her awful singing. Whilst Chantal told her of a similar story of her time playing Cinderella and actually being sick resulting in her understudy having to take over the role.

Her Papa would sit quietly listening, as he wasn't too sure what to add. He had spent some time with Lilly on her own whilst the girls were at work and he had tried to explain why her mother had left him, but it was a difficult story. How do you tell someone the truth that even you, yourself, are appalled at your own behavior?

Lilly met Michael and Paul and liked them both instantly, they were funny and teased her over her American accent just like brothers, reminding her of Jeff and Tim. How different things would have been if they had been brought up together.

Fran took Lilly to meet Audrey. It was strange meeting all these people that remembered her as a baby, but she did not know of them. Audrey asked after her mother and showed her one of the scrapbooks she had been keeping over the years.

"Will you take some of these back with you? I started to keep them with your mother in mind, as I wanted her to know how her two babies had developed over the years. I've got six altogether, and I have written her this letter as well," said Audrey handing over both the scrapbooks and letter.

Lilly looked through the first scrapbook in the privacy of her bedroom. For her, it was heartbreaking to see all the moments that her mother missed during their growing up. Lilly knew she had to go back home, as she was due to start her teacher training course at the beginning of October. She was torn between wanting to stay on the one hand and wanting to get home to see her other family, on the other.

Lilly had sent her mother a brief telegram to say she was going to Jersey and then written her a long letter. She hadn't expected a response as by the time the letter arrived, she would be on her way home, not giving her mother a chance to reply.

Lilly also met her Auntie Angela, her husband Hedley and cousin John. It was so strange having all these relatives; Angela asked her lots of questions about her mother, where she lived and her family. She wasn't too sure if it was out of interest or if she was just being polite.

Her Papa also asked her all sorts of questions too, about her proposed plans to return home, where she would fly from and where to. Initially, she thought this was a bit bizarre as to why he needed such in-depth details, then she overheard him asked her sisters what holidays they had left to take from work.

"Why, Papa?" asked Fran, "You have never taken an interest before, what are you up to?"

"I was wondering if you might like to go and visit your mother?" he responded. "Lilly is planning to go back home in just under two weeks and you could both go with her. I have phoned the travel agents and got all the information."

"I can't afford it, Papa, not with the wedding next year. I am saving hard for that plus I am not sure I can get time off at such short notice," said Fran.

"Same here, Papa! I am saving hard for my wedding too, although I could get the time off, that would not be a problem for me," said Chantal.

"I'll pay for everything! You don't need to dip into your wedding funds, it would be my treat! Anyway, think about it, but be quick, we don't have long to book everything."

Lilly was ecstatic when the very next day, Fran announced, "Guess what Lilly?"

"What?" she asked.

"Chantal and I are coming home with you!"

The next few days were mad with excitement as they planned their trip. However, Lilly was concerned. What if her Mother didn't want to see them? what about her Dad? What would he think? Did he even know? Lilly knew it would take too long to write; she could send a telegram, but that would be restricting. So, the only alternative was to telephone, but what was the time difference? Trying to calculate it in her head - five hours, it must be five hours behind. All these thoughts kept her awake nearly all night.

Lilly estimated that if she phoned at lunchtime, then her mother would just be getting breakfast ready at home. She was on tenterhooks waiting for noon to arrive. Luckily, she was alone in the house as everyone was at work, her Papa apologizing for leaving her on her own but he had to go to a job.

Promptly at twelve Lilly picked up the phone and dialed the number for international calls; her mother answered on the third ring.

"Mama, it's me, Lilly."

"Oh! Lilly, I have been so worried about you, how are you? Where are you? I got your postcards from Italy, but they didn't say much!"

"I am fine Mama, and will be home at the end of next week," said Lilly. There was a bit of an echo on the line, making it a difficult conversation.

"Where are you?" asked her mother anxiously.

"I am in Jersey, didn't you get my telegram?"

Clara felt as though an express train had whooshed through her body and she fell onto the chair by the phone, as Lilly explained that her sisters were coming with her. Clara thought she was going to faint, memories were flying through her mind like a movie being played at double speed. She could barely hear Lilly through the fog in her ears and tears were streaming down her face- her babies were coming home!

"It's going to be okay. Mama." said Lilly, finishing the call.

Lilly was so concerned with her mother's reaction that she immediately phoned Auntie Niamph. Niamph was her mother's best friend, and Lilly couldn't remember a time when Niamph had not been part of her life and her confidante.

"Lilly, lovely to hear from you! Are you home? Your mother has been really worried about you! Lilly, can you hear me?"

"Yes sorry, I can hear you, Niamph! I have just spoken to Mama. Can you go around and make sure she is okay?" asked Lilly.

"Why? What has happened? Are you alright?" questioned Niamph, with concern.

"Yes, I am fine and will be back soon, but Mama has had a bit of a shock! And Niamph, I wanted to ask you about—" The phone went dead.

Lilly sat down her thoughts going to the photos she had taken, one in particular had unnerved her. In the background of a photo she had taken of Jenny showing off an artifact she had dug up, stood Millie. Millie appeared to be staring straight at the camera, but the girl looking down the lens was Auntie Niamph!

PART TWO
NIAMPH'S STORY

CHAPTER 18

"Mommy, Mommy, tell us the story of Bernadette!" squealed Niamph's twin sons, Bradley and Scott, as they jumped up and down on their beds.

"Get into bed, and I'll tell you a short story, as it is way past bedtime and you have school in the morning," said Niamph.

Niamph Hartley struggled to find a new story to tell the boys about their big sister. Over the years she had made up numerous tales, but how could you tell two little boys with no understanding that you gave their sister away to complete strangers?

Niamph had been born in 1926 into a staunch Irish farming family in rural County Westmeath in Ireland, and was one of seven children. Her family were hardworking and cash poor. Her father, Shaun Flynn Senior, and brothers all worked on the farm making just enough money to clothe the family. Although there was no money, the family were self-sufficient, growing all the vegetables they could possibly need and anything left over was taken to the farmers' market and sold. They raised cows, pigs and chickens, plus goats and sheep to keep the weeds down.

Every Saturday her mother, Kathleen, would load the cart with anything surplus to their needs to sell at the market. The summer months were better than the winter months when there would always be more eggs than they required. They occasionally sold milk but more often than not, her mother would churn the milk to produce butter, which was always a good seller. The family had an old nag - as her father described their little horse - and he would be hitched up to the cart that her mother, together with one of the girls, would drive to the market.

Kathleen was a resourceful woman and with the money she made at the market, selling her wares, she would buy tea, flour, soap and at times, yards of fabric to make clothes. There was also a clothes stall at the market - some of the clothes were second-hand - and she would try to get to this stall early to try and pick up a bargain.

Niamph's two eldest brothers, Shaun Junior and Killian, officially left school at aged fourteen to work on the farm. However, before leaving school and during busy times on the farm, the boys had been kept home to help their father, who could ill afford to pay outside labour. Colin, her next brother in age to her, had also left school at fourteen, but he had taken an apprenticeship with a local garage which although the wage was a pittance, at least it brought a bit of cash into the family finances. Niamph's eldest sister Nula was the first girl to leave school and had wanted to get a job, but their mother needed her to stay home and help her, especially with the youngest in the family, Seamus.

Seamus had been born with Down Syndrome when Nula was six. Niamph had been four and their youngest sister Megan was two. From the day Seamus was born, their mother changed; she had never been the type of mother to cuddle her children, but she would kiss them goodnight and make sure they were well fed and clean. But from the day she gave birth to a son with mongolism, she became cold and distant. She would shout and reprimand her children constantly for the slightest misdemeanor. It was as though they were to blame for Seamus' condition.

Niamph and Megan loved Seamus; they would play with him and help him with the simple tasks that he initially found difficult and in return, he would give them all the love, hugs and kisses that their mother and father failed to give them.

Kathleen had a baby every two years since she had married and Seamus's birth had been very difficult as she had been confined to bed for six weeks after the birth. Following his birth, the hospital had carried out a hysterectomy - 'Thankfully!' Niamph had heard her mother once say to another market stallholder – which left her unable to have any more children.

The girls, even at such a young age, were expected to help their mother around the house, and at times help on the farm too. Most of the time it was fun for Niamph and Megan collecting eggs, feeding the chickens, churning the butter, but neither liked sweeping out the cowshed with a broom bigger than themselves or feeding the smelly pigs!

They all went to the local village school that was closely linked to the Catholic church, and the priest - Father Patrick - would often come to the farm and berate her mother for not sending the boys to school.

Shaun married Kathleen, his childhood sweetheart, in 1916. He had avoided serving in the Great War due to a broken ankle that had never healed properly and which left him with a severe limp. The newlyweds moved into the Flynn farmhouse, and Kathleen took over the running of the house from Shaun's elderly mother, his father having died some years earlier.

Niamph doted on her elderly grandmother, who taught her to play the piano and would sit with her and listen to her read, her own mother being too busy to take any interest in their schoolwork. Nula hated that their grandmother favoured Niamph over all her other grandchildren and would often make nasty comments and call her 'Granny's little pet'. Their grandmother like nothing better than getting the family all together for a singsong around the piano, but these gatherings were always boycotted by Nula, with her saying "I'm not getting involved in singing stupid songs around the stupid piano!" and would storm off to bed. Their grandmother sadly died when Niamph was eight years old and she missed her desperately.

Shaun Senior had been an only child. His arrival came as a complete surprise to his mother as she was forty-two and been married for twenty-five years without any sign of a child.

At the outbreak of World War Two, Shaun Junior joined the Irish Home Defence so that he could continue to help his father on the farm and at the same time help defend Ireland. However, by early 1942, all three boys had signed up to join the British Army and were posted abroad. Shaun struggled during these years, relying heavily on the three girls to help him.

Niamph was the only one in the family that loved learning and hated to miss a day at school. She would ask for extra homework and borrow books from the library that she would quite often read to Seamus. Instead of leaving school at fourteen the priest had got her a scholarship to high school, much to the annoyance of her father who wanted her to go to work to help the family finances. He also hated the idea of receiving charity from the church. The priests in Ireland at that time were like God and woe betide anyone not heeding their advice, so when Father Patrick arranged for Niamph to go to high school Shaun just agreed without an argument, but would often moan to Kathleen, "What use is an education to a girl? The only thing they good for is marriage and having babies."

Father Patrick helped with the purchase of a uniform and all the equipment that Niamph needed for high school. Niamph kept her uniform in pristine condition, washing and ironing it herself and hanging it behind the door of the bedroom she shared with Nula and Megan. Megan being younger, admired Niamph's uniform - she didn't want one herself though, as she hated going to school and the thought of going to another school at fourteen horrified her! But Nula was jealous, not of her going to high school but that Niamph was again getting special attention. She would deliberately bang the bedroom door which would result in Niamph's uniform falling to the floor, or she would make sarcastic comments like, "Little Miss Perfect is too special to get her hands dirty!" if she saw her washing her hands after doing a job on the farm. Or often she would remark, "Little Miss Perfect can't do any jobs today, she has *homework* to do!" |Nula would take any chance she got to make Niamph's life difficult, even though Niamph always did her fair share of the chores.

In 1945 when the boys returned unscathed from the war, Nula married a boy she met at church and was only too pleased to move to a village not far from Dublin, to live near his parents. "The further I can get away from this family, the better!" she announced on the day she left home. Over the next two years, Nula had two children of her own.

By 1947 the three elder brothers had married. Shaun Junior had moved his wife into the farm and Killian had rented a cottage nearby with his wife, as there was very little available space at the farm. Colin had taken over the garage in the village, where he had started his apprenticeship on leaving school, and he had married the owner's daughter on his return from the war. During the war, Colin had seen very little fighting as he had been seconded to the servicing and fixing of the army's artillery vehicles.

Megan at fourteen, worked on the farm until the end of the war. When her brothers returned home, she couldn't wait to get away, and on the days, she managed to get off work she would go to the nearby villages and towns, going from shop to shop asking for work. She wanted to do something better than work on the farm and she eventually managed to get a job as a shop assistant at a dress shop in the next town, renting a room with the owner of the shop.

Niamph, however, continued at high school until eighteen. She achieved excellent grades in all her examinations and when the time came for her to leave school, a natural progression was for her to become a teacher. Father Patrick arranged a post for her at a local primary school, initially as a teaching assistant. Niamph loved teaching the little ones to read and write, and her father let her keep a small amount of her wage to herself. Megan would try to persuade her to leave home, but Niamph couldn't bear to leave Seamus on his own with their parents, and brothers. Although now a strapping lad of eighteen, nobody but Niamph had time for Seamus, even though he did his fair share of work on the farm, albeit at a slower pace than his brothers.

CHAPTER 19

After almost four years at the school a new headmaster, Liam Ryan, was appointed, He appeared to take a lot of interest in Niamph and soon promoted her to be a proper teacher rather than an assistant. The promotion came with an increased wage which delighted Niamph, as she was able to buy clothes she couldn't previously afford.

Niamph was now a young lady of almost twenty-two and she had never had a boyfriend as such - she had boys who were friends, but nothing more than that. So, when Liam Ryan started paying her attention she was flattered and it excited her a bit that someone was taking notice of her. She bought herself a lovely new outfit at the shop where Megan worked and when she wore it to school the following week, Liam complimented her.

"That's a smart new outfit you have on today, Miss Flynn. It shows off your figure beautifully!" he said, winking as he looked her up and down. A week later he asked to see her after school in his office.

Arriving at his office, Liam offered Niamph a cup of tea. "Now, Miss Flynn, I just wanted to make sure you were settling into your class?"

"Yes, thank you. They are such good children and it's a pleasure to teach them," said Niamph.

Liam came around his desk and stood behind her, putting his hand on her shoulder, "I would like you to think about putting on a school play for the end of term," he said, "Perhaps, we could go for a drink after work on Friday to discuss it?"

"I would love to do that! I have a lot of ideas," replied Niamph innocently.

Liam waited her for after school on Friday and drove her to a small hotel some distance from the school. They sat in the corner of the saloon bar and Niamph told him all about her idea for a musical where the children could sing and dance. She was so engrossed in telling him of her idea that she didn't realize at first that he had placed his hand on her knee. Feeling shaken, Niamph excused herself and when to the ladies' room. When she returned, she quickly finished her drink and said she had to get home.

As Liam drove her home, he said, "Your idea is brilliant and I can't wait to see the show!"

"You mean I can go ahead and arrange it?" asked Niamph.

"Indeed, I do Niamph! You don't mind me calling you Niamph, do you?" he said.

"Thank you. No, of course I don't," she said.

"You must call me Liam," he said, placing his hand on her knee again.

Niamph asked him to drop her off at the end of her lane as she didn't want her father seeing the car, but before she could get out of the car he leaned over and kissed her on the cheek, saying "See you Monday!"

It became a regular occurrence for Liam to invite Niamph to his office on the pretext of discussing the show, with the compliments become more suggestive. On one occasion, when he grabbed hold of her bottom, Niamph laughingly said with embarrassment, "Liam, you mustn't do that!"

"And why not?" he asked, "I like a well-rounded woman!"

One day Liam asked Niamph to help him after school with some marking and to prepare end of term reports. They sat side by side at a desk. Niamph knew Liam was married, having met his wife when he first joined the school, and also knew that he had two children at boarding school. Niamph had taken an instant dislike to his wife, who she found a bit snooty - she appeared to look down her nose at all of the school staff as though it was below her to speak to them.

The gossip in the staff room was that Liam had been dismissed from his previous role as the headmaster of a private school in Dublin. Although the other teachers speculated as to why he had been dismissed - with the favourite being that he seduced a female member of staff - nobody knew for certain. Niamph tried to take no notice of the gossip as she didn't want to believe that he was nothing more than sincere with his comments.

On another occasion after staying late at school, Liam said "My wife and I lead separate lives you know Niamph. So, if I were to kiss you, we wouldn't be hurting anyone," putting his arm around her and drawing him to her. He kissed her, forcing his tongue into her mouth. Niamph had never been kissed before and found she quite liked it - it gave her a tingle in her stomach. She wasn't sure what to do when he started caressing her breasts over her clothing.

"I should be going now it's getting late," she said, with embarrassment.

"Let me drive you," Liam offered. Niamph realized afterwards that she should have said no as he drove her to a quiet lane and kissed her some more, undoing the buttons of her blouse and groaning as he felt her breasts. When he then started to put his hand up her skirt, Niamph quickly said "No!" and asked to be taken home.

As time went on and Liam kept telling her how attractive she was and how she was the sort of woman he should have married, their relationship progressed from just touching to making love in the back of his car. He made her feel special, and he told her he loved her.

Towards the end of one week just before half term, Liam told Niamph that his wife was going to take the boys to see their grandparents the following week and invited her to his house. Telling her parents that she was going on a course for school, they spent five glorious days together - at least this was how Niamph saw it! They drove out to dinner each evening after spending most of the day in bed. Niamph was in heaven, especially when he said he was going to leave his wife and marry her.

Their affair continued for some considerable time before the inevitable happened.

CHAPTER 20

When Niamph missed her monthlies twice, she stupidly made excuses to herself and tried to ignore the signs, but when she missed her third consecutive period, she eventually faced up to the fact that she was pregnant and didn't know what to do.

After school she went to meet Liam saying she needed to speak to him urgently. She convinced herself that this would be the point that he would actually leave his wife and take care of her and eventually marry her. But when she told him the news, he turned on her.

"You stupid cow! Get out of my office!" he shouted. Niamph ran out sobbing and made her way home in a state of shock, thinking to herself that perhaps Liam was just shocked and that tomorrow he would say he was sorry for treating like he did! She felt sick to her stomach, trying to think about what she could do.

Dinner was on the table when she arrived home. She felt too upset to eat but knew her father would be angry if she wasted the meal placed in front of her. She struggled with each mouthful, then helped her mother clear the table and wash the dishes. Her mother kept looking at her and Niamph suspected that she must have guessed something was not quite right. But all she said was, "You better sort that out young lady, and quickly!"

Niamph didn't want to go to school the following day but she did. Halfway through the morning she was summoned to Liam's office. Niamph was elated thinking Liam had realized his mistake and was going to say how sorry he was, but when she arrived at his office, two members of the school governing board confronted her.

"We understand you are pregnant, Miss Flynn. Unfortunately, we will have to dismiss you as we couldn't possibly have an unmarried mother teaching at the school. I'm sure you will appreciate that it would not set a good example for the children. Please collect all your personal possessions and leave. You will be paid until the end of the month." Niamph was so stunned that she didn't say one word in response.

Over the next couple of days, Niamph tried speaking to Liam - even sending him a letter - but he totally ignored her. She even thought of going to see his wife but quickly rejected the idea, 'Why cause misery to someone else?' she thought.

Over dinner, Kathleen announced to her father, "Our precious daughter is pregnant!"

"Which one?" he asked innocently.

"There is only one sitting at our table!" stated her Mother. Her father looked up from his meal and stared directly at Niamph, not quite believing what his wife was saying.

"You're pregnant?" he asked.

"Sorry, Da!" she said, looking down in shame.

"And is he going to do the right thing and marry you?" he asked.

"He's already married, Da!" said Niamph still looking down, embarrassed at having to tell her father.

"Get out! Get out of my house! I won't have any bastards in my house! Get out now, you are a disgrace to this family!" he shouted at her.

Niamph ran upstairs in tears and packed her few meagre possessions in a carpetbag and left. She walked down the lane leading from her home towards the nearest village; it was pitch black but she felt so distraught she couldn't even cry. After walking for about a mile reality hit her, she had no idea what to do or where to go! When she arrived in the village and saw a bus approaching, she decided to catch the bus to Ballymore where Megan lived.

It was late when Niamph arrived at the shop where Megan lived and worked. She felt guilty as she knocked on the side door which led to the living accommodation above the shop. Eventually after knocking for some time, Megan's employer answered the door, "I am so sorry to knock so late, but please can I speak to Megan?" asked Niamph politely.

"And who are you, young lady?" asked the woman.

"I'm Megan sister, Niamph," she replied.

"Come on in, I know she is not asleep as her light is still on," said the woman beckoning Niamph to follow her up the stairs. The woman knocked on Megan's door, "Come in!" Niamph heard Megan say. She opened the door "You have a visitor," turning towards Niamph, the woman said, "I will leave you with your sister" as she turned and left.

"Niamph, how lovely to see you!" said Megan rushing over to Niamph and hugging her. It was as though the floodgates opened as Niamph fell into her arms and sobbed her heart out.

"Niamph, whatever is the matter? You're shaking, are you sick? What is it? Please Niamph, tell me what has happened? Has somebody died? Please Niamph, tell me!" begged, a concerned Megan.

Niamph tried to speak, but only a faltering sob came out of her mouth.

"Come and sit down, Niamph. And calm down - I will go and get you a cup of tea, just sit down take your coat off and put this blanket around you," said Megan, quickly leaving the room and shouting for Rose.

Mrs Rose Blake was Megan's employer; she was a widow with two married sons who now both lived in Dublin. Megan was like the daughter she had never had and treated her as such. When Megan answered her advertisement for the position of shop assistant, she knew straight away that Megan would fit the job. After accepting the job offer, Megan had asked Rose if she knew of a room she could rent nearby and Rose didn't hesitate and offered her a room in her living accommodation above the shop.

Megan was good company and no trouble, she had made a few friends with the girls at the factory across the road, but she wasn't the type of girl to be out every night. Megan never mentioned her family but Rose had gathered from things that Megan had said from time to time, that she had not had the best of childhoods; her father had been extremely strict and her mother had been cold and showed them very little love. However, Rose knew that a lot of large Irish Catholic families struggled to feed and clothe their children, especially those working the land.

"Rose, Rose!" shouted Megan.

"What is it, colleen?" asked Rose.

"It's my sister, something is very wrong and she is very upset! Is it okay if I make her a cup of tea? It might calm her down," said Megan.

"You go back to her and I'll make the tea," said Rose, so Megan quickly returned to Niamph who had now stopped crying and was a bit calmer.

"Tell me, Niamph, what's going on?" asked Megan. Niamph started to tell her when Rose bought in a cup of tea for them both.

"Rose, this is Niamph my sister next up from me." said Megan.

"Hello Niamph, are you okay colleen? You look very pale, here drink your tea I have put some sugar in it as you look like you have had some bad news. As it's late, do you want to stay the night with Megan? If so, I will make up a bed on the settee," said Rose.

"Thank you," said Niamph taking the cup of tea and holding it between her two hands to warm herself up. "If it's no trouble, yes please I would like to stay the night," confirmed Niamph.

"Niamph can sleep with me, it will be like old times," said Megan looking at Niamph. "It will saving you having to make up a bed on the settee, Rose."

"Okay, I will leave you to chat. Goodnight!" said Rose.

"Goodnight Rose and thank you!"

Niamph continued to tell Megan everything that had happened right up to that evening when their father had thrown her out.

"Oh Niamph! How could you have been so stupid? But in a way, I can understand - we haven't had much love in our lives so when someone comes along and starts to show you affection, then you cling on to it. Rose has taught me a lot since living here and I soon realized that a lot of boys are not interested in me for me! But one day I will find the right person. You thought he was the right one, but he just used you. What are you going to do? I wish I could help you, but I don't know how I can," said Megan.

"I don't know; I thought I would ask Nula," said Niamph.

"Well good luck with that, I can't imagine she would be of any help, but you never know! Let's get ready for bed as it's getting late and I have to be up for work in the morning," said Megan.

Megan snuggled up to Niamph to keep each other warm like they had done nearly all their lives, and both had a good night's sleep. Rose made them breakfast in the morning before opening the shop. Niamph thanked Rose for letting her stay and said goodbye to Megan, promising to keep in touch before making her way to get a bus to Dublin and seek help from her elder sister.

Nula lived with her husband Cathal and two young children. Cathal had lived with his family in the village near the Flynn's, before moving shortly after the war to Dublin. Nula, seeing the move as her opportunity to get away from her parents and the caring of Seamus, suggested to Cathal that they get married so that she could move with them to Dublin. They now lived with his parents in a large house on the outskirts of Dublin. The house had a workshop attached to it from which Cathal and his father ran a furniture-making business.

Niamph arrived at Nula's house just before lunch. Her knock on the door was answered by Nula, "Niamph! What brings you to my door? Come in!" said Nula.

Niamph entered Nula's house for the very first time. Walking into the kitchen she was amazed at how homely and neat everything was. Nula's two sons looked shyly up at Auntie Niamph. Nula invited her to sit at the table and made her a cup of tea.

"What brings you to Dublin, Niamph? How are Ma and Da?" asked Nula.

"Same as always," said Niamph and started to explain to Nula why she had come to see her. Before Niamph had got a quarter way through the story, Nula stopped her. "You are not going to tell me you are pregnant, are you?" she laughed.

Niamph felt embarrassed and merely answered, "Yes."

"Well, well little 'Miss Perfect' is up the duff! I suggest you drink your tea and go Niamph! I don't know how you could even contemplate asking for my help. What did you ever do for me? As far as I am concerned you can get lost!" said Nula, smugly.

Niamph didn't finish the tea she just got up and left. 'Why did I think she would help me? I should have known,' she thought to herself. She was back to square one and so made her way back to the bus station, unsure of what to do next. She had very little money and sat waiting for a bus racking her brain for inspiration when she thought of Father Patrick.

It was early evening when Niamph arrived at the parochial house. She was exhausted from all the travelling as well as hungry. The housekeeper answered the door; Father Patrick was just about to have his dinner and invited Niamph to join him. "I wondered if you would come and see me Niamph," said the priest.

"You have heard then, Father?" asked Niamph.

"Unfortunately, I have. Mrs O'Dea from the board of governors came to see me and told me," said the priest.

"I don't know what to do, Father. My family have disowned me, and I don't know which way to turn," she said, sobbing quietly.

"Crying won't help, Niamph! Eat your dinner. You can stay here the night and let me think of a solution," he said.

The following afternoon Father Patrick returned home and told Niamph to collect her belongings as he was taking her to Tullamore and he would explain on the way.

It was a long drive and the priest explained that he had spoken to the Mother Superior of the order of the Sisters of Saint Vincent de Paul, who was willing to take Niamph into their unmarried mother's unit.

"This order of nuns run a laundry service for the surrounding area, and they also take care of the unmarried mothers and arrange for the adoption of their babies. The expectant mothers are required to work in the laundry, unless they can afford to pay for their board and medical expenses, which I presume you cannot?" said Father Patrick.

"That's right, I can't. I don't have much money at all," replied Niamph.

"Then you will have to work in the laundry with the other girls. I am sorry but this is the best I can do, Niamph," he said.

"Thank you, Father, you have done more than I could have asked for!" said Niamph.

It took almost two hours for them to get to the convent and Niamph was conscious that Father Patrick had to drive back again for evensong. Mother Mary Joseph met them when they arrived and invited them into her office. "I cannot stay Mother as I have a long drive back, so I will go and leave Niamph in your safe hands," he said, hurrying off.

"Go, Father, Niamph will be well cared for by the order," confirmed Mother Mary Joseph. Father Patrick left, wishing Niamph good luck and instructing her to contact him if she needed him for anything.

The Mother Superior's attitude changed quickly after the priest had left, it was as though she put on one face for him and another for those inside the convent. The Mother explained to Niamph that she would join all the expectant mothers in a dormitory upstairs where she would stay until the baby is born, then she would be moved to another dormitory to look after her baby until she left the convent. During her time at the convent, she would be expected to work in the laundry to pay for her board, food and medical expenses. "There will be a small wage each week to enable you to pay for any extras you may require," the Mother explained.

The Mother handed her some papers to sign, which Niamph signed without really reading them fully. She could hardly take anything in, everything was happening to her so quickly - one minute she was happy at school and now here she was in this convent. Although the Mother did explain that her baby would be handed over for adoption to a good Catholic family of their choosing, Niamph couldn't quite envisage a baby yet, especially one that was hers'.

"We choose the families very carefully and place the babies where they would be best suited," the Mother continued to tell her. Niamph had no preconceptions of her pregnancy, that the thing growing in her abdomen was an actual baby, at this stage it was just something that was to be dealt with. She would hand this little thing over and would leave to get on with the rest of her life, or so she thought.

Mother Superior rang a bell, and another nun appeared. "This is Sister Mariana and she will take you up to the dormitory. After morning prayers and breakfast, you must make yourself known to Sister Therese and she will allocate you a position in the laundry. We use only surnames here so you will be known as Flynn from now on. You are excused, now go with Sister Mariana," she said.

Sister Mariana took her upstairs and showed her which bed would be hers. There were eight wrought iron beds in the room each with a thin mattress and one pillow . Her bed was unmade and sitting on top of the bed she could see a bath towel, sheets, and blankets. Besides the bed was a low bedside cabinet with a small cupboard, next to which was a closet with hanging space and shelving. The room had three long thin windows with no coverings overlooking the front driveway and the whitewashed walls held a simple cross with an effigy of Jesus nailed to it, hanging at one end of the room. "There is just enough time before dinner for me to show you where everything is," said Sister Mariana, who sounded much kinder than the Mother Superior.

Sister Mariana showed Niamph where the bathrooms were. There were three bathrooms in total to be shared by all the girls, and another communal washroom with a row of sinks and a row of toilet cubicles. The Sister explained that there were presently fourteen girls staying at the convent and twenty nuns.

Making their way downstairs, Sister showed her to the dining room where all the girls were standing behind their chairs in readiness for dinner. Niamph found a vacant seat and stood behind her chair like all the others. One of the nuns, who she found out later was Sister Angelica, was just about to say grace. Niamph followed the lead of the other girls - she bowed her head, put her hands together and joined in when they recited in unison "For what we are about to receive, may the Lord make us truly thankful, Amen!"

With a roar of scraping chairs, they all sat down. The nuns were sat at two long tables and the girls were all sat on another. The young girl to Niamph's right whispered, "Hello, I'm Gwen or 'Lynch'." "Hello, I'm Niamph or 'Flynn'," responded Niamph. The girl to her left in turn, whispered, "I'm Bridie or 'O'Connor'."

The meal was a meagre affair; there was a portion of a stew of undeterminable meat with three boiled potatoes and a small pile of cabbage, and a small bowl of rice pudding followed the main course. A glass of water accompanied the meal. When the meal was finished, the girls each took their plates and placed them on a trolley at the end of the dining room. Later, Niamph was informed that there were two girls employed in the kitchen who did all the washing up of the dishes.

Niamph followed the girls up to the dormitory where she met some of the others. The girls either side of her were both very young, sixteen-year-old Sarah 'Healy' and fifteen-year-old Maddie 'Burke'. They explained to her how they had time after dinner to do what they wanted, "But you can't leave this floor," said Maddie, before lights out at nine.

Niamph made her bed up, put her belongings away in the closet and made her way to the bathroom to wash before changing into her nightdress. She met Gwen in the bathroom, "I'm in the bed opposite you! Do you know what job you will be doing yet?" she asked.

"No," replied Niamph, "I have to see Sister Therese in the morning."

"Try to get into the pressing room - that's one of the easier jobs," said Gwen.

Gwen informed Niamph that she was from Dublin and that she was twenty-one and six months into her pregnancy. Niamph didn't like to ask her why she was at the convent, besides the obvious; she felt she didn't want to ask too many questions on her first day.

Niamph had been provided with a beige sack dress and white apron to wear, exactly the same as all the other girls. She started work the next morning not in the pressing room but at the rinsing tubs. She and two other girls were tasked with rinsing the washed items two or three times until all the soap suds had gone, then they had to pass the items through huge mangles ready for drying. Another pair of girls would take the wet items and hang them on washing lines in an outside yard to dry.

By the end of the first week, Niamph was completely exhausted; her hands were red raw and chapped from being in water nearly all day and even though the three of them had taken it in turns to operate the mangle, her arms ached.

The girls had no work on Saturday afternoons however they were all expected to change their beds, to each wash their clothes and clean their dormitory and bathrooms. On Sundays, they were all transported to the local church for Mass. The nuns all participated in taking communion, however, the girls having committed a mortal sin were prohibited from attending confession, never mind taking communion. Niamph was given to understand that there would be no forgiveness until after the birth of their babies.

They received their pittance of a wage on Sunday mornings before church and they were all expected to place some of it on the collection plate. Niamph soon learned that most of the girls donated a halfpenny or just pretended to put something in the collection plate. One of the girls always had a collection of halfpennies for the girls to change one of their pennies that the nuns had given them in their wage. The nuns never gave them halfpennies.

Sunday afternoons was their own time. They were even permitted to go to the convent library and take one book on loan. Niamph had loved reading since she was old enough to read on her own. There were only three girls in the library which surprised her, as there was not much else to do on their afternoon off. There was not a vast selection of fiction, so she chose David Copperfield by Charles Dickens, even though she had read it before. That evening she lay on her bed reading to herself.

"Niamph?" asked Maddie. "Are you reading that book or just looking at the pictures?"

"There aren't any pictures, Maddie," she replied, showing her the page she was reading. "How are you reading it then?" Niamph was bemused at Maddie's question, not really understanding what she meant.

"I'm not sure what you mean Maddie? I am reading the story to myself," she explained.

"Oh!" exclaimed Maddie, "You mean in your head?"

"Yes, exactly. Don't you read Maddie?" asked Niamph.

Maddie looked at bit sheepish and replied, "No, I can't read! My Da didn't let me go to school. Will you read to us, Niamph?"

And so, began an evening ritual whereby Niamph would read to the girls. When nine o'clock arrived they would all sigh, disappointed that they would have to wait for the next evening to continue the story.

Niamph suggested to Maddie that she teach her to read, "Oh! Would you? That would be grand!" replied Maddie. And so slowly but surely over the next two months, Niamph taught Maddie her alphabet, and by the time Maddie was ready to leave the convent, she could read several easy words and write her name.

Niamph was sad to see Maddie leave and even sadder to know that she was returning home to her abusive father. Maddie had confided in her, telling her that after her mother had died when she was twelve, her father had sexually abused her which had resulted in her pregnancy. It was only the intervention of her new sister-in-law that arrangements had been put in place for her to have her baby at the convent. "He wouldn't dare touch me again, my brothers will look after me," she told Niamph confidently.

Many of the girls had had their babies since Niamph had arrived at the convent. It was quite a traumatic experience watching the girls when they realized that their babies had gone. Some of them didn't care much and left before the babies were even handed over, but others sobbed uncontrollably, totally heartbroken and inconsolable at the loss of their baby. It was at these times that Niamph feared having her baby and how she would react when her baby was taken away.

The doctor, together with a midwife, would visit every two weeks to check the girls depending on the stage of their confinement. Three weeks before Niamph's due date she started to suffer from swollen legs and ankles. She was in a lot of pain and very tired which resulted in her being unable to complete a day's work. When the doctor examined her on his next visit, he confined her to complete bed rest, telling the Mother Superior that she was at risk of pre-eclampsia. "I will be back next week to check on this girl, but if she complains of any other symptoms phone me straight away," he said.

Five days later she was rushed to the hospital in an ambulance, after the other girls reported to the Mother Superior that Niamph was vomiting violently. The doctor was waiting for her at the hospital and after examining her ordered an immediate cesarean section.

When Niamph woke up some hours later she had a beautiful, healthy baby girl. She fell in love with her straight away holding her until the nurses insisted that she be put back in her cot so Niamph could rest. Niamph stayed in the hospital for just over two weeks, feeding the baby every day and when she was allowed out of bed, she would bath and change her. When the nurses asked what she was going to call her, she stated "Bernadette!". She had read the story of St. Bernadette several times, and she hoped that the Virgin Mary would watch over her baby.

On returning to the convent, Niamph she was ordered by the doctor not to do any heavy work for at least another four weeks. She was put to work in the nursery helping Sister Marie-Joseph look after the babies - she could hardly call it work as she loved every minute and cried when each baby left the nursery to start his or her life with their new family. Sister Marie-Joseph had a camera and would take a picture of each baby with its mother as a memento.

Nothing could have prepared Niamph for that fateful day when an American couple came to collect Bernadette. With just one hour's warning Mother Superior told her to get the baby ready for hand over!

"I'm not ready, Sister!" said a shocked and emotional Niamph to Sister Marie-Joseph.

"Unfortunately, you will never ever be ready my dear, but you must be brave for Bernadette's sake," responded the Sister.

"I can't do this! I can't do this!" she screamed, sobbing and holding Bernadette so close that she also started crying.

"Niamph, you must try and calm down! Here, let me take the baby? Go and wash your face. You have to go downstairs and hand your baby to Mother Superior," said Sister Marie-Joseph in a calm and controlled voice.

Niamph fell to the floor in a crouching position, hugging herself and sobbing uncontrollably. "Please Sister, don't make me do this? How will I live without her - how Sister? I can't do it," she sobbed.

"Niamph, this is what you agreed to! You know you can't look after her, you have to let her go!" said the Sister gently, taking her arm and helping her to stand up.

"I know Sister, but nobody prepared me for this hurt! I can hardly bear it!" said Niamph totally overwhelmed with emotion, so much so she didn't know what to do with herself.

The Sister took her hand, dried her face, and handed her Bernadette. "Say goodbye Niamph. You have to go down to Mother Superior, she will be waiting for you."

Niamph slowly made her way downstairs, removing Bernadette's tiny bonnet on the way and putting it in her pocket. Mother Superior was waiting for her "You just need to sign this form Flynn, and I will take the baby."

Niamph gently kissed Bernadette on the forehead and handed her over to Mother Superior before she ran from the room and locked herself in the bathroom. She felt sick - she wanted to scream but was too fraught with emotion! She washed in face in cold water and made her way to her bed in the dormitory and wept until she fell asleep.

Later that afternoon, Mother Superior summoned her to her office. "Now Flynn, you have spent almost eight weeks without contributing to your keep, so you will need to continue working here until you have repaid the convent the amount you owe."

"What do you mean?" questioned Niamph, "I thought I would be free to leave?"

"I am sorry, but that is not the way it works. From now on you will be paid, less your board and lodgings, and you can use what is left to start repaying what you owe us before you can leave," stated Mother Superior.

Niamph was speechless and when she told the other girls, they couldn't quite believe it. She now realized why the two girls in the kitchen remained at the convent long after the birth of their babies. She was a prisoner in a vicious circle, how would she ever be able to repay the amount she owed from the meagre wage she received?

Over the following two weeks Niamph negotiated an increase in her wage with Mother Superior, stating that as she didn't need to see the doctor, she was saving them money, and she also didn't need to take time off for check-ups. However, it still took nine months before she was able to leave the convent. Each night she slept with Bernadette's photo on her bedside table and her little bonnet under her pillow. She would smell the bonnet taking in her baby's scent. Initially, she would cry herself to sleep every night, but gradually she began to come to terms with her loss, although she would never forget.

Niamph refused to attend mass on a Sunday saying to Sister Marie Joseph "I have attended church since I was a baby, Sister. I assisted our parish priest with the readings of the Stations of the Cross every evening during Holy Week since I started school. When I was older, I gave up my spare time and helped the children prepare for their first communion and confirmation. I now look what God has done to me; He has taken my baby, made my family hate me, and abandoned me here! So, I am finished with Him."

"Niamph, you can't blame God for has happened to you! He can't be all things to all people and look at how He sacrificed his own son? Let me ask you to look at your situation another way - is not your baby's new mother saying, 'Thank you God, for giving me this beautiful baby'. I understand you are angry and upset at this moment in time, but I beg you not give up on your faith," said Sister Marie Joseph.

"You are right. I am angry and perhaps in time, I will return to church but not at this present time, Sister," said a defiant Niamph.

Mother Superior suggested to Niamph that she could tidy up the library and catalogue the books on a Sunday instead of going to church, in exchange for a small payment. Niamph jumped at the chance of earning some extra money as well as carrying out a fairly enjoyable task, which took her some months to complete.

CHAPTER 21

Niamph left the convent fourteen months after she arrived with exactly the same possessions she went in with, plus her precious photo and bonnet. She had already made up her mind as to what she would do and having had eight months to think about her future, she decided to go to America. But as she currently had very little money and no job, she made her way to Father Patrick in the hope that he would again help her.

It felt strange leaving the convent as she had been there so long without going any further than the church. It was like she had been set free from prison, but she was suddenly all alone in the world as she'd had no contact with anyone in her family since arriving at the convent, being told on her arrival that correspondence with the outside world was not permitted. Niamph wondered if anyone from the family was concerned about her, especially Megan whom she wanted to see as soon as she could. Niamph removed her sack dress and apron for the last time and put on her own clothes for the first time in over a year. Her clothes felt much too big, she hadn't realized how much weight she has lost since having her baby. With tears in her eyes, Niamph said goodbye to all the girls and left.

Niamph managed to get a lift into the nearest village with one of the laundry delivery drivers and boarded the first of three buses that would take her to Castlewood. Everything appeared different than she remembered, more colourful, but she presumed that anything would be more colourful after the drab convent. Father Patrick welcomed her with open arms and after Niamph told him of her plans he promised to try and help her; he was astonished that she had remained at the convent for such long time and promised he would question Mother Superior the next time he had any contact with her.

Niamph stayed with Father Patrick for ten days during which time he would sit with her discussing her loss of faith, eventually persuading her to attend mass and take communion after hearing her confession. Niamph felt it was the least she could do as it was a way of repaying the priest for what he had done for her, even though she was still angry with God for not being there in her hour of need. However, she thought trying to convince herself, 'Perhaps the Priest is being guided by God, and this is the way He is helping me'.

A colleague of the priest who had a parish in Liverpool, England, had said that he would give Niamph a letter of recommendation for a teaching position at a school in New York, run by the church for Irish immigrant Catholic children. Father Patrick also said he would give her a reference and agreed to help her with her fare to New York. "You can repay me Niamph, by taking up your faith again,' said Father Patrick. So, at the end of August 1951, Niamph would make her way to England. On the night before she left the parochial house, Niamph sat down and wrote a letter to the lady who had taken her beloved Bernadette. "I know I am not allowed to contact the person who adopted Bernadette, but I saw her name on the papers! Can you please ask Mother Superior to forward to this letter, Father?" asked Niamph of Father Patrick. "I will send you my address when I arrive in New York, just in case she replies," said an ever-hopeful Niamph.

"I will Niamph, but don't expect a reply! You must try to forget, and get on with your life, Niamph," replied Father Patrick.

Before leaving Ireland Niamph went to see Megan, the only family member she cared for and felt the need to see before leaving for America. Megan was surprised and delighted to see her. She was horrified to see how thin she was and to learn what had happened to Niamph since the last time they had seen each other. Megan cried as Niamph told her all about Bernadette, feeling her heartache as though it was her own.

Rose offered Niamph two dresses that were on the sale rail, which Megan quickly took and paid for out of her savings. "You'll need some clothes for the journey and to start your new job, Niamph, so please take these from me!" said Megan.

"Thank you, Megan, I will repay you once I am settled," promised Niamph.

"I don't need repaying Niamph, just be happy," responded Megan.

Niamph stayed with Megan for two nights before making her way to Dublin ready to embark for Liverpool. While Megan was at work, Niamph used the shop's workshop to alter the clothes that were too big for her. The two sisters hugged each other tightly and said a tearful goodbye, with Niamph promising to write as soon as she was settled in America - and it was a promise that she would keep.

The ferry from Dublin to Liverpool went overnight, and Niamph luckily managed to get a pair of vacant seats that enabled her to lie down in the fetal position and get some sleep. It was a fairly smooth crossing and before arriving in Liverpool, Niamph bought herself a cup of tea and a buttered roll, not sure when her next meal would be.

Liverpool docks were nothing like Niamph had ever seen before! Everyone was bustling about their business and shouting to each other. She had written down the address of the Liverpool priest and asked one of the porters for directions. "You can get a bus Miss, it's not a long walk to the station. And it's cheaper than getting a taxi

- turn right, and it is at the top of that road!" he said pointing to a busy road immediately in front of the docks. Niamph thanked him and made her way in the direction he had pointed to the bus station, which as he had said was a fairly short walk. At the ticket office, they explained which bus Niamph needed to take, so she purchased her ticket and waited for the bus to arrive.

As Niamph alighted from the bus, there in front of her was St Matthew Roman Catholic Church standing on one corner of a crossroad junction; it was an imposing sight with a row of stain glass windows on either side and a huge front entrance with a large wooden door. Niamph went round to the back of the church and immediately saw the parochial house. Father Francis greeted her warmly and called his housekeeper, who showed her to her room and told her to come down to the sitting room when she was ready.

Niamph spent two days in Liverpool before departing for America. She explored the city, walking the streets and seeing buildings damaged by the war awaiting repair or rebuilding. There were still a lot of old buildings, like the Liverpool Playhouse on Williamson Square, that were remarkably undamaged, the three-story building with its impressive façade and two domed towers on each of the front corners of the roof. Niamph loved the city with its friendly people and architectural history and even thought to herself that she could have happily settled here if she had not made up her mind to go to America.

Niamph departed for New York in September 1951 on the M.V. Georgic and with her carpetbag holding her meagre possessions she made her way to the Liverpool docks, filled with excitement at the prospects of starting a new life but also apprehensive at what the future would hold.

As she waited patiently in the queue among the hundreds of people waiting to board the ship, a girl of around the same age as her with a baby in a pushchair stood in front of her. Niamph estimated that the little girl in the pushchair, was about the same age as Bernadette would be. She made faces and cooing noises at the little girl, who was peeking around her mother, smiling and showing off her baby teeth. When Niamph spoke to the little girl, the mother turned around, "Oh! Hello, I wondered who Lilly was laughing at."

"Sorry," said Niamph "I was trying to distract your daughter. I could see she was getting restless."

"That's okay," said the young woman, "She doesn't like being restrained in her pushchair, she wants to get out. Hopefully, it won't be long before we board. My name is Clara by the way."

"I'm Niamph, are you going to New York?"

"Initially yes, but only for a night before getting a train to North Carolina," replied Clara.

The queue started to move slowly forward and the porter helped Clara with the pushchair up the ramp, another steward examined her tickets and directed them to her cabin. Niamph was just behind her.

"Where is your cabin?" Clara asked.

"It is in third class, I am sharing with some other people. It was the cheapest I could get!" responded an embarrassed Niamph, not wanting to tell anyone that she was in the cheapest class available but felt compelled to tell the truth. Niamph could see that Clara appeared to feel sorry for her, as she said, "Why don't you go and find your cabin and drop off your luggage and then come and find me? I'm in cabin 401B," said Clara. looking at her boarding card, "Then we could go and explore together."

They were called third-class cabins but actually they were more like a dormitory, however instead of beds, there were several two tiers bunks each with an individual identification number. Each bunk had a curtain that could be closed once inside. There were both men and woman in the cabin and Niamph could have cried at the lack of privacy she would have to endure during the voyage. She quickly put her bag on her bunk and made her way to Clara's cabin.

Niamph knocked on the cabin door and Clara let her in; it was a small cabin with two single beds. Clara was just telling Niamph that she would prefer to share a bed with Lilly as she was scared that Lilly will fall out of bed in the night, when they heard the ship's engines start.

"Quick the ship is about to disembark! Let's go up top and watch it leave!" exclaimed Niamph.

They quickly found their way to the deck, taking it in turns to carry Lilly. They fought their way forward to find a space near the railings, people were crowded everywhere on the deck all waving goodbye. Niamph with a heavy heart watched the dock disappear, it was as though she suddenly realized that she was leaving everything she knew behind and was somewhat scared of what the future would hold. She wanted to shout, 'Let me off I have made a mistake!' but knew it was too late. With tears welling up in her eyes she returned the waves goodbye, but not to anyone in particular just to her old life. Together with Clara she watched the dock slowly disappear and then with a sense of wary excitement they made their way below deck, Niamph trying to make light of the situation saying, "Let's find the cafeteria, I am starving."

They walked around and around several of the upper decks and on passing the formal dining room, Niamph stated, "I don't think you will see me in there, not on my budget."

"You're right and I don't think Lilly will be welcome in there, either!" said Clara. They soon found a cafeteria, which was self-service. Clara explained to Niamph that she had vouchers that she could exchange for meals for both her and Lilly. They walked up and down to see what was available. Niamph was looking at the prices with a frown on her face, concerned that the small amount of money that she had would not stretch very far.

"Let's find a table first and then decide what we will have?" suggested Clara.

At the table Clara questioned Niamph about her finances. "I don't have much money at all, but I can afford one dish. I will just have to be careful and keep to a budget. I just want to keep most of my money for when I arrive in New York," she said.

"Tell you what! I have vouchers for both Lilly and me, and Lilly is not going to eat very much. So, why don't you take Lilly's voucher and we will give her something from each of our plates? We will just need to choose something easy for her to eat," suggested Clara.

"Thank you, Clara, that is really kind of you - but you don't have to do that, after all, you have only just met me!" said Niamph.

"Don't be silly, It's fine! Let's find out what the vouchers get us," said Clara.

They approached the front desk and asked about the vouchers. The attendant explained that there was a voucher for each of the three days onboard which entitled them to a breakfast, lunch and dinner at any of the restaurants onboard. She said that the voucher would be marked each time it was used.

"So, we can go to the formal dining room if we want?" queried Clara.

"Yes, the voucher entitles you to eat anywhere on this deck, but not the first-class deck," replied the attendant.

Niamph then asked the attendant about third-class passengers with no vouchers, "In that case," the attendant informed her, "you will need to go to the concierge desk and purchase food vouchers of your choice."

"That's settled then!" said Clara, "Let's go and choose what we are going to eat!"

Clara asked the waitress for a highchair for Lilly and settled her in the chair with a bread roll to chew, while she and Niamph went to get their food. They returned to the table with their plates of food, a drink, and an extra dish for Lilly.

Niamph took great delight in helping feed Lilly and encouraging her to drink from a cup, so much so her own food nearly went cold but for Clara's intervention.

After dinner, they walked back to Clara's cabin. "I need to get Lilly ready for bed, she is getting tired," said Clara.

"I will go back to my cabin and see you in the morning," said Niamph.

"No, don't go yet come in and keep me company for a bit, it is still early. Sorry, am I being pushy? Only stay if you want to," said Clara.

"I would like nothing better than to stay, thank you!" replied Niamph.

The cabin shared a bathroom with two other cabins, and as it was only early evening, no one else was using the bathroom, so Clara was able to bath Lilly.

"Please, Clara, can I give Lilly her bath?" begged Niamph.

"Yes, if you want to, but you might get as wet as Lilly likes to splash a lot! It will give me a chance to unpack," said Clara.

Niamph gave Lilly her bath and played splashing with her until the water was getting too cold to continue. She wrapped Lilly in a big towel and took her back to the cabin. Clara passed her Lilly's nappy and nightgown. Lilly's eyes were beginning to close as Niamph dressed her, so Niamph kissed her goodnight and together with Clara, they tucked her up tightly in one of the beds. Lilly was soon sound asleep.

Clara was intrigued by Niamph's interaction with Lilly, which appeared to be more than just a liking for children.

"Do you have any children, Niamph?" asked Clara, "You seemed to enjoy taking care of Lilly." Niamph tried to answer but was too choked up to speak and tears began welling up in her eyes.

"Sorry Niamph! I didn't mean to upset you, are you okay? Come and sit down," said Clara, quite concerned by Niamph's reaction. Niamph composed herself as she sat down on the bed. Clara put her arm around her shoulders and tried to comfort her. Silent tears were slowly falling down Niamph's cheeks.

"Please don't cry."

Niamph started to speak with a bit of a croak at first, as she told Clara that she had a little girl almost the same age as Lilly.

"Where is she?" asked Clara.

"She was adopted by an American couple when she was six weeks old! All I have left of my Bernadette is a bonnet and a photo," explained Niamph.

"I don't understand! Why did you let her be adopted? Where is your husband? What about your family?" questioned Clara.

"I don't have a husband and I come from a very strict Catholic family. Having a baby outside of marriage is a mortal sin and a disgrace on the family, so I had no option but to let her go," explained Niamph.

"I still don't understand what happened - why didn't the father marry you?" probed Clara.

"I will have to start at the beginning for you to understand the end," explained Niamph, as she told Clara the entire story.

"So, now I am going to a Catholic convent school in New York to teach there," finished Niamph. Clara was horrified at Niamph's story but she knew only too well how people could treat each other so badly. She asked Niamph if she would like to share her cabin for the journey.

"As I said before, I was going to share with Lilly anyway, so this other bed is yours if you want it?" offered Clara.

"You don't need to ask me twice!" said Niamph and left to retrieve her luggage.

The rest of the voyage passed in a flash. Niamph and Clara became firm friends, each night sitting in the cabin and telling each other their life stories.

Niamph was speechless at Clara's bravery, not only during the war but also at her decision to leave her abusive and violent husband. She tried to understand why Clara had left her two daughters behind.

"I was scared, Niamph, as to what would happen next; I thought he was going to kill me! I miss my little girls more and more each day." This time it was Niamph's turn to comfort Clara as she heartbreakingly, sobbed on her shoulder.

They discussed the future and how they would both like to get their daughters back; they cried together and laughed together. All too soon they arrived in New York, they had packed the night before and were up on deck to watch the ship sail into the dock. Clara's future husband's brother was meeting her off the boat, and Niamph was to make her way to the convent where she was to work.

The women exchanged addresses and promised to write to each other, both crying as they hugged each other goodbye. Niamph squeezed and kissed Lilly to which Lilly vocally objected! Going through immigration, they lost sight of each other amongst the milling crowds.

New York Harbour was a mass of people and noise. There were porters offering their services shouting at the top of their voices, dockers shouting to each other, stewards attempting to organize the passengers in the right direction, each shouting to try to make themselves heard above everyone else. Niamph was disorientated and just followed the crowd towards what appeared to be the exit. As she got outside everything seemed a bit quieter. She had the address of the school so now she just needed to find which way to go. Luckily, a porter seeing her looking a bit confused asked if he could help her. "I am going to the Church of the Annunciation in Manhattan, can you tell me the best way to get there?" she asked.

"Well Ma'am, that must be at least 40 miles from here, so a cab would be your best option! It would be very complicated to get a bus or tram as none go from here direct, you would have to change several times," replied the porter.

Just as she quietly assessed the situation, a priest and two nuns approached the porter and asked him to get them a cab to upper Manhattan.

"Are you going near Convent Avenue by any chance, Father?" asked the porter.

"Yes, why do you ask?" asked the priest in a thick Irish accent.

"Well, this young lady here is going to a church there. You couldn't perhaps let her share your cab, could you sir?" asked the porter.

The priest turned around to face Niamph and asked, "Where exactly are you going, young lady?"

"I am going to the Church of the Annunciation, Father. I don't have much money and am not quite sure how I am going to get there," she replied, honestly.

"Well, you are in luck young lady, because that is exactly where we are going! You are most welcome to join us," the Father extending his hand to Niamph. "I am Father Joseph, and this is Sister Amata, now who are you and why are you going to the Church of the Annunciation?" asked the priest.

"Thank you so much, Father! My name is Niamph, and I am taking up a post of a teacher at the school attached to the Church," Niamph said, as she gave her luggage to the cab driver. She climbed into the cab, sitting in the back with Sister Amata whilst the priest sat in the front next to the driver.

Father Joseph explained that he and the Sister had just returned from a visit to Ireland and without realizing, they had been on the same ship as Niamph, 'Not in third class, I bet!' thought Niamph to herself.

"If we had known you were on the ship you could have joined us; I hope you didn't find it too lonely being on your own? It's a long, arduous trip when you don't know anyone," said the Priest.

Niamph was so in awe of her surroundings that she wasn't really listening to the priest as the cab made its way along the docks travelling towards Upper Manhattan. Niamph had thought that Liverpool had been busy, but the volume of traffic and the noise in New York was deafening to Niamph's ears. The streets gave the impression that they were encased by the huge buildings, from her viewpoint in the cab the sky was obscured by the height of the buildings. It wasn't until the priest announced that they were nearing their destination that the buildings seemed not as tall and more evened out.

The imposing limestone building of the Church of the Annunciation came into view occupying an entire block; the frontage displayed a large arched window above a triple pillared arched entrance. Father Joseph instructed the cab driver to stop outside the rear of the building where a large gravelled courtyard surrounded on three sides by various limestone buildings of varying shapes and sizes.

They all alighted from the cab. Sister Amata quickly bade her farewell and made her way to the right-hand side of the courtyard, which Niamph presumed was where the order of nuns lived. Father Joseph led her to a door directly in front of the courtyard entrance, with the door opening before he had time to knock.

"Now, Niamph let me introduce you to Mr. Wilson? He is the headmaster of the lower school and he will look after you. Goodbye and good luck! No doubt I will see you at Mass on Sunday," he extended his hand to Niamph's and shook it warmly.

"Hello, Miss Flynn, I presume? I was expecting you! Come in, let me take your bag," said the headmaster.

CHAPTER 22

Peter Wilson was fifty-five years of age with receding greying hair, combed back from his forehead. He was a handsome man and had a good physique for his age, standing at almost six foot tall. Peter was married to Susan and they had two grown-up sons aged thirty and thirty-two. Their eldest son Simon lived with his wife and two children in Lower Manhattan, where he practiced medicine. Susan doted on her two grandchildren.

Peter and Susan's youngest son, Douglas was an engineer and was currently working in Australia on a revolutionary reservoir scheme in the Snowy Mountains. Douglas had no intention of marrying, as he like nothing more than traveling to extreme places around the world, putting his engineering skills to good use.

Peter had worked at the school since graduating from university where he had met Susan at their very first lecture. They married soon after graduating and joined the newly opened School of the Annunciation. Susan was the same age as Peter and her once brunette hair was now a demure silver-grey, and the slim figure of her youth was now lost to a more rounded appearance, although she remained fit due to her love of playing tennis.

When the couple first joined the school, there were twenty-six pupils aged between five and eight years old, all children of poor immigrants that had travelled from either England or Ireland. Susan taught the five to six-year-olds and Peter the older ones. The school had been the idea of Father Nicholas, an Irish priest who had taken over the running of the Church in 1914. When he had seen the immigrants' children running around the streets barefoot and not attending school, he decided to do something about it and converted part of the church buildings into classrooms and thus establishing the school.

Within ten years the school had increased in size dramatically to over one hundred pupils and eight teachers. The school although run by the church initially for the poor of the parish also took in fee-paying children. The school had established an excellent reputation and parents who could afford it, were more than willing to pay for their children's education. The fees received enabled the church to put more funds into the development and expansion of the school.

Peter took great pride in being able to recognize from a very early age those children with potential, and he would nurture these children and encourage them to go on to the high school after leaving the church school. One of these such children was a boy from the East End of London called Maxwell Lyle. He had outperformed all of the other children in his class and by the age of eleven was running his own stall at the local market every weekend. His father, Eric Lyle, would spend all week going around the more affluent areas of New York collecting any unwanted items. At the end of each day, he would sort through the collected items, the better pieces were kept for resale and the unusable items would be dumped.

Maxwell's Mother would painstakingly clean the items for resale, washing and pressing any clothing and polishing other pieces until they gleaned.

Maxwell had the 'gift of the gab' and he would flatter the old ladies and flirt with the young girls who visited his stall, and not a weekend went by when all the items on his stall were not sold.

With Peter's guidance, Maxwell soon learned how to keep accounting records and to maximize his profit margins. By the time Maxwell was twenty-five years of age, he was a wealthy man and had opened a department store of his own. It was a prestigious store over three floors, employing more than seventy people.

It was at this time that Maxwell decided he wanted to help his community and approached Peter with the offer to open a high school attached to the Church, so that pupils could make a seamless transition from junior school. With the agreement of the Church, Maxwell purchased eight acres of land adjacent to the back of the church and set about building a state-of-the-art high school. The school took two years to complete. Peter, Susan and Father Benedict, together with an accountant and a retired university lecturer, formed the Board of Governors. The school was named 'The Lyle Academy' and soon became a leading high school in Manhattan.

Peter was planning for his retirement and he had purchased a run-down house that he was slowly renovating it in readiness to retirement at sixty. He was looking forward to being able to relax on the stoop of his new home and read all the books he presently didn't have time to read, no longer have to worry about writing endless numbers of end of term reports.

One of Peter's role within both schools was the employment of staff. Following a telephone conversation between Father Michael, a colleague of Father Benedict and a fellow priest in Liverpool, he had engaged a new young teacher, Niamph Flynn, to take over from a teacher who was leaving to have a baby.

CHAPTER 23

Peter introduced Niamph to his wife Susan, and explained that Niamph would be welcome to stay with them until such time as she was able to find accommodation of her own. Susan showed her the room that she would call home for the time being.

The room had a double window that overlooked the courtyard but the wood paneling around the walls gave the room a dark and dingy appearance, despite the amount of light from the window. There was a double wardrobe in one corner and a dressing table with a full-length mirror attached to one side sitting next to the window. A double-sized bed occupied the far wall, with a small cabinet on either side of the bed. All the furniture was in dark oak wood and the only decorative item was the eiderdown on the bed, which was in bright yellow.

Susan closed the door behind her, leaving Niamph to unpack her few possessions. Niamph was suddenly overcome with an overwhelming a sense of loneliness, as though a dense fog was swallowing her. She gently stroked her one prized possession, the framed photo of Bernadette. She had thought that coming to America would make her feel closer to Bernadette, but instead she felt further away. Close to tears, she looked up and caught sight of her reflection in the mirror. She was shocked at how pale she looked and how lackluster her hair appeared.

'For goodness sake, Niamph! Snap out of this self-pity! Just look at the state of you,' she said, chastising herself. 'Your new life starts now, today, this very minute.'

She placed the photo in the top drawer of one of the bedside cabinets and made her way downstairs. Susan was in the kitchen preparing dinner, and rejected the offer of help from Niamph.

"Go and sit down with Peter. I am certain you have lots of questions to ask him," said Susan.

"Ah! Niamph," said Peter, as she entered the living room. "I hope you find your room satisfactory? I am sure it won't be long before you find yourself a home of your own, but take your time. It's important to find the right place, one where you will be happy," said Peter "Now, come and sit down."

Peter informed Niamph that she would start teaching in a couple of days, at the beginning of the school week.

"You don't have far to go as the school is next door, through the gate to the left of the courtyard. I will introduce you to everyone and take you on a guided tour," Peter explained.

Susan soon announced that dinner was ready and the three of them sat down to eat. Susan described the local area and how the schools had evolved over the years, especially after Maxwell Lyle's involvement.

"You will no doubt meet him, he likes to attend our Board of Governors' meetings, which are held once a month. He often walks around both schools to see what the children are doing. In fact, his own children attend the school," said Susan.

Niamph insisted on helping Susan with the clearing the table and washing the dishes, "I want to start as I mean to go on, Susan. I can't expect you to wait on me and I'm extremely grateful to you both for inviting me into your home. I promise I won't be any trouble, and I will endeavor to find something of my own as soon as I can," said Niamph.

"Take things slowly, Niamph. Finding just the right place that is within easy travelling distance of the school and in a good area won't happen overnight. Talk to the other teachers; explore New York and the right place will find you," stated Susan.

"Thank you, for being so understanding. In fact, if you point me in the right direction for the buses I will start exploring tomorrow!" replied a more upbeat Niamph.

Niamph rose early the next morning and sat in the kitchen with Susan to eat breakfast, after which she set off for her foray of New York. She caught the bus outside of the church, which took her to the main bus station in Lower Manhattan, where she obtained a bus timetable and a map from the tourist information centre next door to the station. Marking on the map the bus station, so at least she would be able to find her way back to catch the bus to return home.

The streets in Lower Manhattan were all sequentially numbered and the buildings were in blocks, making the city effortless to navigate. Unlike Liverpool, where the lanes and streets went all directions, making it easy for you to get lost. Niamph made her way using her map, to Central Park where she stopped and sat on a bench to read the map further. She noted that there was a Jewish Museum was not far from where she was and she decided to make her way there.

The building reminded Niamph of a grand French Chateau that she had seen in history books, with its imposing mansard roof. She later established that its façade was made of limestone from Indiana and carved in a Gothic revival style. The architect had based the building on a classic châteauesque style, thus, her first assumption was correct. She spent two hours viewing the various exhibits. She was mesmerized by everything, it was like nothing she had ever seen before and vowed to come back so that she could see the exhibits that she had missed on this visit. She was by this time very hungry, so she made her way to a café that she had seen on her way into the museum. She had very little money left and what she did have would have to last until her first payday, so she chose the cheapest things on the menu being a sandwich and a coffee. The sandwich turned out to be huge and she was later to find out that everything in America was bigger than expected. She arrived home elated at her first expedition.

CHAPTER 24

Niamph's first day at school arrived; she was surprised at how old the building was although the classrooms and hallways were all brightly decorated with the children's artwork, including illustrated poems and short stories with the names of the children above or below the work.

Peter introduced her to all the staff gathered in the staff room in readiness for the day ahead. There were ten teachers, plus Peter; six men, and four women. Peter had already explained to her that Susan no longer taught but instead acted as the school secretary. Niamph was to take over Grade 1, the six to seven-year-olds, from the current teacher Jennifer Martin.

Miss Martin was a plain sort of woman. Niamph guessed that she was about the same age as her and she informed Niamph that she was six months pregnant. She was taller than Niamph and had short brown mousy hair, and she wore horn-rimmed spectacles.

"Good morning children, this is your new teacher Miss Flynn," The children at this point all stood up, and in unison said, "Good morning Miss Martin, Good morning Miss Flynn," then they all sat down again.

There were twenty-three children in the class, ten boys and thirteen girls. Each had a little desk of their own and there were two lines of hooks on one wall, each with a child's name above.

Niamph's role for the next two weeks was to shadow Miss Martin and she was surprised on that first day that the children were not more advanced in their reading and writing. They spent the first part of the morning chanting the alphabet which in Niamph's opinion was not the best way to teach them. The children who knew the alphabet were the ones shouting the loudest, whereas those who were struggling appeared to be opening and closing their mouths in the hope that no one could hear them give the wrong answers.

That day flew by. Niamph sat with a number of the pupils helping them to copy the letters that Miss Martin had given them and although the majority could copy them relatively easily, there were a number who found the task painstakingly difficult. One little boy by the name of John, was trying desperately to hold his pencil in his right hand to do his writing.

"That's good. John hold your pencil like the other children, not in your left hand," said Miss Martin loudly from the front of the class. Niamph could see the boy struggling and so offered to sit and help him. He whispered to Niamph, "I can't use this hand, can I use my other hand?"

Niamph's heart went out to him; she had always maintained that if a child was left-handed so be it, why make them use their right hand? Luckily it was the end of the lesson so she didn't have to respond to John, but thought she would tackle Miss Martin later.

Unfortunately, Miss Martin left promptly at the end of the day giving Niamph no opportunity to raise the subject. So, at dinner that evening when Peter asked her how her day had been, she voiced her concerns.

"I know I am new to the school, but I do have a few questions, Peter," said Niamph.

"I am listening. Ask me anything and I will try and give you an answer," replied Peter.

"Well, firstly, I presume that the children have to achieve a certain level of, say reading and writing, by the end of each term or year. Is there something written down, so I can ensure that my pupils reach these goals? And does each pupil have a record of how they are progressing?—"

"Hold on Niamph, one question at a time!" laughed Peter, stopping Niamph in full flow.

"Like every school in the state, we have to abide by the rules set out by the education authority, and that includes the level of knowledge that each child should reach at the end of their school year. Therefore, the answer to your first question is yes, and in fact, I am in the middle of preparing a pack for you setting out this criterion. Now with regards to your second question, yes, each pupil has a report book. Miss Martin should have these and they should be up to date. However - and this is between you and me - Miss Martin has been causing me some concern, and if she hadn't announced her pregnancy last term then I would have had to review her position at the school," said a serious Peter.

Peter explained that the school policy was for each form teacher to take their class of children through from kindergarten through to Grade 6 when they would move to Middle School. That way the children could form a bond with their teacher and not have to change to a new form teacher each year. Of course, the children did have other teachers who specialized in subjects such as PE and music.

"Miss Martin joined us just over a year ago and took on the children joining the school for the first time in kindergarten, but unfortunately, those children have not progressed as they should have. Although I have spoken to Miss Martin on several occasions in this regard, she always refers to the children that have done well. Now those children will do well no matter what, it is the ones that are not doing well that are causing me concern," said Peter.

"I am telling you this Niamph because I want you to take on this class and show me that you are capable of bringing these children up to the level of knowledge that is expected for their age. How you do it is up to you; we are not the type of school to say, 'at this school we do it like this!' - you must do it your way, but obviously within reason."

"I hope I will be able to prove to you that I can do this Peter. And thank you for having faith in me, it means a lot," replied Niamph.

Niamph was so pleased that she had spoken to Peter about her concerns as it now gave her the confidence and enthusiasm to go forward. She suddenly had a goal, one that she intended to reach.

Miss Martin left the school two days later and didn't return. Niamph now had full control over the class and she immediately dismissed the chanting of the alphabet and timetables in favor of individual learning. She put the children's desk together enabling them to work in pairs, however, this left her with the problem of there being an odd number in the class but she soon solved this problem by putting three desks together, with John joining two little girls.

Niamph encouraged John to write with his left hand and this transformed him from an introverted little boy to one that soon took leadership of his team of three. She made the classes fun and interactive. Yes, of course, there were still those that struggled, but she would sit patiently with these pupils until they had grasped their letters and numbers, setting pieces of homework for them to complete at home.

Parents collecting their children at the end of the day would often stop and speak to Niamph saying how thankful they were for the effort she had put in to help their child. The day that John's mother approached her was the day that Niamph realized she had made a difference to the children.

"I want to thank you Miss Flynn, and say how grateful I am to you. John is so much happier now. I had a problem trying to get him to go to school before - he hated it - especially when Miss Martin tried to make him write with his right hand. Now he can't wait to get to school, so thank you!" said a happy Mrs. Newcombe.

When Niamph had been in Ireland, she loved to take her pupils on nature walks which was easy as it was a village environment with countryside all around. In New York however, it was a different matter. When she broached the subject with Peter, he informed her of the various parks in the area that she could visit. So, with the help of Mr Garcia, the school janitor who drove the school minibus for her, they made their first trip a visit to Crotona Park. Niamph walked the children through the park pointing out the trees, bushes, flowers and creatures, naming them and telling the children all about them. She encouraged the children to collect as many items as they could fit in their bags, before sitting on the grass by the duck pond to have their packed lunch before returning to the classroom.

The following day in art class Niamph set them up in teams to make a collage of their day at the park. She was astounded at the number of different items they had collected from duck feathers to a dead beetle, and at the end of the lesson - with more glue and paint on them than on the paper - each team came up with a completely different theme. Their collages took pride of place on the classroom wall much to everyone's delight.

All was not perfect in her class, as there was always one child who didn't conform and that was Sebastian. Niamph couldn't work out if he was just naughty, seeking attention or an exhibitionist. After a few months of teaching, Niamph detected a pattern to his disruption of the class; whenever she asked each pupil in turn to read from the blackboard, and it approached Sebastian's turn, he would begin his antics - standing on his chair or banging his ruler on his desk, or he would make faces at his friends to make them laugh. Anything that would result in Niamph reprimanding him and making him sit at the front of the classroom as punishment.

Like a flash of lightning, it came to Niamph one evening, whilst marking homework in her room, that perhaps he couldn't read the blackboard. With this in mind, she waited to speak to Sebastian's mother after school the following afternoon.

"Mrs. Bailey, can I ask you, has Sebastian ever had an eye test?" questioned Niamph, as she went on to explain Sebastian's behavior and her theory that perhaps he couldn't see to read from the blackboard.

Two weeks later, a bespectacled Sebastian walked into the classroom - her theory had proved correct. Sebastian remained the class clown, but his behavior vastly improved.

Niamph felt proud of what she had achieved in that first term at the school, as she completed each pupils' end of term report and updated each of their report books. All of the pupils had improved massively more than she had anticipated, and it just proved, she thought to herself 'All they had needed was encouragement and a little help'.

CHAPTER 25

When Niamph received her first pay packet at the end of her first week at school, she started to make plans for her future. Susan refused to take any money from her for her stay, saying that it cost no more to feed three people than it did two and the room was standing empty anyway. She hoped to be able to save at least half her wages which would help when she found accommodation of her own and needed to buy things. With winter approaching, she would have to buy herself some warm clothing and the remaining money she would use to explore New York.

Each weekend Niamph would catch the bus to the station and from there she would explore a different area. She visited as many of the sights of New York as she could from the Empire State Building to the Statue of Liberty. She liked nothing more than browsing through Bloomingdale's department store; the majority of the clothing was beyond her budget, although she did manage to buy a beautiful calf-length navy blue wool coat reduced by fifty percent because it had a button missing. Realizing that the belt hid one of the buttons, Niamph knew she could easily remove this button and put it in the missing one's place and sew a different button under the belt, no one would ever notice.

She would have loved to live near Central Park but soon discovered that accommodation in this area was the most expensive, every week she would scour the local paper for accommodation. It wasn't until early 1952, having been in New York for nearly six months and saved sufficient funds, that she commenced her search for a home in earnest.

The search was not as easy as she originally thought it would be viewing property after property, they were either too small, too dirty, too expensive or some she didn't even enter, after walking down a street that appeared too dubious for her liking.

Three weeks before the end of term she arranged to see a three-roomed apartment in Englewood. The only problem was that it was on the other side of the Hudson River, which would make her journey to school each day a bit longer. With this in mind and a preconception that she wouldn't like it anyway, she made her way early one Saturday morning to view the apartment.

The journey took thirty minutes and two buses, following the instructions given her by the landlord to Front Street. At the junction of the street, she noted that a flea market was in progress in a community centre. 'I'll go there after,' she thought to herself. The street had rows of three-story houses on either side of the road with wrought iron rails running the length of each building, each had steps going down to basements and another set going up to the ground floor. There were troughs of flowers hanging from the majority of the railings making the area look pretty.

Lime trees lined the street, planted at approximately eight-foot intervals. Children were playing noisily in the streets and adults sat chatting on old chairs, or on their steps outside of the buildings. The entire place was buzzing, with music coming from the buildings making Niamph smile as she approached number nineteen. On reaching the building, she was met by a smiling slim black man wearing a colourful woolly hat over his dreadlocks.

"Hello, Miss Flynn is it?" he asked.

"Yes, and I presume you are Mr. Ramirez?" replied Niamph, shaking his extended hand.

"Follow me, the apartment is on the first floor." Niamph followed him up the steps and through the entrance. Behind the door she could make out a row of letterboxes each numbered, with a shelf below with large piles of unopened mail.

The entrance hall was clean and tidy; the walls were painted in white, and the flooring was rather scuffed wooden parquet. They climbed the wooden stairs up to the first floor. The apartment with the number five on the outside of the door, was one of four on that floor. Mr Ramirez opened the door; Niamph was astonished at how bright and airy the entire room was, a complete contrast from the ones she had seen previously. It was a large room approximately thirty-foot square with full-length windows filling the front wall that overlooked the street. The room was partly furnished with a bed in one corner, a settee and coffee table sitting in the middle of the room. Mr Ramirez showed her the small kitchen at the back of the room, next to which was a small bathroom. The kitchen had a gas stove and waist-high cupboards running along one wall. A sink and draining board with cupboards underneath stood next to the stove and there was a small table and one chair in the corner. The only downside was that the kitchen had no windows. The bathroom had a bathtub, toilet and washbasin with a mirror over the basin - again there were no windows. Niamph loved it and she started to visualize how she would furnish it, changing the curtains that looked past their best.

"Well, Miss, what do you think, do you want it? It is a week in advance and a week's deposit," he said. Niamph didn't want to sound too enthusiastic, but wanted to shout, "Yes please, yes please!".

Niamph walked over to the bed and examined it, "The bed is a bit..." but before she could continue, he said,

"If you take the apartment now and pay me, I will provide you with a new bed."

"In that case, yes, I will take it!" she said, trying to contain her excitement.

"When do you want to move in, Miss?" he asked.

"Next weekend if that is okay with you?" replied Niamph, "But I might move some of my things before that."

Mr Ramirez gave her a rent book and asked her to sign a single page, one-paragraph agreement and then handed her the keys - one to the front door and one for her apartment. He explained that for security purposes, the front door was locked at ten o'clock each evening and opened again at seven o'clock each morning, so she would need the key during those times to access the building.

"I keep one key to your apartment for emergencies and I will use this to deliver your new bed by next week. I will come every Saturday morning to collect the rent. If you are going to be out, please leave the rent with Mrs Osborne at number one; she is always home," he then left Niamph in her new home.

Mr Jose Ramirez's family originated from Jamaica but he and his brother Tarone had been born in the United States and had served their country in the Armed Forces during World War II. Their father, a successful tailor, had died in 1948 and left his sons an inheritance, enabling them to buy several properties in New York which were the foundation of their property development company. They now bought run-down properties and renovated them, either selling them for a profit or retaining them in their letting portfolio. The most profitable was the apartment blocks they had purchased, as these provided them with a regular income.

Mrs Faye Osborne lived on the ground floor and she could be found every day sitting in her window that overlooked the front of the building, watching all the comings and goings. She was a widow of about eighty years of age, if not older, and very rarely ventured out of her apartment. She relied on her daily help to do all her cleaning and shopping. She was understood to be a wealthy woman, but when looking at her and her surroundings, you would never have come to that conclusion.

Niamph was soon to find out that Mrs Osborne was the nosiest person on the planet. If she couldn't immediately see what you were bringing into your apartment, then she would openly ask you what she had missed.

She soon settled into her new life and would write long letters to Megan, with Megan writing back giving all the news from home. The exchanges would take at least two months from the time Niamph dropped her letter into the mailbox, until the time the reply arrived at her apartment. Niamph also regularly wrote to Clara and this exchange only taking three weeks at the most.

Once a year on Bernadette's birthday, Niamph wrote to Father Patrick enclosing a letter for Bernadette, but no reply was ever received.

One weekend in early January 1953 on a rather cold day, Niamph sat watching the skaters in Central Park while intermittently reading a book, when a man sat down on the bench next to her. He made her jump when he said, "It's bit chilly today!" with an accent of a mixture of American and Irish.

When Niamph replied, "Yes, it is."

The man responded in a rather surprised manner, "I detect an Irish accent, do I not?"

"Yes," laughed Niamph in response, "And I detect a bit of Irish in yours." They sat and chatted for some time, explaining that he had been in America for five years and that he worked as a porter at Fulton Fish Market and lived with his two brothers in the Bronx.

"Let's go and get a hot chocolate, it is too cold to be sat here!" he said, grabbing her hand. They ran to the café at the edge of the park, finding a table in the warmth of the café. They spent over an hour in the café chatting and arranged to meet the following week at the same place. On the bus home, Niamph realized that although she knew his entire life story, he knew nothing of hers.

His name was Patrick 'Pat' Sheehy and was originally from Tipperary. They would meet every Sunday during term time, sometimes just going for a walk or going to the cinema to see the latest movie. Niamph loved wandering around the flea markets picking up items for her apartment, and Pat would delight in joining her. During the school holidays and whenever Pat had a day off work, they would venture outside of New York visiting the surrounding areas by tram.

Over the years, Niamph slowly but surely fell in love with Pat. She met his brothers, their wives and children, as they all shared one big, three-story house near where they all worked in the Bronx, with Pat living in the two small rooms that made up the attic.

Niamph's apartment was her haven; she had repainted it and bought several prints at the flea market and hung them on her walls. She had lovely rag rugs on the floor, which had again been picked up at the flea market. In fact, her entire flat, apart from her bedding, was purchased at various flea markets.

Niamph enjoyed listening to her little radio whilst doing her marking and schoolwork at her small desk, that again she had purchased at the flea market on the corner of her street and which the stallholder had kindly delivered for her. Life was beginning to get happier and more settled. She had the framed picture of Bernadette by her bedside, which she kissed each night before going to sleep.

The first time that Pat had visited her flat she had discreetly put the picture in the drawer of the bedside cabinet, as she didn't want to tell him about Bernadette until she felt the time was right. However, this proved to be an error of judgment.

Niamph had been in New York for six years when Pat asked her to marry him; she couldn't have been happier, she loved him so much. 'The man of my dreams!' was how she described him in a letter to Clara.

Late one Sunday night at the beginning of January 1957, after a lovely meal with Pat's family, they sat on the settee in Pat's attic home and discussed their future. When Pat mentioned children, Niamph felt it was the right time to tell him about Bernadette.

"I need to tell you something Pat, about my past. It's important that there be no secrets between us." She then proceeded to tell him the story of her pregnancy and subsequent adoption. As Niamph talked, Pat became quieter and quieter. She thought he was digesting her words and what had happened to her, until she noticed he was clenching his fists and soon started to bang them up and down on his knee.

Niamph had misread the situation. Pat suddenly stood up and started shouting at her, calling her all sorts of horrible names. He kept saying how he hadn't laid a finger on her to protect her for their wedding night, before he pushed her down onto the sofa slapping her and trying to tear at her clothes. Niamph thought he was going to rape her and assumed she must have screamed at that point although thinking back she couldn't remember doing so! All of a sudden, Pat's brother was hammering at the door, and then he burst into the room.

"What the hell is going on up here?" he yelled, stopping in his tracks assessing the situation and staring at his brother.

Pat turned to Niamph and said cruelly, "Get out! Get out, you are nothing but a slut! Get out - I never want to see you again!" Niamph quickly grabbed her bag and coat and ran down the stairs in floods of tears. Slamming the door loudly behind her before running home.

Niamph cried all night, tossing and turning in bed trying to sleep. She could not quite believe what had happened - why one minute was saying he loved her, then the next he was calling her names! All because she had made a mistake when she was young. What sort of a man was he that could turn from a loving person to an angry monster in a matter of minutes?

Niamph dragged herself out of bed the next morning to go to school, covering the dark shadows under her eyes with makeup. In the early hours of the morning she had decided that she would have to leave New York. She couldn't stand to be there any longer; even though the chances of bumping into Pat were remote, she didn't want to take the risk. But where would she go? Certainly not back to Ireland!

PART THREE

MILLIE'S STORY

CHAPTER 26

Millicent Barbara Henderson was born on 1st July 1950 to Grace and her oil magnate husband Samuel II, also known as Sam Junior; she was their third child. The baby girl arrived at a New York City hospital and was taken to Boston just over six weeks later to be introduced to her two brothers, Samuel Walter III - known as Walt - and Lawrence - known as Larry.

Walt was intrigued by the sudden appearance of the baby girl, as at the age of eleven although he wasn't fully aware of the details of pregnancy and childbirth, he did have friends whose mothers had had babies and he was aware that they grew very fat before the baby was born, whereas there had been no evidence of his mother gaining weight or getting fat.

'But what do I know' he thought to himself, 'This is just another nuisance in my life!'. He already had Larry to annoy him, who was now five years old. Why not introduce another kid? He sometimes felt that his parents did not consider his feelings at all.

Walt would be going to junior high school in Boston North in September - it was the same private boarding school his father had attended - where he would be a weekly boarder coming home each weekend. He was looking forward to time away from his pesky little his brother and now a screaming baby sister!

By half term, Walt had asked his parents if he could be a full-time border, as he couldn't stand the incessant questions from his brother or the constant smell and crying of the baby. "I think you are overly exaggerating the situation Walt, but if it makes you happy then we have no problem with you boarding full-time," said his mother.

Walt wanted to ask his mother how she could possibly know he was exaggerating as she was never around; the nanny had full responsibility of the baby and Larry, whilst she was at some charity event or playing bridge with her cronies.

Walt's father was a second-generation oil magnet, his grandfather Samuel, had made his fortune in the Pennsylvania oil business in the middle eighteen hundreds and the business had been passed down to his two sons, Samuel Junior and Ethan. The business over the last hundred years had changed dramatically, diversifying into banking, financial services, and latterly, politics. Although the brothers ultimately ran the businesses, a network of family trusts owned them. These financial vehicles were set up to protect their wealth for future generations and render them more tax efficient.

Samuel Senior had dedicated his life to mining and found oil quite by accident in 1859, and virtually overnight became an extremely wealthy man. He had not married at this point in time, but he soon found a host of women vying for his attention. The one that caught his eye was the beautiful socialite Meredith 'Missy' Woods. Missy was almost forty years his junior and looking for a rich husband - and she found one - managing to get this wild disheveled man down the aisle in record time! By the age of sixty-two, Samuel had two sons, a huge house in Boston, a summer lodge in Maine, a ranch in Wyoming and a wife that liked nothing more than to spend money and socialize.

Samuel had spent the majority of his life attempting to make his fortune, and he was not going to let a frivolous wife fritter it away, so he sought financial advice and set up the family trusts to protect his wealth.

When Samuel Senior died at the grand age of ninety-six, he had already handed over the running of the businesses to his two sons. Having no interest in mining, they sold the oil fields to a publicly owned oil company and the family trusts received not only a multi-million-dollar payment, but also shares in the oil company. Samuel II became more involved in the banking and finance sector, whereas Ethan was more interested in the arts.

Ethan created a charitable trust to purchase works of art and paintings, which were then displayed in public galleries in major cities around America. Ethan also created a realty trust to purchase the premises that housed the galleries, thus adding realty to their empire.

Missy liked nothing better than attending corporate events at the galleries and mingling with the rich and famous, in the latest couture. At the age of fifty-five, she was still a striking woman with long wavy auburn hair styled loosely on top of her head, and adorned with jeweled pins. She would always wear beautiful handmade floor-length dresses in layered silk and on some occasions, she would carry a cane for effect. In cold weather, she would have fur-trimmed capes and hats to match her attire.

Missy had very little to do with her sons, instead employing a succession of nannies to take care of them. She was distraught at having grandchildren, always thinking of herself as twenty and certainly not a grandmother! Missy died after a short illness at the age of sixty-five.

Ethan had become involved in politics at university and now at the age of forty-five, he was a senator in the House of Representatives. He married Shirley in 1926, the daughter of a former senator and they had one son born in 1930, who they named Wesley.

CHAPTER 27

The house in Boston where the family lived the majority of the time, had been commissioned by Walt Senior in early 1885. He purchased just over three acres of land and gave a builder a rough sketch of the house he envisaged on the plot. It took ten years to complete, and when Missy got her hands on it in 1897, she extended it to double the original size and renamed it 'Grove Hall'. It was now a formidable residence, the original square colonial house now having extensions on either side. The front veranda commissioned by Samuel now displayed a pillared marble entrance with marble steps leading up to double mahogany doors.

The front door opened onto a vast hallway with an elaborate curved staircase leading up to the first floor. On either side of the hallway were a library to the left and a drawing room to the right; at the rear of the hallway, there were doors leading to the kitchen, dining room, a study and Missy's personal little sitting room. The dining room was huge with a table big enough to seat twenty people, with two sets of double patio doors leading on to a large veranda that overlooked the vast cultivated gardens. The dining room also had a double door leading to the kitchen, which was another vast room with a breakfast room attached for the children to eat their meals, and another set of patio doors leading to the rear veranda.

The first floor held the nursery with a door leading to the nanny's quarters; there were six additional bedrooms - some with a small bathroom attached - and the master bedroom that not only had its own luxurious bathroom, but a dressing room as well. The second floor held the staff quarters and several storage rooms.

Missy had arranged for the laying of plush carpets in all the upstairs rooms and the drawing room, with highly polished parquet flooring in the remaining rooms. All the downstairs rooms were furnished with expensive and modern furniture and the walls were adorned with original paintings. Every surface appeared to hold an antique vase or ornaments. Missy loved the house, employing an army of gardeners to keep the grounds in pristine condition - she had even ordered the erection of an orangery to grow exotic fruits and plants.

The house was not very child-friendly and Nanny had her work cut out keeping the children from running around inside the house, for fear of them breaking an expensive ornament. At least outside they could run around, as the only things that could get broken were an odd plant or two that were easily replaceable.

Samuel didn't like the showroom home, and in 1906 when his sons where seven and five, he bought the ranch in Wyoming where he could take the boys during the school holidays. Here, they learned to ride like cowboys and loved nothing more than hanging out with the real cowboys who worked the ranch for Samuel. Missy hated the place; in retaliation and on a whim, she bought a summer lodge on Moosehead Lake in Maine, which was a beautiful homely log cabin on the bank of the lake, with a mooring. However, after spending one summer there, Missy found it too remote and soon took herself back to Boston, whereas Samuel and the boys loved the remoteness, enjoying sailing on the lake and camping in the woods.

By 1916 the boys no longer wanted to go to the ranch or Maine, preferring to stay in Boston and hang out with their friends. Samuel Senior now aged seventy-eight preferred to stay in Wyoming. Here he could live a more casual life than Missy expected of him when he returned to Boston. He didn't want to dress up in a formal suit and socialize, he just wanted to smoke his pipe and ride his horse, so by the time Samuel died, he and Missy hadn't lived together for almost twenty years.

When Sam II started courting Grace Doyle in 1929 and brought her home to meet his mother, Missy knew she was the right sort of wife for Sam and encouraged the courtship. They married in 1932 at St Stephen's Catholic Church in Boston. Samuel Senior being too frail to attend the society wedding in Boston and was never to meet his new daughter-in-law. Grace turned her nose up at a honeymoon in Wyoming preferring to go to Europe. On their return from honeymoon the couple took up residence in Grove Hall, and Missy moved to a plush apartment overlooking Haymarket Square that she had purchased for herself.

Grace was originally of Irish descent; her grandfather Calhoun Doyle, was a staunch Catholic who had arrived in Boston from Ireland with a small amount of money in his pocket. He set himself up as a small trader, selling rejects of factory-made clothing from a wheelbarrow and within fifty years he had his own mills and factories, producing garments of all descriptions and was wealthy beyond his wildest dreams. Grace was his eldest grandchild - the daughter of his eldest son Padraig.

Grace had been brought up like a princess. She had been an only child and given everything she asked for and more. She had been tutored at home by a succession of tutors; none had stayed more than two years finding it hard to cope with this precocious spoilt little girl. Samuel II, at the age of twenty-nine, was one of the most eligible bachelors in Boston and on meeting him at the first society ball of the season, Grace set her sights on him. 'This is the man I will marry!' she thought to herself - and marry him she did, two years later!

Grace soon took over Missy's role as a society hostess, a job she had been born for and relished every aspect. After four years of married life, Grace was disappointed not to have become pregnant, as she was expected to produce an heir to inherit their joint wealth. She sought out a respected gynecologist in Boston and tried all the methods recommended by him, but to no avail. When adoption was first suggested, Grace spoke to their local priest, Father Theodore, as she knew the church was heavily involved in adoption at that time. Father Theodore told her about a convent in Ireland that cared for unmarried mothers that the church worked with at close quarters. The church assisted in finding suitable Catholic families that could offer these children a home. The priest explained that American couples were the preferred choice for the adoption of these children, as the Sisters at the convent felt that the children would have a better quality of life in America.

"Nothing to do with money then?" questioned a sarcastic Sam when Grace broached the subject of adoption with him.

Grace and a reluctant Sam travelled to Ireland in early 1939 and returned with a baby boy, Samuel Walter Henderson III, known as Walt, at last making them a family. The intervening war years prevented Grace adopting another child, and it wasn't until late 1945 that they were able to travel to the same convent in Ireland returning with another baby boy, whom they named Lawrence Samuel, to be known as Larry.

Grace wanted to complete her family with a girl and it took several years to convince Sam, but in August 1950 they again made the journey to Ireland, this time returning with a beautiful baby girl, who they named Millicent Barbara.

CHAPTER 28

Millicent's name was soon shortened to Millie and during her first year of life, she was looked after by a wet nurse. Once weaned, she was handed over to Larry's nanny, Nanny Margie.

Marjorie Kennedy had joined the family when Larry was one year old; she had come over from Ireland in 1946 when her local priest had recommended her for the job as the nanny for Grace's son. She was eighteen when she arrived and was now twenty-three. She longed to get married and have children of her own, but had little opportunity at Grove Hall. The nearest she got to romance was flirting with one of the gardeners, but their days off never seemed to coincide so it hadn't progressed beyond snatches of conversation when the children were playing in the garden.

Margie loved her job. She had her own room and was paid a good wage, most of which she saved and was accumulating a sizeable sum in the savings bank.

Larry now attended a private primary school not far from their home. A driver would take him each morning and pick him up at the end of the day. He was a loving, gentle little boy and Nanny Margie's favourite, he loved nothing more than listening to a story, sitting on Nanny's knee. Like his brother he had dark hair and a pale complexion but was the complete opposite in nature. Nanny didn't like Walt much - she found him brash and rude - and was thankful that she didn't have to look after him. Whenever he came home from school, he rarely ventured up to the nursery section of the house. Instead, he remained in the kitchen with Mrs Grant the cook, and took his meals with his parents.

Millie was an adorable little girl and Margie knew that she was adopted, although Grace never actually said as much to her. There had been no evidence of a pregnancy, Grace had just turned up with the baby late one evening with a wet nurse in tow. Margie valued her job too much to ask questions and therefore kept her assumption to herself. However, she did wonder whether the two boys were also adopted, as although there was some similarity in all three children, such as dark hair and a pale complexion, all three had very different personalities.

Margie found the family dynamics very strange; she had been brought up in a loving but poor Irish family where they sat down altogether to eat a family meal each day. Whereas at Grove Hall, the children ate their meals with Margie in the breakfast room each day. She presumed this was how rich people did things, but she still felt that it was not quite right. However, this changed as the children grew up and started high school, their parents having decided that they were mature enough to eat with them.

Every evening before bedtime, Margie would take the children downstairs for time with their parents. When Millie reached the age of two things started to change in the household, Grace began to take more interest in the children even giving Margie an extra day off every other week and taking charge of Millie herself, even collecting Larry from school.

It was on one of these days off that Margie started courting John, the gardener, and it was two years before she plucked up enough courage to tell Grace of their courtship and their intention to get married. But she needn't have worried as Grace congratulated her and even offered them accommodation in one of the workers' cottages. By the time Millie started her schooling, Margie had a baby of her own and no longer looked after Grace's children.

With the departure of Margie, Grace felt that the children were too old for a nanny and instead employed a male tutor. Thirty-year-old Jonathon Stiles would arrive each morning to tutor Millie and to help Larry with his homework. At weekends he would keep them entertained with trips to the swimming baths, where he taught them to swim, or trips to the cinema to see the latest movie. Depending on the weather he would take them to play in the nearby park, and on rainy days they would visit museums. He also taught them how to ride a bicycle and would take them on long bike rides, returning them home exhausted.

Grace was convinced that Jonathon was homosexual but kept her thoughts to herself. She was also a little bit in love with him; he had chiseled features, dark hair combed back in a quiff and an athletic body, unlike Sam whose hair was now receding with flecks of grey and his body had become a bit flabby. But at fifty-seven, what did she expect?

Larry, at the age of twelve, followed in Walt's footsteps and started as a weekly boarder at junior high school. He also decided to become a full-time border after the first term. Millie missed him terribly and was lonely with just Jonathon; she desperately wanted to go to school, but her mother said that girls of her status didn't go to school.

The summer that Millie turned ten and Larry fourteen, Grace decided to spend the summer holidays in Maine, asking Jonathon to join them. "The lodge is right on the lake and we have a small sailboat, so you could teach the children to sail. I'm sure you would enjoy it," said Grace.

After some thought Jonathon agreed. 'I've nothing much else to do these summer holidays' he thought to himself, his relationship with his latest boyfriend had recently come to an amicable end, and he had been dreading being on his own during the summer months. Plus, he was being paid to go on holiday!

Grace wanted to get away from Boston and Sam, she was convinced that he was having an affair - not that she had any evidence, it was just that he had changed so much over the last six months. He had dyed his hair to cover the grey streaks and started going to the gym. When Grace asked him about this midlife crisis as she called it, he dismissed her saying "I'm just trying to improve my lifestyle. I was getting too fat sitting behind a desk all day, and the doctor said I should lose weight and get fit!" he explained. Grace didn't believe him as they attended the same doctor, who was also a friend, and he hadn't said anything to Grace about seeing Sam.

Grace ordered the lodge to be cleaned and aired in readiness for their arrival and asked for the larder to be fully stocked. They employed a local couple, Mr and Mrs Clark, to look after the lodge which they did - along with several other lodges nearby.

At the beginning of August, they packed what they need for a month and made their way to Maine. It had been a long time since Millie had been to the lodge and she hardly remembered what it looked like. Larry was excited to be going as he loved the outdoors, telling Millie what they would be able to do.

"We will be able to go swimming, canoeing, and make a camp in the woods and sleep there overnight," he explained to Millie. No sooner had they arrived than Larry dragged Jonathon out to the boathouse to check on the sailing boat and the canoes. They washed the boat and quickly painted it ready to test the following day, but unfortunately the canoes had perished and were beyond repair. Grace unpacked with a reluctant Millie who had wanted to go out and help the boys.

Larry came indoors. "Mom, we will have to get some new canoes! Those in the shed are no good, will it be okay if I go to the boatyard and get some more tomorrow?" asked Larry.

"Yes, go and see Mr Clark he will help you get some. Why don't you get two doubles, then we can all go canoeing together?" suggested Grace.

"You want to go out on the lake in a canoe, Mom? Well, that will be a first!" laughed Larry.

"Don't be so cheeky! Just because you haven't seen me in a canoe doesn't mean that I haven't been in one!" responded Grace.

"Well, I can't wait to see you!" said Larry.

"It's getting late, why don't you two come in now and help us get some dinner together? Then we can have an early night ready for an early start in the morning? It's been a long day."

Mrs Clark had left them a chicken salad in the fridge, so Grace and Millie prepared dinner for the four of them, while the boys laid the table. The lodge had six bedrooms and previously when the family had spent time at the lodge, Grace had employed a local lady to come in to cook and clean. On this occasion, Mrs Clarke had been unable to find a cook only a cleaner, but promised that if required she would come and cook a meal for them.

Although Grace knew vaguely how to prepare a meal, Millie had never been allowed by Mrs Grant to do any cooking. She had only been allowed to watch, so this was a new experience for Millie and she liked it. "Now Millie, this is only a salad and this is about my limit! I can't cook so don't expect much from me!" Grace said before Millie could comment.

"Do you have a barbecue?" asked Jonathon.

"Yes, there is a brick one built out the back, why?" asked Grace.

"Well, so as long as you can prepare a salad, I can cook the meat on the barbecue. Larry and I will inspect it tomorrow, and go and see what they have at the shop," suggested Jonathon.

"We could go fishing and cook the fish," said an enthusiastic Larry.

"You two are going to be busy tomorrow! Now come and sit down!" said Grace. They sat down to a lovely chicken salad with crusty bread all prepared by Mrs Clark, and put on the plates by Grace and Millie. 'And that,' thought Millie to herself, 'Is what Mom called preparing dinner!'.

The next day the boys went to buy some new canoes with Mr Clark; they also got some charcoal, lifejackets and fishing rods together with all the reels, hooks and lines recommended by the shop assistant, and loaded all their purchases into Mr Clark's truck.

Mr Clark set up all the rods for them and showed them how to bait their hooks and cast the rods. He also showed them what to do when the line got tangled, as he thought to himself 'That they will undoubtedly do!' He helped them carry the canoes down to the lakeside and on seeing the sailing boat, he said: "I think it might be a good idea to get some new sails. I'll get these this afternoon for you, now is there anything else you need?"

"A tent please, Mr Clark! Millie and I are hoping to go camping in the woods," said Larry.

"Okay, my boy, I will see to it!" said Mr Clark - thinking to himself, 'These townies have no idea what they are doing!' Seeing the expression on Mr Clark's face, Jonathon assured him that he was an accomplished sailor having spent a lot of his childhood at the lakes in Michigan.

Grace and Millie came back from shopping loaded with groceries and filled the pantry and refrigerator with their purchases. Grace felt quite pleased with herself, but as Millie said later to the boys, "The lady at the shop told us what to buy and even added some items we would never even have thought of buying."

That evening they ate burgers in buns with a salad; Grace had never eaten a burger before and wanted to use her knife and fork until she saw Jonathon pick the bun up and eat it with his hands.

Mrs Clark had made up four bedrooms for the family and at the end of their first day, Grace invited Jonathon to have a drink of champagne with her on the veranda, after the children had finally gone to bed. They sat in the moonlight on the swing settee that Mr Clark had set up on the grass outside the lodge. It was a beautiful warm night and after two glasses of champagne, Grace suggested they go for a swim.

"I will just go and change into my swimming shorts," said Jonathon.

Taking Jonathon by the hand and leading him towards the water, she said: "No, let's go skinny dipping!" and began taking off her clothes. Jonathon was a bit surprised by Grace's suggestion, but after a couple of drinks he thought, 'Why not?' and took off his clothes and dived into the water.

"Come on then!" he shouted, "This was your idea! It's absolutely invigorating – well, cold actually!"

Grace didn't dive in but instead gently walked in from the bank. "My goodness it is cold!" she declared, lowering herself into the water and swimming towards Jonathon.

Jonathon could clearly see her naked body in the moonlight, thinking to himself 'Not a bad body for a woman of her age'. They swam around for a short time before Grace said, "I think we should get out now, I am sure something is swimming around my feet!"

"Don't be such a cissy!" joked Jonathon, diving beneath the water and grabbing hold of her ankles. Grace screamed as he pulled her under the water.

"You! You…!" she spluttered when she surfaced.

"What?" he asked, grabbing hold of her to stopping her from going under the water again.

"That's not fair! You're a better swimmer than me," she said, holding on to him for support. As she held on to him, she could feel his gradual erection against her body, and looking into each other's eyes they kissed gently. As they parted, Jonathon was about to apologize, when Grace took hold of him wrapping her legs around his body. He held her tight and they kissed again, Jonathan exploring her mouth with his tongue.

"I think we should get out now," he gently whispered in her ear, sending shivers down her body. They collapsed onto the grass, kissing passionately and exploring each other's bodies with their hands. Eventually, Jonathon lay on top of her and they made love. It was the most fantastic sensation that she had ever experienced; in her thirty years of marriage, she had never achieved an orgasm! 'What having I been missing?' she thought to herself. Afterwards, they lay in each other's arms looking up at the stars for some time in total silence.

"You are the first woman I have ever made love to," Jonathon said in a whisper.

"And what did you think?" Grace asked, "Because for me it was amazing - in fact, so amazing I want to do it again!"

Jonathon turned to her and kissed her. "Then let's go to bed … now!" he said, pulling her to her feet and almost running into the lodge. He carried her into her bedroom, closing the door quietly behind him so as not to wake up the children, before lowering her on to the bed. He started kissing her on her stomach and slowly making his way up her body before making love to her, this time more urgently, and exhausted they both fell blissfully asleep.

Early the next morning, Jonathon slipped out of her room and into his own room, before the children were awake.

Millie noticed an immediate change in her mother; she was suddenly laughing a lot, joining in with the activities and she even hugged and kissed her. The change in Grace mystified Millie, but she relished in it. Her mother had never been tactile with any of her children, but now she appeared to be a totally different person.

Having been home tutored Millie was oblivious to the ways of life and relationships. Although Jonathon had tried to get her involved with other children by taking her to a swimming club and a reading club at the library, she was still very naïve. However, Larry being at school with other boys of his age and sharing playing fields with the girls' school next door, was very aware. Going to an all-boys' school all they seemed to discuss, at the age of almost fifteen, were girls and sex. So, when he saw Jonathon sneaking into his mother's room late one night, he immediately guessed what was going on.

Millie and Larry had the best holiday ever that summer; they spent days sailing on the lake - almost drowning at one point when the boat overturned, but thankfully they were wearing their life jackets. They paddled their canoes until their arms ached, Millie sharing with her mother, and Larry with Jonathon. They all patiently fished with Larry catching a huge - according to Larry - Lake Trout, which Jonathon gutted and barbecued for their dinner. Millie and Larry also made friends with some neighbouring children and they all went camping together in the woods, leaving Grace and Jonathon alone in the lodge.

All too soon it was time to leave. On their last night, Grace lay in Jonathon's arms feeling sad that this would be their last night together. She was totally in love with him, and the feeling of emptiness left her distraught, especially at the thought, that she may never enjoy these moments again. She knew the relationship couldn't last, she would never leave Sam even if he were having an affair, a divorce in their society was out of the question.

"What happens now, Grace? Will I see you when we get back?" asked a concerned Jonathon.

"I don't think I could bear to lose you, but you must understand that I could never leave Sam either," replied Grace.

"I do understand Grace, but I want to carry on seeing you," he said, kissing her.

"We will work something out. I want to carry on seeing you as well!" she said, returning his kiss.

CHAPTER 29

Grace had reluctantly agreed that Millie could go to school and had enrolled her into a nearby private girls' school.

Grace was busy when they got back to Boston after their holiday; organizing Millie for school, she took her shopping for her new school uniform, buying her a satchel and all the pens and pencils she wanted. This was the first time she had been properly shopping with her mother - they even went to lunch. Millie loved this new relationship that was developing with her mother.

Even more, Millie loved school. Having been home tutored she was much more advanced than her fellow pupils in English, Mathematics, History and Geography but she lagged behind in the other non-core subjects like Art, Science and especially PE. She didn't know how to play netball or hockey and had to learn quickly. She soon made a best friend in Sophie; Sophie Petty was also new to the school having moved to Boston from New York, and they soon became inseparable. Sophie came from a different background to Millie, both her parents worked hard running a restaurant so that their two children could attend private school; to them education was the way to a better future and encouraged both the children to work hard at school.

Three weeks after they arrived back from Maine, Sam went away on business for the weekend, giving Grace a chance to meet up with Jonathon. They arranged to meet at his apartment; it was a small one bedroomed apartment with a galley kitchen off the small living area and a tiny bathroom - all Jonathon could afford until he got a new job. They spent two glorious nights together, with Grace making an excuse to Mrs Grant that she had to go away for a charitable function.

"Jonathon, your apartment's a bit small can't you get a bigger one?" she said to him seriously.

"Oh, Grace, you are such a snob! What's wrong with my apartment? We only need the bed," said Jonathon. She hit him playfully objecting to what he said.

"What I mean is that there is no room for me even to leave a change of clothes! And your bathroom, well how can we both fit in that little bathtub?" she laughed.

"I know it's small, but I will get a bigger one as soon as I start my new job, which by the way is in two weeks at Taylor's College teaching English to foreign students!" Jonathon informed her.

"That's great, but would you let me buy you an apartment?" Grace asked.

"Oh, Grace how could I possibly let you buy me an apartment? What would happen if we broke up? It's very generous of you, but I don't think it is a good idea," he said seriously.

"It would be a present with no strings attached! If we broke up - please God I couldn't bear the thought of that! - then it would be yours to do with as you please." she promised.

Two months later, using some of the inheritance left to her by her father that was tucked away in a trust fund, Jonathan moved into a plush two bedroomed penthouse apartment. As far as Grace was concerned it was perfect as she could drive into the basement car park and get the lift directly up to the apartment without meeting anyone.

Grace was the patron of a charity set up by her father many years before his death. Its main objectives were to provide education and welfare for underprivileged children. Over the years with all her contacts, the charity had become well renowned throughout America. Grace would travel all over America, hosting fundraising events and visiting centres set up by the charity. When three months into their relationship, she was told that the head of fundraising was retiring, she put Jonathon's name forward for the position. In her opinion, with his educational background he was perfect a perfect candidate, and luckily enough, the Trustees agreed and offered him the job.

It was the perfect arrangement, Jonathon would accompany Grace on her various visits and partner her at fundraising events, so the arrangement suited them both very well. Jonathon was still uncertain about his sexuality and would often seek out male company, which for obvious reasons he kept secret from Grace, avoiding bringing them back to his apartment at all costs.

Grace now slept in a separate bedroom from Sam, saying that his snoring prevented her from having a good night's sleep, which he accepted without a fight. She still suspected that he had a mistress, but as she no longer loved him, she didn't really care. Although part of her still felt betrayed, and would often think to herself, 'What's wrong with me?'.

Jonathon had furnished his apartment to suit Grace, as he still felt it was more hers than his and would consult her when buying anything new. "I don't know why you ask me! If you like it, then buy it! And if you like it, then I am pretty sure I will like it as well." She would say.

In 1965, with summer fast approaching and long school holidays ahead, Grace suggested to Millie that perhaps they could go to Maine again for their summer holidays. Millie was now fifteen, and Grace felt that this would be the last year that Millie would want to go on holiday with her.

Larry had from the age of seventeen preferred to go to summer camp with his friends, rather than go away with the family. It had been two years since they had all been to Maine, the previous year Sam had arranged a family holiday in Florida, but in the end only Millie had gone with them. It had been a tense time as Grace had to sleep in the same hotel room as Sam, although unbeknown to him, she had requested twin beds so at least she was able to avoid any physical contact.

"Daddy wants to go down to the ranch this summer, but it is up to you? Either come with me to Maine or go with Daddy to the ranch," Grace asked Millie.

"I think I would prefer to come with you, but Larry won't want to come, and I would be on my own. Unless, perhaps Sophie could come as well?" asked a hopeful Millie.

"Well, you can ask her, but her parents may have arranged something else!" agreed Grace.

"I will phone her now!" Millie disappeared into the study and came back about five minutes later.

"Mom, Mom she can come! It'll be a great time with Sophie, I can't wait!" said an excited Millie.

"Would you mind if I invited Jonathon to come with us?" asked Grace.

"No, he is good fun, and he can cook like last time!" replied Millie.

"There is just one thing Millie. Please can you not tell Daddy that Jonathon is coming with us? It can be our little secret," suggested Grace.

“Okay, but why not tell Daddy?” she asked curiously.

“Trust me, he wouldn’t be happy!” laughed Grace, trying not to make a big deal out of it.

So it was that at the beginning of August they made their way to Maine arriving early evening. Mrs Clarke had again prepared the lodge for them making up four bedrooms, but Millie insisted that she and Sophie share a room. The girls chose which room they wanted and dumped their luggage on the floor and made to go out, “Where do you think you two are going?” asked Grace.

“We thought we would go and see who's about down at the marina! it’s still light outside, please Mom? replied Millie.

“Okay, but come back when it gets dark, Mrs Clark has left us a salad for dinner, so you can eat when you get back.” said Grace.

Millie and Sophie ran to the marina where there was a group of teenagers about their age, they soon joined them and introduced themselves. The group was all on holiday, some of them Millie knew from previous visits, and they were soon making arrangements for the next day. They stayed and chatted to the group until it got dark and then made their way back to the lodge.

Grace was waiting for them. “Oh, there you are, I was beginning to get worried,” she said.

“It’s okay Mom we met up with a group all about our age. We are going out with them tomorrow, you don’t mind, do you?” Millie asked.

“No, that is fine. It’s good that you make some friends your own age to go about with, although Jonathon might miss having someone to go canoeing with," said Grace.

"Don't worry about me! I will enjoy relaxing and I might go fishing, although I will have to go and get some bait first," said Jonathon.

"We'll need to stock up with food, so I will come with you. Then I can relax in my deckchair and read a book while you're fishing," suggested Grace.

"Sounds perfect to me," said Jonathon.

During the month they were in Maine they hardly saw the girls, each morning they would take what they needed for the day and disappear, or sometimes their group would come to the lodge to meet them. On those days they were usually canoeing on the lake in front of the lodge, Jonathon would light the barbecue and cook burgers and sausages to feed them all. "It's the least I can do because I am sure the other parents must be feeding Millie and Sophie when they are gone all day!" said Jonathon.

With the lodge being fairly private, Grace and Jonathon were able to swim and to sail together and then disappear into the lodge to make love. Some days they would just relax, read and drink copious amounts of champagne.

"This is the life," said Jonathon, "Beats work any day; I could get used to this!" Grace laughed, thinking 'Welcome to my world!'

Millie and Sophie had each found themselves a boyfriend from the group and the four of them would go for walks hand in hand. They had wanted to go camping in the woods but Grace fearing the worst, explained that they were too young to be camping out all night with two boys.

"You are such a spoilsport, Mom! What do you think we are going to do?" asked Millie.

"It's not you I am worried about, it's those boys! They are a bit older than you. Anyway, my answer is still no!" said Grace to a huffing and puffing Millie.

Jonathon laughed at Grace, "You are such a spoilsport Mommy!" he teased, "And what exactly do you think those boys are after?"

"I think you can guess at that, after all, you were a sixteen-year-old boy once upon a time!" she responded knowingly.

Millie and Sophie flounced off to tell the boys they couldn't go camping and suggested that they go to the cinema instead. On the way back home after the cinema, leaving the boys to go one way and Millie and Sophie the other, Sophie asked Millie, "What exactly is your relationship with Jonathon?"

"He was my tutor until I went to school, and now he works with my mom," replied Millie, "Why do you ask?"

"So, he's not your mom's boyfriend then?" asked Sophie.

"Of course not, Mom is married to my Dad, silly! What makes you say that anyway?" asked Millie.

"Well, it is just that the other morning when I went to the bathroom before you were awake, I saw Jonathon coming out of your Mom's bedroom and he was only wearing his underpants," said Sophie.

Millie went quiet, not knowing what to say. "Oh!" was all she replied. Suddenly everything fell into place; Millie now knew why her mother didn't want her father to know that Jonathon was coming on holiday with them. How her mother had changed from the distant and cold person she was before that first time they came to Maine with Jonathon, to the happier, more loving and tactile mother that she was now; how she had happened upon Jonathon giving her mother a shoulder massage, her mother giving the excuse that she had a crick her neck. Her Mother and Jonathon were having an affair!

The remainder of the walk home Millie was very quiet. "I wish I hadn't said anything to you now!" exclaimed Sophie, "I have obviously upset you and that is the last thing I wanted to do."

"I am sorry, Sophie! It is just that, well…I should have guessed! And in fact, if I am honest with myself? I did know but chose not to believe it," explained Millie.

"It won't affect our friendship, will it? You are my best friend, and I couldn't bear it if you didn't want to be my friend anymore," implored Sophie.

"Don't be silly, you are my best friend as well, and nothing will ever change that! Can I ask just one favour though?" said Millie, "Please can you not tell anyone else, especially your parents?"

"You should know me better than that! I would never betray a confidence, and I promise I will not tell anyone else," replied Sophie.

Millie changed the subject and they started discussing the forthcoming new term at school. The junior high school they attended demanded that each pupil participate in at least two extracurricular activities. They both loved tennis and would play this all year round, either outside during the summer or inside during the colder weather, so this remained their first choice. The previous term they had chosen to learn to play chess but they were both useless at it, so decided they needed to choose something else for the coming term.

There were several choices, Millie was already an accomplished piano player and therefore didn't want a music-based activity. Sophie had said she would like to play the guitar, but as she wanted to do something with Millie, she decided against this activity.

So, the activity they had chosen to start together was archaeology. They had attended a talk on the subject at the end of the previous term, given by a university lecturer by the name of Professor Alan Wilson and thought it might be quite fun; they would get to go on the occasional digs and visit museums. Millie had shown an interest in the history of man and evolution when Jonathon had taken her on various visits to national historical parks and museums when she was younger, and she longed to learn more. Her enthusiasm had rubbed off on to Sophie, who was now as eager as Millie to get started.

At the end of their long summer holiday, a driver had picked them up from the station and dropped Jonathon off first and then Sophie. Millie waved goodbye to Sophie. "See you Monday at school!" she shouted from the car window.

Sam was waiting at the door to greet them, he gave Grace a peck on the check. "Lovely to have you both home, did you have a good time?" he asked.

"It was the best! We met loads of people our age and did lots of swimming and sailing. Mom cooked on the barbecue, would you believe?" said an excited Millie.

"Well, you both look very tanned," he said hugging Millie, "I missed you!"

"How did your holiday go Dad? Not as good as ours I bet?" asked Millie.

"Well I rode every day and went out with the work hands to check on the cattle, looked at all the improvements made since I was last there, discussed the future improvements to be made and generally did nothing but relax and not think about work," he explained.

"Were you okay on your own Dad? You weren't lonely without us?" quizzed Millie.

"What do you think?" he asked, "Now let me help you upstairs with your cases."

Larry came home two days later, now in his second year at university where he was studying Economics and Marketing, in readiness to join his father in the family business.

Millie knocked on his bedroom door. "Come in!" he shouted, and on seeing Millie he asked her how her holiday with their mother had gone.

"We had a great time, how was yours?" she replied.

"Fantastic, you can imagine all boys together - or perhaps you can't being a girl!" he joked.

"Larry…er…can I ask you something?" asked Millie, hesitantly.

"Of course, Ask me anything you like!" said Larry looking towards Millie and seeing the concerned look on her face.

"No, let me guess - you are going to ask me about Jonathon?" he stated.

"How on earth did you know that?" she answered.

"Well, you've just come back from holiday with Mom. Just the two of you - and Sophie of course! - and I bet 'The Jonathon' went as well?" he said.

"You are psychic sometimes, but did you know…?" she asked, hinting with her eyes.

"Yes, I guessed some time ago. Well, after our last holiday together in Maine I became suspicious, then when the charity employed him and I had to attend an event, I saw them looking all lovey-dovey." Explained Larry.

"What about Dad, does he know?" questioned Millie.

"I doubt it, but don't worry about Dad. He has a bit on the side - you know his secretary, Jessica? - she goes everywhere with him, part of her duties as secretary. I bet she went on holiday with him to the ranch," said Larry.

Millie started to cry gentle tears that flowed down her cheeks, she couldn't quite believe what she was hearing.

"Don't cry Millie," said Larry, putting his arms around her and holding her.

"What will happen to us if they divorce?" she asked tentatively.

"That will never happen, Millie, not in their society. Everything is for appearance, so there is no need to be concerned, life will just carry on as before. I suggest you keep this to yourself that would be the best course of action," said Larry.

"What about Walt, does he know?" raised Millie.

"You know Walt, he is only concerned for himself, so I doubt it! I can't be sure, but I wouldn't recommend you tell him. You know you can talk to me anytime Mills, don't you?" offered a concerned Larry.

Millie knew that she could always talk to Larry. Ever since she was a toddler, she had sought out Larry, she loved his sensitivity and he would always praise her piano playing even when it was initially awful. He would read bedtime stories to her making up the story if the book he was reading from was too long, and he wanted her to get to sleep. He would cuddle her if she fell to try and make her feel better, and he would even participate in playing childish games with her. Even though he was five years older than her, he never dismissed her.

Unlike Walt, as soon as Millie became aware of feelings, she felt he hated or was perhaps was jealous of her. When she was a toddler, he would pinch her to make her cry and then tell Nanny that she was crying over nothing, again. When she was older, she learned to stay out of his way.

Walt was obnoxious and arrogant; he appeared to think that everyone was beneath him, especially when it came to her and Larry. He had scraped into university and studied accountancy but had not achieved the results expected of him by their father. He had gone into the family business and been placed in the accounting department but was not well-liked by his colleagues, Millie had often heard her father saying to Walt that he had to curb his arrogance and not throw his weight around as if he owned the place. "You have to earn respect," she had heard her father say. It was only when she was older that she understood what her father was trying to instill in Walt. But nothing much changed, Walt was the boss's son, and over the years he had remained in the same position in the office while other more deserving employees had been promoted and moved on.

Walt no longer lived at the family home. Instead, he had acquired an apartment nearer to the office, where he resided with a live-in housekeeper. He would come home every other weekend for Sunday lunch with the family, chatting to his mother and father mostly about business, and ignoring Millie and Larry, only speaking to them if he had to. So, there was no way that Millie would mention anything to Walt about their mother's affair.

CHAPTER 30

Five years into their relationship it was still as fresh as that first day. As soon as Grace would arrive at the apartment, they would be tearing each other's clothes off and making their way to the bedroom. Jonathon taught her all aspects of lovemaking which she never thought possible, even buying her a few sex toys to experiment with.

Grace was now fifty-six but felt no different from when she was seventeen, and her heart still missed a beat when she saw Jonathon. Her enviable figure had remained the same since her early twenties, and she could easily pass for someone ten years younger.

However, Jonathon now aged forty had started to experience a series of illnesses. At first it was a constant cough and a head cold that took weeks to shake off, and he would be tired for long periods. He would put it down to the stress of work or unhealthy eating, and when he began to lose weight Grace demanded that he go to the doctor for a check-up.

Jonathon didn't like going to the doctor, thinking it was a complete waste of time and he would miss crucial appointments. As a consequence, it took almost a year before he was diagnosed with leukemia. Grace was devastated and paid for the best specialist in the business to get treatment. The first round of chemotherapy left him drained and unable to look after himself, so Grace employed a fulltime nurse to look after and care for him during that time. She would visit as often as possible.

A year after the treatment, he was given the 'all clear,' and their life resumed to as it was before his illness. They celebrated with a holiday in the Caribbean before Jonathon returned to work. Grace told Sam that she had booked a spa holiday on her own, where she could get pampered every day and it was not something he would enjoy, leaving him bemused as he knew Grace didn't like her own company.

They enjoyed a full week together lying on the beach, swimming and each night making love, which she had missed during the time he was having treatment. Grace loved him more than life itself and couldn't even contemplate losing him. For Jonathon, it was perhaps slightly different; although in his own way he loved her, it was not all-consuming and he felt at times a bit overpowered by her constant attention, especially after his illness. Jonathon was glad the holiday was only for a week as more than that was not something he wished to contemplate. He liked their arrangement whereby he only saw her once or twice a week and the occasional weekend on business, he couldn't imagine himself married to anyone.

CHAPTER 31

Millie, at the age of eighteen, started at the University of Boston sharing a room with Sophie on the campus. Her mother had wanted her to rent an apartment near to the university as she felt that campus was not in keeping with their status, but Millie didn't want to be different; she wanted to be like everyone else.

"But who will do your washing Millie? and how will you feed yourself?" asked her mother.

She was right of course, Millie had never lifted a finger to do anything around the house; Mrs Grant did all the cooking, and there were maids who picked up Millie's washing from the bathroom floor and miraculously, it would turn up washed and ironed neatly laid on her bed. She didn't really know what a washing machine was, never mind actually use one.

"Don't worry Mrs Henderson, I will teach her how to look after herself!" said Sophie, "But don't expect me to pick up after you, Millie, you will have to do your bit! Cooking is easy, especially if we live on beans on toast."

Millie knew that Jonathon hadn't been well; she had caught her mother crying inconsolably one afternoon and when she tried to comfort her, the entire story had come tumbling out. She didn't know what to say, realizing how difficult it must be for her mother to keep her emotions under control in the presence of her father, and all the time being worried sick about Jonathon.

At one point she heard her father say, "For God sake woman, pull yourself together, what is the matter with you?" to which her mother replied, "I think it is the menopause my hormones are all over the place. I will go see the doctor, see if he can give me something."

Millie knew that her father's affair had ended as on one occasion when Walt was having Sunday lunch with them, he had asked his father about his secretary.

"What's happened to Jessica, Dad? I went up to your office, and there was a new woman there?"

"Oh! She decided to leave for pastures new about a month ago. She wanted to work part-time but that is no good to me, I need a fulltime secretary. So that was it, she left!" explained her father.

"After all these years! Staff! You can't rely on them, can you? No loyalty these days." responded Walt. Millie and Larry looked at each other, dying to know more, but unable to ask. Now Millie understood why her father had been so grouchy the last couple of months. She had just thought he was having a difficult time at work, but now she knew different.

In a way Millie felt guilty at leaving her mother alone with her father and going off to university. Her father had started spending more time working from home and she knew this irritated her mother, as she couldn't sneak off to see Jonathon as often as before.

Larry now worked in the marketing department of the family business and was a respected employee, unlike Walt. He had moved into his own apartment, which he told Millie that more often than not, was shared with his girlfriend, Izzy. He had been dating Izzy since his last year at university and he confided in Millie of his intention to ask her to marry him. Millie liked Izzy a lot. She was funny, and she adored her brother. Izzy came from a hard-working family and had taken up a teaching post at a local primary school. She was very down to earth; she would joke about how she had to teach Larry to iron his shirts and cook a meal. There was no way that Izzy was going to be a stay at home wife like Grace.

To everyone's surprise, Walt brought a woman along to one of the family's Sunday lunches and her name was Muriel. She was older than Walt by several years although nobody said exactly, Millie just guessed. She was a perfect match for Walt; snooty and obnoxious, she was a tall thin woman with a pointy nose and thin mousey hair. Millie instantly disliked her, especially when she asked Millie what she was going to study at university. When Millie replied, "Archaeology," she dismissed her with her nose in the air as though she was a bit of dirt on her shoe saying, "How extraordinary."

There was a full society wedding for Walt and Muriel when they married six months later, Millie was glad that she wasn't asked to be a bridesmaid - Muriel already telling her that she was far too old. Muriel's mother organized everything, only asking Grace for a list of guests and friends from their side of the family. This suited Grace as Jonathon was in the middle of his treatment at that time, and she could think of nothing else.

Millie and Izzy sat next to each other in church, "I bet you are glad you weren't asked to be a bridesmaid? Look at those awful dresses - you would have looked like a walking blancmange!" said a giggling Izzy. "Anyway, when you are my bridesmaid or should I say, 'Maid of Honour', we will go and choose together - something classy!" said Izzy.

Millie was surprised, "Has Larry asked you?"

"Yes'" said an excited Izzy, "Last weekend, but don't tell anyone yet! Larry wants to wait until after Walt's wedding before making the announcement. He doesn't want to take the limelight off Muriel."

Millie was ecstatic, not only to be asked to be Maid of Honour but that her favourite brother was to marry a girl that had become a good friend. Sophie remained her best friend, but Izzy was a close second.

"When will the wedding be, soon, I hope?" asked Millie.

"We hope perhaps next spring, but it won't be posh like this! My parents couldn't possibly afford anything near this extravaganza; it will be a small and intimate, with just the family and friends that we are close to," explained Izzy.

"I don't blame you! It makes you wonder if Walt even knows half these people," whispered Millie, as the ceremony was about to commence.

The reception was held in a marquee at Walt's golf club. There were over five hundred guests with champagne flowing, as soon as your glass was empty a waiter was behind you refilling it. Millie and Izzy got a little bit tipsy and were told off by Grace for giggling too much.

"Muriel's parents must be well off to afford all this," commented Izzy.

"I think her father is some sort of banker and she is their only child, so not short of a cent or two," remarked Millie.

Millie, together with Larry and Izzy, circulated amongst the guests speaking to the people they knew and trying not to drink too much more, as instructed by Grace, which was difficult as there appeared to be no soft drinks available.

The family was staying overnight at the hotel attached to the golf club and Larry had to virtually carry

Millie to her room. In the morning, she struggled down to breakfast, feeling the worst for wear.

Izzy said, "You look how I feel, and that's not good. Fancy bacon and eggs for breakfast?"

"Please don't even mention food, my head is about to explode! All I want is water and aspirin," mumbled Millie. Larry suggested she have something to eat as it would make her feel better, handing her a glass of water and two pills.

Muriel and Walt were honeymooning in Europe; they had organized a tour of Italy, France and Germany, ending with a cruise up the Rhine.

"It sounds fantastic," said Izzy, "I hope you are taking notes, Mr Henderson!" she joked to Larry.

"Shh! We agreed to wait before saying anything, but I guessed you would tell Millie, 'your partner-in-crime'! You two are unbelievable sometimes, I saw you laughing at the bridesmaids yesterday!" said a disapproving Larry.

"No, we weren't laughing. Honestly, we were just grateful that we hadn't been chosen to wear one of those awful dresses!" explained Millie.

CHAPTER 32

On her eighteenth birthday, Millie's father had presented her with a car and during the holidays she had learned to drive. So, in the October after she was eighteen, Millie started at the University of Boston signing up to study the History of Art and Archaeology. Sophie had initially wanted to do archaeology with Millie, but her parents wanted her to join them and help run the family restaurant eventually, so reluctantly Sophie had signed up to study Hospitality Administration.

Sophie was disappointed as it meant that she couldn't live on campus with Millie, as they had intended. Instead, she would commute to lectures from home and when not studying or attending lectures, she would be working in the restaurant.

Millie, on the other hand, didn't want to commute, she wanted to be on campus with other students so she could learn to live independently. Suddenly she found herself all alone, living and cooking in a communal area and then retiring to her own room to sleep. She quickly learned to cook the simplest meals for herself by watching and asking her co-students, some of whom were only too happy to teach her and luckily, she was a quick learner. When it came to washing her clothes she felt embarrassed the first time she visited the communal laundry, she read and re-read the instructions on the washer and in the end had to ask one of the other girls. Gill was on her course, she had seen her in the lecture room but never spoken to her. "Hi!" said Gill to Millie on entering the laundry room. Millie watched her intently as she loaded the machine with her washing and switched it on. Gill turned around and noticed Millie watching her intently, "Are you okay?" asked Gill.

"Well kind of, except I have never used these machines before and don't really know where to start," explained Millie.

Gill laughed, "Really? I'll show you it's easy when you know how." So, Gill explained the stages of working the machine "Oh! It is easy, except I don't have any powder. Where can I get some?" queried an embarrassed Millie.

"You can borrow some of mine today, but you can get it at the campus shop," informed Gill.

"Thank you, that is very kind of you," Millie responded. They sat and chatted until the machines finished, and then Gill showed Millie how to use the dryer.

"Didn't your mom ever show you how to do your laundry?" asked Gill.

"My mom wouldn't know how to do it herself! We have helpers who do everything like that," explained Millie.

"Wow! My mom would love that - she hates washing and ironing!" said Gill.

Again, Millie felt embarrassed to admit neither she nor her mother did any work around the house. Until she met Sophie, Millie had always assumed that everyone had servants.

"Doesn't your mother have any help?" asked Millie.

"No, my parents couldn't afford such a luxury. I have two brothers and we all have to do chores in order to get pocket money, in effect, we are the 'help' so to speak," explained Gill.

"I presume you can't iron either," said Gill, "I'll show you how when the tumble drier has finished drying the clothes" Gill and Millie soon became firm friends. Gill had a room in the block next to hers, and they regularly got together at mealtimes with Gill showing Millie how to cook more complex meals and what to buy. In turn, Millie would drive Gill to the shops and on trips at the weekends.

They also would sit and study together, exchanging information and ideas. When their professor took them on excursions and digs, they would share the sleeping accommodation. In no time they had a big circle of friends; by the end of the first year Gill had a serious boyfriend and she would spend more time with him than with Millie, which Millie didn't object to, as she was now a firm fixture in their group. That summer their professor, Alan Wilson, took six of them on a dig for four weeks at a native American site in Georgia. They enjoyed every minute; Millie was especially fascinated with the tools used by the native Americans and was ecstatic to uncover several tiny arrowheads and some intricate items that appeared to be some kind of buttons.

Millie only went home for two weeks that summer to be a bridesmaid at Izzy and Larry's wedding. The wedding had been initially planned for the spring, however, Izzy's father had been very ill at that time so they decide to postpone the wedding so he would be able to walk her down the aisle. As promised, Izzy let Millie choose her bridesmaid dress which was a simple long powder blue silk dress with 'leg of mutton' sleeves, and had a low back and scooped neck. The bodice fitted to the waist and then gently fell to the floor in a sort of A-line design. She looked beautiful with her long dark hair held back with a hairband of flowers, but not as beautiful as Izzy. Izzy was blonde and very slim. As she was slightly shorter than Millie, Millie chose to wear flat shoes whereas Izzy wore white satin ballet shoes with a kitten heel.

Izzy's dress was a simple fitted garment made from ornate Italian silk with sleeves to the elbow. Her hair had been put up in a mass of curls with small white flowers pinned into the curls and her bouquet was made up of the most delicate wildflowers. Her father walked her down the aisle to a waiting Larry, who had turned to watch her walk towards him, gasping at the vision of her loveliness. By the time he took her hand, he had tears running down his face. In fact, the entire congregation appeared to be in tears when they saw Larry crying.

Much to Grace's displeasure, the reception was a small intimate affair with no more than sixty guests. It was just what Izzy and Larry had wanted, not the flamboyant show that Walt and Muriel had put on. The guests were made up of immediate family along with friends of Izzy and Larry, not those of their parents. The speeches were funny and informal, and in the evening, there was a live band which everyone twisted and shaked to until it was time to go home. Millie having learned her lesson from Walt's wedding, drank only a moderate amount of alcohol.

CHAPTER 33

After almost five years in remission, Jonathon's leukemia returned. He was too tired and weak to show any emotion, whereas Grace was angry at him for not telling her six months earlier that he was beginning to feel unwell again. The cancer leaving him so sick that the doctors didn't want to start any treatment until his body was strong enough to withstand the harsh chemotherapy treatment required to kill off the disease. That time never came for Jonathon, as he died three months later.

Grace was so distraught she didn't know what to do with herself. She wanted to scream at Jonathon, 'Why? Oh, why didn't you tell me earlier?' and went from anger to crying inconsolably. She stayed in his apartment that first night holding his pillow tightly and breathing in his scent; she couldn't sleep, only dosing now and then. She would wake up and remember he was gone, only to start crying again. She didn't know how she was going to go home and act normally when all she felt like doing was crying. She couldn't eat; as soon as she put food in her mouth she wanted to vomit. She felt empty, her heart completely broken. But she had to go home, carrying in her handbag one of Jonathon's dirty shirts, which night after night she held close to her.

Sam was shocked to see the state of her the next morning at breakfast. "You look terrible, whatever is the matter, are you sick?" he asked.

She tried to stop herself from crying and muttered, "I feel a bit under the weather, I might just go back to bed."

"Do you want me to call the doctor?" asked Sam with concern.

"No, I'll be fine. Just a bug, I guess," she replied knowing that she had to go to the hospital to organize for Jonathon's body to be removed to a funeral parlour.

Grace waited until Sam had gone out before making her way to the hospital. When she arrived, she was met - to her complete surprise - by Jonathon's parents and sister.

"Hello, you must be Grace. I'm Jonathon's mother Mabel Stiles, and this is my husband Howard and our daughter, Alice. Sorry to meet in such sad circumstances," she said.

"The hospital phoned us yesterday, as we were down as his next of kin. I must say this is a terrible shock for us; we didn't know he was ill. We weren't very close, and haven't seen Jonathon for several years. He only phoned now and again," explained Mabel.

"I am so sorry, but he never spoke of you otherwise, I would have phoned you myself," said Grace, as unable to control her emotions started to cry. "I am sorry, but it is such a shock for me. I can't seem to be able to control myself," she said, dabbing her eyes with her handkerchief.

Mabel put her arms around Grace "I am sorry too, my dear. I can see you are clearly very upset, come and sit down. Unfortunately, we need to discuss the arrangements."

The hospital had organized a funeral director to speak to them in a side room at the hospital. Grace let Mabel take control of the discussions, she was glad that she didn't have to get too involved and after signing all the paperwork, Mabel asked Grace if she could accompany them to Jonathan's home.

Grace had asked her driver, Lionel, to take her to the hospital as she felt too traumatized to drive herself. She knew he was waiting for her in the car park and had to take the risk of asking him to take them all to Jonathan's apartment. She felt vulnerable in the car and hoped they wouldn't talk too much and alert Lionel of what exactly was going on.

They arrived at the apartment, and Grace told Lionel that he could go home and she would get a taxi back when she was ready. She hoped and prayed that Sam wouldn't be home and question Lionel as to her whereabouts. Grace let them all into the apartment with her key and they were astounded. "How on earth did Jonathan manage to buy such a lavish apartment?" asked his mother.

"He obviously rented it, Mom! There is no way he could have afforded to buy a place like this," exclaimed Alice. Grace didn't know what to say so said nothing; they all looked around making various comments as they went from room to room. His father went directly to Jonathan's desk that was in the corner of the living area and started opening all the drawers, removing item by item and reading each piece of paper.

"Would you believe it?" he shouted to Alice, "He actually owns this apartment and he has left it to you in his will."

"What, me?" asked Alice, in disbelief.

"Yes, you! He has left not only a will but detailed plans for his funeral. Come and have a look," said Howard.

"There is an envelope addressed to you, Grace," he said, handing her the envelope. Grace placed the envelope in her handbag, not wanting to read it in front of his parents.

Howard read the will out loud to them and along with a letter detailing how he wished to be cremated at a private family funeral. They spoke in such a matter-of-fact way that Grace felt as though they were invading her and Jonathan's private space; she just wanted to go and leave them to it but felt obliged to stay. When they said, they would stay at the apartment rather than a hotel, she felt desolate. She was screaming inside 'Get out! Get out!', eventually saying that she would have to leave and promised to phone the apartment the following morning.

"Well, if you have to go, my dear, then you must. We should have the date of the funeral tomorrow. Good-bye for now," and without another word Mabel continued what she was doing, as Grace left the apartment.

Grace hailed a taxi outside and couldn't wait to get home. As it happened Sam hadn't come back, so she was able to speak to Lionel and ask him to be discrete. Lionel had been with the family over fifteen years and he knew his place, he would never have divulged Grace's whereabouts even if he had been asked, and felt a bit disappointed that Grace had even asked.

Jonathon's funeral was held five days later. Millie and Jonathan's work colleagues were a bit upset that the funeral was to be private but as Grace explained, it was the family's decision. As Grace watched the coffin slowly move towards the curtains that would take the coffin to be cremated, she felt as though she would faint. Sitting down quickly with her head in her hands, she sobbed as quietly as she could.

She had nothing left of Jonathan, not a photo not a memento – nothing! Just his shirt and her memories. Grace never saw the apartment or his family again.

Millie phoned her that evening to make sure she was okay; Grace was very quiet on the phone and Millie could make out that she was crying. "Thank you for phoning, but I will be fine. It was just a shock," said Grace.

"Mom you don't need to be secretive with me! I knew about you and Jonathan; I've known for a long time, I just want to make sure that you are coping?" asked Millie.

"Honestly, darling, I will be alright, don't worry," said Grace trying to reassure her daughter.

"Well, if you need me or want someone to talk to Mom, please - I beg you - just phone! I can be home in a couple of hours. Promise me Mom, I can't bear for you to be alone with no one to talk to." implored Millie.

"Thank you, darling, but I will be just fine," repeated Grace.

It was over six weeks later, at Christmas, that Millie saw her mother and although she greeted Millie with a hug and a kiss, Millie could see that Grace was still hurting inside.

On Christmas morning when they were exchanging presents, Sam presented Grace with a beautifully wrapped small flat parcel. "Happy Christmas, darling!" he said, giving her a peck on the cheek.

"I thought we said no presents? I feel guilty now because I have only bought you this small gift," handing him a square box with a ribbon tied around it.

"I thought you said no presents," he repeated, taking the box.

Grace opened her parcel and inside were some cruise line tickets, "What is this?"

"I'm taking you on an around the world cruise! I think you need a holiday, my dear," announced Sam. Grace didn't know what to say.

"That is just what you need Mom! You'll have a great time!" declared Millie.

"Thank you, Sam. You are right of course, a relaxing holiday is just what I need, and I will need an entirely new wardrobe to take with me," she proclaimed.

"That's the spirit! I will need a new dinner suit too as mine is getting a bit tight," Sam laughed patting his stomach. The three of them were by themselves for Christmas lunch; Walt and Muriel had gone to New York for the holidays, and Larry and Izzy had gone to her parents. It was a quiet time, they went to their close neighbours for pre-lunch drinks and then came home for their own lunch. As usual, Mrs Grant had put on a lavish feast but refused to eat with them, instead preferring to have her lunch with Margie and her family.

They were invited to Larry and Izzy's for New Year's Day lunch. Millie loved going to Larry's, his house was cozy and homely so you could relax. They had no servants, although Izzy admitted that she had a cleaner that came in three times a week.

"I have so much marking to do for my class and projects to prepare, that I find doing all the cleaning and especially the ironing is just too much work," said Izzy "I want to enjoy my weekends with Larry not spend it doing housework."

"No one should be wasting their time with housework, my dear," said Grace.

Izzy provided a delicious lunch after which they retired to the living room, "We have an announcement," said Larry, catching everyone's attention. Izzy had a broad smile on her face, and Millie guessed straight away what Larry was going to say.

"We are having a baby! Well, Izzy is not me!" announced a very proud Larry.

"Oh! Congratulations darlings!" said Grace, hugging them both at the same time. "I am going to be a granny! I am so delighted for you both!"

"Congratulations!" said Sam, "A new life into the family, Grace!" he said putting his arm around Grace and kissing the top of her head, then turning to Izzy. "Well done my girl!" he said giving her a gentle hug and kissing her cheek before taking Larry's hand and shaking it with both of his hands "Well done son!"

Millie screamed in excitement. "When is it due? Auntie Millie – it sounds so good – Auntie Millie!"

"If you let me get a word in," said Izzy, "The baby is due around the second week in August."

"What do you want?" questioned Millie, with excitement, "A boy or a girl?"

"Well, one of those and we don't mind which, do we Larry?" responded Izzy.

The rest of the afternoon was taken up with baby talk. Larry had never seen his mother so excited about anything before - perhaps this announcement came at the right time. He told Izzy later, "It will give Mother something to look forward to!".

"Just so long as she doesn't interfere too much, you know what she is like," said Izzy.

"No, I don't think she will interfere, she will just suggest you have a live-in nanny, as she did with us," stated Larry.

"Well, I don't want a nanny, do you?" asked Izzy.

"Not at all. I want us to look after the baby, put him to bed and read him stories, not some nanny. I want us to be a proper family," responded Larry.

"So, do I, and less of the 'him'!" said Izzy putting her arms around Larry.

CHAPTER 34

Millie went back to university in January. This was her last semester and her Uncle Ethan had already offered her a full-time job in one of the Trust's art galleries. It was obvious to her that her father had suggested this to his brother, as it was not often that her Uncle and Aunt Bonnie came up to Boston, spending the majority of their time in New York or Washington. However, they came to Boston and spent two days between Christmas and New Year with the family, and it was on one of these days that he took Millie to one side and asked her if she would be interested in a position in one of the galleries. Millie jumped at the chance as she knew a number of the galleries included a natural history department. Ethan explained that she could choose where she wanted to go and suggested that she visit some of the galleries before making her decision.

"These are part of your inheritance Millie, so it's a good idea for you to see how the galleries are run and how we try and make them self-funding. Your brothers are looking after other sectors of the business, so it is good that you have an interest in the arts," said Uncle Ethan.

Uncle Ethan was three years younger than her father, and he and Bonnie had four children. They were Millie's first cousins, but she didn't know them very well. There were twin boys, Freddie and Ben, who were now forty-three, Ella who was thirty-nine and then Nat, thirty-five. All four were married with children of their own; the boys all worked in various areas of the family business and Ella was a stay-at-home mom.

Millie didn't have to think about Uncle Ethan's offer, it was exactly what she had wanted and accepted without any hesitation.

"I am not sure which gallery I would like to work in though, but it would have to be one that has a collection of native American artifacts," she stated.

"That's no problem, Millie, there are several available. What I will do when I get back home is send you a selection, and I suggest you visit each of them and decide from there," suggested Ethan.

"Thank you Uncle, but will there be a vacancy if I say, choose one in Chicago for instance?" asked Millie.

"Don't worry about a vacancy Millie, I will sort that out. You just concentrate on finding the right place for you," said Ethan.

Millie had four months to prepare for her final examinations and two months to submit her completed course work to her tutors. She and Gill studied hard as they both wanted to gain a good grade in their degree. They hardly socialized during this time, instead spending each weekend in the library or with their tutors.

When they came out of the examination room following their final paper, they both breathed a sigh of relief. "I never want to take another examination in my life!" exclaimed Gill.

"No, neither do I," said Millie "Let's celebrate!"

An end of exams prom party had been organized in the main hall of the university for the following day. Millie and Gill helped decorate the room in readiness for the party, while others laid out tables and chairs. A live band had been booked, and everything was ready to go.

All the girls dressed in their prom dresses looking very glamorous and the boys looked dashing in their dinner suits. Gill was escorted by her boyfriend Victor, and his friend Alfie had asked to escort Millie. They had a fantastic time and were very hungover the next morning.

Millie had received a message from Professor Wilson asking to see her that afternoon in his office. Wondering what he wanted, she made her way over to the main building and met Gill on her way. "Are you going to see prof as well?'" asked Millie.

"Yes, I wonder what he wants us for?" questioned Gill.

"Well, we are just about to find out," responded Millie. Waiting outside his office where two other students from their course Joe and Harry, who they knew quite well and had been on digs with them in the past.

"What do you think he wants?" Millie whispered to Joe and Harry, just as the professor called them into his office.

"Thank you all for coming. The reason I have asked you here is to invite the four of you to accompany me on a dig during the summer. I have been invited to participate in a dig in Northern Italy. I can take several helpers with me, and I thought that perhaps you four might be interested," said the professor. They all looked at each other in surprise.

"I, for one, would be really interested!" exclaimed Millie, and the three others soon joined in with 'So would I!"

"That's fantastic! I am anticipating leaving here on 25th July. We would fly via London to Milan; it's a long flight so remember to bring a book with you to read, or something to occupy you on the flight. I will let you know how much the flights are before I book them, so you can check with your parents that they are agreeable with the cost. You will need to bring sufficient money with you to cover anything else you might want to do," said the professor.

"Such as?" asked Joe.

"Visiting the local hostelries! Or you might want to go sightseeing," the professor replied. "And you will need a passport, so make sure you apply for one now if you haven't already got one."

They left the professor's office excitedly discussing the trip. Millie was staying on campus until after her graduation but decided to drive home that weekend so she could organize her passport.

CHAPTER 35

Grace and Sam departed on the SS Oceanic, for their cruise. It departed from New York in early February. Grace had five large suitcases containing more than sufficient outfits for their four-month cruise. She didn't want to be seen wearing the same outfit more than once, so with the help of a designer had purchased mix and match outfits that would appear to look different each time she wore them.

Grace felt apprehensive on entering their verandah suite to see the large double bed. She hadn't shared a bed with Sam for over ten years and seeing the look on Grace's face, Sam gently took Grace's hand saying, "It will be okay, don't worry."

The cabin, located on the first-class deck, was one of the best on the ship with a balcony, sitting room and bedroom with an en suite bathroom. They had been allocated their own steward who insisted that they go to the top deck and watch the ship depart while he unpacked their cases.

Sam and Grace made their way up to the open deck area and waved to no one in particular as the ship left New York harbour. They looked around to see where the dining room was ready for their evening meal before making their way back to their cabin and getting lost in the process.

The steward had left them a bottle of champagne on ice; Sam poured them both a glass, lifting his glass and clinking it against Grace's toasting, "To us and the future!"

Their steward had pressed their outfits in readiness for dinner and escorted them to the dining room. They sat at a table with three other couples from different parts of America and the conversation was easy. Two of the other couples, Sheila and Ralph, and Ruby and Willie, were on their second and third cruise whereas the third couple Earl and Gladys, like Grace and Sam, were on their first. Sheila gave them a few tips and the ladies were soon making plans for visits to the spa.

Grace and Sam later retired to their cabin. Grace nervously changed into her nightgown and got into bed with Sam. However, she worried needlessly as Sam merely kissed her goodnight, turned over and went to sleep. Grace didn't know whether to be disappointed that he had just turned over and gone to sleep, or not. Over their first week, Sam gradually made more advances towards her; at first, they would talk about their day and he would linger over the goodnight kiss, then he held her close to him while she slept. By the end of that week, as he stroked her body gently, Grace responded by putting her arms around him and kissing his neck. Maybe, because they no longer had the inhibitions they had had when they were younger, their lovemaking was the most satisfying she had previously achieved with Sam. Not the lust she had experienced with Jonathon, but a pure love of mutual respect.

Sam and Grace danced the nights away and walked hand-in-hand around the decks in the early evening. During the day they would either relax in a deck chair or visit all places that the ship docked. They also played the silly on-board games and even participated in a fancy dress evening, dressing up in cowboy and cowgirl outfits.

They dined at the Captain's table one evening, with the Captain asking Grace how long they had been married. "We married in 1932 so almost forty years," she replied, "Why do you ask?"

“Sorry, I thought you were going to say something like six weeks. I thought you were on honeymoon!” exclaimed the Captain. Sam laughed at the Captain’s comment, thinking to himself ‘Yes, it feels like we are on honeymoon’.

All too soon the cruise was over and they arrived home tanned and happy, Grace immediately moved back into the master bedroom to be with Sam. Everyone remarked on the change in the couple since returning from the cruise, even Mrs Grant commenting to Lionel, “Thank goodness those two have buried the hatchet, it was becoming unbearable at times!”

“Perhaps now everything will get back to normal,” replied Lionel.

CHAPTER 36

Millie arrived home late on a Friday evening following her meeting with the professor. She excitedly told her parents over supper about the invitation to take part in a forthcoming dig.

"Italy is fantastic, darling, you will love it! We stopped in Genoa on our cruise; it was such a pretty place," said an enthusiastic Grace.

"Where exactly will you be going?" asked her father.

"It's a site in Lombardy called Bagnolo, which is in Northern Italy. We fly to Milan and then a minibus will take us to the site," explained Millie.

"I am sure you will have a great time, and then you have decided to work at one of Ethan's galleries, I hear?" said her father.

"Yes, I'm not sure which one yet; I need to look at all papers Uncle Ethan has sent me," replied Millie, "Plus I need to get a passport. I've got the form but I need my birth certificate to go with it."

"No problem, I will get it out of the safe for you in the morning," replied her mother.

"Thanks, Mom, I'm going to go to bed now as I'm absolutely exhausted from the drive down," said Millie, bidding them goodnight and making her way to her room.

Millie got up late in the morning and had her breakfast on her own, while Mrs Grant chattered away to her. "Your mother has already left; she was going to the hair salon and then to have lunch with one of her friends,"

Mrs Grant informed Millie, "And your father is in his office."

"Ah, that's good. I will go and see him after breakfast," said Millie. As Millie ate her breakfast, she told Mrs Grant all about the forthcoming trip to Italy, "I will have to go and see Larry and Izzy tomorrow before I go back to university, to explain that I won't be here when the baby is born. That is the only downside of going to Italy; I really wanted to be here to see the baby," declared Millie. "But I might not get a chance like this again, especially after I start work."

After breakfast, Millie made her way to see her father in his study, "Hi Dad, Mom has gone out and she has forgotten to give me my birth certificate. I would like to get my application for my passport to the Passport Services Office as soon as possible, can you get it for me?" asked Millie.

"It's in the safe," he said, just as the telephone on his desk rang, "Hold on, let me just take this call."

Millie could see the safe door was open so she looked inside and soon found a large brown envelope with 'MILLIE' written on it. She removed the envelope and sat on the floor to look at the contents; there were further smaller envelopes inside with one labelled '*BIRTH CERTIFICATE*'. 'Ah, this is what I want!' she thought to herself and started to put everything back into the larger envelope when writing on another envelope caught her eye. It stated, '*ADOPTION PAPERS*'.

Millie's heart missed a beat and with a sense of foreboding she opened the envelope - her heart now beating as though it would jump out of her chest at any moment. There were several items in the envelope; the first one she looked appeared to be a legal document, she slowed began to read it. It was mostly a printed document with spaces that had been completed by hand:

> I, *Niamph Ellen Flynn* do hereby relinquish my baby for adoption and agree not to make any contact with the adoptees and hereby give my consent to the Mother Superior of the Order of the Sisters of Saint Vincent de Paul of Tullamore, County Offaly, Ireland to act in all matters relating to the adoption.
>
> Baby's Name: ***Bernadette Flynn***
>
> Date of Birth: ***1st July, 1950***
>
> Signature of Mother: ***Niamph Flynn***
>
> Signature of Adoptee: ***Grace Henderson***
>
> Dated: ***9th September, 1950***
>
> Witnessed: ***Mother Marie-Claire***

Millie read and re-read the document not quite believing what was in front of her, she was adopted! 'But how can that be?' she thought to herself, 'why hasn't anybody told me? It must be a mistake.' But Millie knew it wasn't a mistake; there was her mother's signature and her date of birth!

Millie then saw another crumpled piece of paper, which looked like it had been screwed up and straightened out again; it was a letter.

Dear Madame,

I know I should not be contacting you, but I just want to make sure that Bernadette is happy and settled into your family.

Please, could you send me a note just telling me she is happy and if possible a photo? You can write to me, care of Father Patrick at Church of Our Lady, Castlewood, Co. Westmeath, Ireland.

Yours most sincerely

Niamph Flynn

"Millie, what are you doing?" shouted her father, making her jump.

She looked up at her father with tears running down her face, "Oh! Darling, you shouldn't have looked in there," said her father, gently.

"When were you going to tell me, Daddy? I am nearly twenty-one, don't you think I should have been told by now?" whispered Millie, still in total shock.

"Come here, darling," said her father, putting out his hands to her.

"No!" she shouted, "You can't just give me a hug in the hope it will go away! I want to know why you haven't told me?"

"There never seemed to be the right time to tell you. And as time went on it didn't seem quite so important..." "Important to whom?" Millie interrupted.

Millie ran from the study crying with the papers held in her hand, shouting, "You have ruined my life!" She quickly went to her room and grab her application form before running out of the house with tears still pouring down her cheeks.

Millie drove straight to the agency for the Department of State and delivered her passport application form, and then made her way to Larry and Izzy's house. Larry answered the banging on the door, and Millie barged passed him, now feeling very angry at the situation. "You are not going to believe this Larry!" she sobbed.

"Calm down, Millie, what's happened? Why are you so upset?" asked Larry, concerned that something dreadful had happened.

"What's all the shouting?" asked Izzy, coming down the stairs.

Millie fell into Izzy's arms sobbing her heart out, "Whatever is the matter Millie?" asked Izzy with concern, looking over Millie's shoulder at Larry. Larry put his hands up in the air, as if to say, 'Don't ask me?'.

"Come on, sit down! Take a deep breath and tell us what's happened," encouraged Izzy.

"Did you know I was adopted, Larry? I found out this morning," questioned Millie.

"Oh Millie, how did you find out?" asked Larry. Millie then realized that when she had looked in the safe, there were other envelopes with Larry and Walt's name on and it suddenly occurred to her that they were all adopted. "Did you know Larry?" she asked, feeling ashamed with herself.

"Well, I kind of guessed when I was younger. Walt was always making nasty innuendos, his best one was 'Well, you aren't really my brother!' It wasn't until I was older that I started to wonder and then one day when Walt made another remark, I asked him what he meant and he told me," said Larry.

"Did you ask Mom and Dad?" asked Millie.

"No, I thought if they wanted to tell me, they would," explained Larry. "Anyway, as far as I was concerned, Mom and Dad are my mother and father; nothing will change that. So, to be honest Millie, I don't see what your problem is."

"I can't explain how I feel. I just somehow feel cheated…perhaps cheated is not the right word, I feel I have been denied the truth. Look at this, my real mother is called Niamph. I don't even know how it is pronounced, it must be Irish," said Millie.

"Let me look, Millie," said Izzy. "You pronounce it 'Neve', I had an Irish friend at junior school with that name. You would never guess the pronunciation if you didn't know," said Izzy. Izzy then went on to read the adoption document and letter, "How sad is that? I wonder if your mother ever replied?" questioned Izzy.

"I doubt it, it looks like she screwed it up and was ready to throw it away, and then changed her mind," said Millie.

"Well, at least she kept it," said Izzy.

"Look, Millie, you need to go and talk to Mom and Dad, allow them to explain. You mustn't just jump to conclusions," said Larry.

"You are right, as always. I will go home and speak to them," said Millie, leaving to go home. But she didn't go home. Instead, she went to see Walt. Arriving at his flat without any warning was not something Walt and Muriel approved of, but Millie didn't care - after all she was family!

Muriel answered the intercom and let her in through the main door to their block of apartments. "Well, this is an unexpected surprise!" said Walt, waiting at their apartment door for her. "Come on in."

Millie had only been to Walt and Muriel's apartment on a few occasions. It was like a show house, she hardly dare sit down on their pristine sofa.

"What do you want, Millie?" asked Walt, in his usual welcoming manner.

"Walt, I found out this morning that I am adopted. Did you know?" she queried hoarsely, trying not to cry in front of him.

"Of course, I knew! We are all adopted Millie, is there a problem with that?" responded Walt.

"Did Mom and Dad tell you?" asked Millie.

"No, of course, they didn't! I guessed at first, especially when you arrived virtually unannounced when I was twelve! But then one day when I was looking for something in the safe and I found my documents," said Walt.

"Did you tell Mom and Dad that you knew?" she asked.

"There was no point, obviously if they had wanted me to know they would have told me. Anyway, does it matter? Ah! But presumably you have a problem with it, is that right?" he asked meanly.

"I don't know. It's such a shock; it's like my world has been turned upside down!" she sobbed.

"For goodness sake Millie, why does it matter? Better to be in this family than some grotty Irish slum, the bastard daughter of some Irish whore!" spat Walt, cruelly. Millie was shocked at Walt's attitude and quickly made her excuses and left. She made her way home with a sinking feeling in her stomach, knowing that she would have to face her mother. All the way home, she kept going over and over in her mind what she would ask her mother.

Grace was sat in the living room reading a book when she arrived home, "There you are darling. Come and sit down; we need to talk. I will just go and get Daddy," said Grace. Millie sat down thinking to herself 'Daddy? She thinks I am still five - Daddy indeed!' Her mother and father came into the room together, "Are you okay, Millie? I was concerned when you left without talking to me," her father asked, with concern.

"I am angry Dad! Why didn't you and Mom tell me I am adopted? Why have you lied to me all these years? Why didn't you tell me? How do you think I feel finding out like that?" questioned Millie, trying to control her emotions but failing dismally.

"We didn't lie to you Millie. Yes, we failed to tell you, but to us it didn't seem important. You are our daughter and that is it. And answer me this, have you been unhappy in this family?" asked Grace.

"No, I haven't," replied Millie quietly.

"We have given you everything Millie. You have wanted for nothing so I can't see a problem. Yes, we adopted you from a mother who couldn't keep you or didn't want to keep you, and yes, I am sorry we didn't tell you. I am going to lie down; I have a terrible headache," said Grace leaving the room.

Millie's father came and sat next to her on the sofa, putting his arm around her, "Millie, let me tell you something. When your mother and I got married, we thought children would automatically come along but unfortunately, they didn't. After five years of marriage, we sought medical advice and soon discovered your mother would never be able to have children of her own. Can imagine how she felt? She wanted to be the same as everyone else, not different. All of our friends had children, Ethan had children, and when she realized she wouldn't have any, she became desperate for a child. It didn't bother me, but perhaps men are different to women when it comes to children.

"Anyway, unbeknown to me, she made inquiries about adoption and Father Theodore made the arrangements. I must admit I was reluctant to adopt at first, but when Walt arrived, she was a changed woman and as long as she was happy, so was I. Then after Walt she wanted another, but there was war in Europe, and she particularly wanted a good Catholic baby from Ireland, the same as Walt. So, we had to wait for Larry. Later, she wanted a daughter and so we chose you," explained her father.

"I understand what you are saying Dad, but it doesn't change how I feel. I just wish you had told me. I feel as though my life has been one big lie."

"Oh, Millie come here," he said, stretching his arms towards her, but she just turned her back on him and went to her room.

Millie left early the next morning after a sleepless night and returned to university. She had intended staying long enough to pack up all her belongings before returning home, but now she decided to go home after her graduation. Then she would only have a few days at home before her departure to Italy, which suited her just fine as the less time she spent with her mother at the moment, the better. She was still angry and upset, and she knew she needed to calm down and take stock of the situation, but found it very difficult. Her entire mind was occupied with thoughts of Niamph; who was she and why did she give her baby away?

CHAPTER 37

The relief that Niamph felt when she arrived at Clara's home in North Carolina was beyond words; she fell into the safety of her friend's arms and was warmly welcomed into the family. She had missed having a female friend to confide in and someone she could freely talk to about Bernadette. In turn, Clara could talk about her two elder daughters, Chantal and Francine, and they would cry together and laugh together. They became like sisters and the closest of friends.

Niamph had felt guilty leaving the school in New York before the end of the school year, but the headmaster had been very understanding given the circumstances. She had spent six wonderful years at the school, seeing her class of children grow from shy five-year-olds to confident eleven-year-olds.

Looking after Clara's children, especially Lilly, was the perfect job for Niamph. Whenever Lilly passed the next hurdle in her growing up stages, Niamph would imagine Bernadette doing the same.

Niamph loved Clara's children as though they were her own. She would sit patiently helping them to read and write, and then as they grew older help with their schoolwork. One of her greatest achievements was teaching Clara's second child Jeffrey, to play the piano - he was a natural.

Niamph had been in North Carolina in a short time when by pure chance, she met James Hartley, the local newspaper editor and owner. She was taken by surprise when he asked her out to dinner, and even more surprised when she discovered that he was an old friend of Carl, Clara's husband. Niamph flabbergasted herself when James asked her why she had left Ireland to come to

America, by telling him it was to leave behind the heartbreak of giving her baby up for adoption.

She hadn't meant to be so abrupt, it just came out of her mouth. In the back of her mind a little voice was telling her not to get attached to anyone who didn't know about her past, as she had already gone down that road and look where it had got her? On their second date, she told James all about Bernadette and he told her all about his fiancée who had died. They soon became an item and their relationship grew from strength to strength; he was her soulmate and second-best friend after Clara.

They married in September 1960 after a long courtship, neither of them wanting to commit themselves to a relationship, especially after the heartache they had both endured. Their twin boys, Bradley Charles and Scott Bernard, were born exactly a year after their marriage making their family almost complete.

Niamph continued to write to Bernadette each year on her birthday, sending the letters to Father Patrick. In all the years that she had written she had never received a reply, but this year a letter arrived back. She could hardly breathe as she eagerly tore open the envelope with the Irish stamp on it, only to be utterly disappointed that it was not news of Bernadette. The letter from Father Patrick informed her that he was retiring from the parish church and his replacement was to be a Father Theodore.

'*I have told him all about you Niamph, and he has promised to continue receiving and keeping your letters safe, until such time as you tell him not to. God be with you, my dear girl,*' he wrote.

Niamph sat down and cried - when would the yearning to see her daughter again go away? She didn't want to stop thinking of her, as she did almost daily, she just wanted the desperation in her heart to diminish.

The only person that Niamph kept in touch with from her past life besides the now elderly priest, was her sister Megan. Megan now lived in the South of England in a place called Devon; she had married an English man by the name of Trevor, and they had two children. She wrote at least twice a year, like Niamph, Megan had found happiness and family stability. Other that Megan, she had no word from her family and had no idea if her parents were even still alive. At times she did wonder about her family, but given the way they treated her, these fleeting thoughts would be filed away in the depths of her mind - she didn't want to be reminded of those times.

CHAPTER 38

Lilly was looking forward to going home now; she was torn between the sadness of leaving her Papa and the yearning she had for home, her Mama, and her dad - in fact, everyone in Raleigh.

The three sisters were leaving on Monday morning, just three days away. Lilly had told them all about the farm and surrounding area, Chantal and Fran were nervous and elated all at once; the only plane they had been on was a small 10-seater to Guernsey, so the thought of a large plane going across the Atlantic was extremely daunting. They had both purchased new suitcases for the trip and had laid out their clothes ready to pack. They felt a bit disloyal to their Papa and tried not to ask Lilly too much about their mother in his presence.

Lilly was going with her sisters and their boyfriends to a dance at the local Young Farmers Club the Saturday night before leaving. She was excited to be getting dressed up and had bought herself a new dress for the occasion, even though the girls had said to her that it was a casual event. She had purchased a striped cotton shift dress, that tied at the waist, in purple, lilac and white, which she thought would be perfect.

When they arrived, Lilly realized how casual it actually was! It was in a huge barn with hay bales for seats, a makeshift bar was at one end and a stage with a live band at the other. The place was packed with boys and girls all around the ages of 18 to perhaps 30, and the boys got them a drink each, which was a local cider. Lilly had never tasted anything like it before. Initially, she found the taste bitter but after the first glass, she began to enjoy it.

The girls all danced together for the first couple of songs and then gradually the boys, who were drinking pints of beer joined in, and Lilly thought to herself that they needed a couple of beers to lose their inhibitions. A boy by the name of Bernie asked Lilly to dance, and Fran shouted over the music to her, “Watch him, he can’t be trusted!” then laughed.

Lilly thought Bernie was quite nice; they danced and he bought her a few more drinks - not cider this time, but gin and tonic. When he took her outside for a bit of fresh air Lilly began to feel the effects of the drinks. She had never been this drunk before but it felt quite liberating, as Bernie lead her behind the barn and started kissing her, she had never felt like this before.

After about ten minutes of trying to hold back his marauding hands, Lilly suggested they go back inside. Fran grabbed her hand and took her on to the dance floor, and they danced until the band stopped for a break.

“Let’s get another drink,” Fran said, dragging Lilly over to the makeshift bar.

“I think I have had enough, but I suppose one more won't matter!” Lilly was thirsty after all the dancing and it was a warm evening, so virtually downed the drinks in one gulp.

“Steady on!” said Fran as Bernie came over and asked Lilly to dance again.

While the band was getting back on the stage ready for the next song, Bernie got Lilly another drink, together with one for himself. Lilly now felt really tipsy; it was a slow dance and Bernie took her in his arms holding her much too close, but at that moment, she didn’t have a care in the world.

After this point, Lilly's memory became a little hazy; she remembered going outside, but the next thing she remembered was waking up in bed the next morning.

Chantal knocked gently on the bedroom door. "Wake up sleepy head! It's almost eleven," she said much too cheerily, coming into the room with a mug of coffee. Lilly's head was thumping and she could scarcely lift it off the pillow.

"I feel like death!" Lilly said, trying to sit up.

"I'll go and get you an aspirin! Then I suggest you have a bath and I will make you something to eat."

As Lilly lay in the bath, she thought to herself that she must have fallen over as she felt battered and bruised all over, especially around her private parts. In fact, she was so sore that she could barely wash herself.

In the kitchen Chantal had prepared bacon, eggs, and toast. Lilly didn't know if she was going to throw up, but Chantal assured her that this was just what she needed for a hangover.

"How did I get home? I don't remember even leaving the dance?"

"We had to literally carry you! Fran and I had to undress you and put you to bed. We left you snoring away!"

"Thanks, that's nice to know. I am sure I don't snore at all," laughed Lilly.

Lilly spent the entire day wrapped up in a blanket on the settee, much to the amusement of her sisters. Luckily, her Papa was helping a friend with a job and therefore didn't see her in such a state. By the time he came home in the early evening she was feeling a lot better.

The next morning all packed and ready, their Papa drove them to the airport. They were catching a plane to London and meeting up with Jeff, before flying out the next day to Charlotte, via New York.

Lilly hugged and kissed her Papa goodbye, with tears streaming down her cheeks. "I'll write, and I will see you next year when I come over for the weddings." Didier was visibly upset seeing his three girls board the plane.

Jeff flew in to London from Germany, where he was playing with his group 'The Jayjays' who were doing a tour of Europe. They met up at the hotel where they were all staying the night. Chantal and Fran were delighted to meet their half-brother, especially with him being a 'popstar', so to speak. To Lilly, he was just her little brother. They all chatted easily throughout dinner that evening, and then in the hotel lounge until late into the night. Jeff had laughed at the story of his big sister getting so drunk she had to be put to bed, and he held her tight and let her cry on his shoulder when she told him about her journey to France and the discovery of an entirely new family.

All too quickly they were saying goodbye with the promise from Jeff that he would attend his sisters' weddings in Jersey the following year.

CHAPTER 39

The girls were nervous boarding the huge plane; they were in awe of its size and the number of people getting on. They had a row of three seats together and Chantal couldn't quite believe that in less than twelve hours she would see her Mama again - a moment she had been waiting over twenty years for.

The flight went quicker that Chantal thought it would; they read, played cards and slept during the eight-hour journey to New York, where there was a short stopover before they changed to a smaller plane to take them to Charlotte. From there, it was a train journey to Raleigh where Tim was to pick them up.

They were stunned by the vastness and beauty of the countryside as they travelled on the train to their destination. Chantal and Fran were used to travelling no more than six or seven miles to anywhere in Jersey. Here, the journey just went on and on and Chantal tried to imagine her Mama traveling this way all those years ago.

Tim was waiting on the platform as the train arrived. He was the polar opposite of Jeff, over six foot tall with a tanned, solid, muscular body, obviously from the all the manual work he undertook on the farm. He reminded Fran of Mike, whereas Jeff was at least two inches shorter and slightly built with no tan. They both had brown wavy hair, Tim's was bleached by the sun and by the way he kept pushing it back with his hand, was a bit unruly. Jeff's hair had been long and straggly, way past his shoulders and it had looked like it needed a good wash and cut, but Chantal presumed it was the typical rock star image.

Tim welcomed them with open arms, giving each of them a bear hug. "I am so pleased to meet you! Wow,

wow!" he said, looking at the three of them standing together "I can't believe I have three beautiful big sisters!"

"Flattery will get you anywhere, little brother," said Lilly, playfully hitting him on his back.

Tim helped the girls with their cases and put them in the back of the car. Lilly sat in front with him, Whilst Chantal and Fran sat in the back, taking in the countryside as they drove to meet their mother.

Chantal was so nervous that she felt sick. The butterflies in her stomach were working overtime, so she tried to calm herself by breathing slowly in and out. When Fran spoke to her, she found it hard to reply to, with the words getting jumbled in her brain. She listened to the conversation between Lilly and Tim, as he was telling her about how their mom had explained about Chantal and Fran.

"I asked her why it was such a secret and why she didn't tell us before now, and seemingly it goes back to when she first arrived; she didn't want our grandparents to think badly of her. Apparently, Dad had told them that her husband had died and she was on her own with you when they met, but Dad knew along about your father and the girls. He told them they had married in England, but in fact they have never married, so you know that makes Jeff and me—"

"Don't Tim! Anyway, let's look forward. You can't change the past so now we need to look to the future with our new family."

Suddenly they had arrived and there was her beloved Mama waiting outside for them - older than she remembered, but still her Mama. Chantal was crying, big sobbing tears before she even got out of the car. They ran towards each other hugging and both crying. Clara parted from Chantal holding her hands and taking a good look at her, "My lovely girl! I can't believe you are here!" she cried, taking her in her arms again.

Fran came around the car to her mother. She was a bit more hesitant until her mother turned to her, "Frannie, my little Frannie!" she sobbed embracing Fran. At this point Fran became overcome with emotion and hugged her mother back.

"Hi, Mama!"

"Oh Lilly, come here, I have missed you!" she said, taking hold of youngest her daughter. Whispering in her ear, "I am so sorry, I should have told you the truth years ago! I am so sorry."

Niamph had been excited to meet Clara's two daughters, she felt as though she knew them. Clara had taken them to meet Niamph, explaining on the way how she had met her all those years ago on the boat traveling from Liverpool to New York. Over tea and cake, Niamph chatted easily to the girls telling them all about the journey to America. She skirted over her time in New York, but told them how she had found happiness and a family in this town, "All due to your wonderful mother!" While their mother was out of the room, she told them of the heartache their mother had experienced over the years and the guilt of leaving them behind. "So, this is fantastic, you two here! I am so happy that Lilly came looking for you." When they left Niamph sat down with a heavy heart, contemplating how she would feel if she ever met Bernadette.

The two weeks holiday in America with their mother was going far too swiftly; Fran loved the farm and she spent days with Carl and Tim finding out all about the crops and even helping them out. She felt at home; after all she would, in less than a year be a farmer's wife. There was no comparison between Mike's dad's farm and Carl's;

for one, it was at least twenty times bigger and she was fascinated at how tobacco was grown - she couldn't quite equate it with cigarettes. Whereas Carl employed between thirty and forty men depending on the season, Mike only employed one full-time worker and seasonal workers, when they were required. She took loads of photos to show Mike - she was missing him desperately, as this was the longest, she had ever been away from him.

Fran rapidly built up an easy relationship with Tim and her stepfather. However, it took some time before she was able to speak freely to her mother. She tried to feel the same connection as Chantal but was finding it quite difficult, and it wasn't until Chantal told her one night in bed about the memory boxes their mother had kept that she was intrigued and wanted to know more.

The day following their arrival, Clara had sat down with Chantal and attempted to explain why she had done what she did.

"I know most of what happened, Mama. I recall something of those times and Papa told me his side of the story, so you don't need to explain. I understand why you left, but what I don't understand is why you left us behind? I remember crying myself to sleep at night, hoping that when I woke up you would be there."

"Oh, Chantal I am so sorry! I wanted to take you both, but I had no money and was at my wit's end! I thought your Papa would end up killing me if I didn't go! I was so scared, I had nobody to talk to and Jersey is so small, I knew the only way to get away was to leave the island - it was a tough decision! Then afterwards, I was frightened to write in case your Papa came looking for me and took Lilly away! I so wanted to get in touch, hence the reason I started writing to you, but never posted the letters."

Clara took a box out of the cupboard and handed it to Chantal. It was a boot box covered in pretty floral paper with her name written inside the lid. Chantal opened it tentatively and there inside the box were neat rows of envelopes intermingled with photos. Her mother pointed to one end and stated, "They start here."

Chantal took out the first envelope dated April 1951, opened it and started to read.

My dearest baby,

It is difficult for me to write this letter and I know perhaps you will never read it, but if you do, then all I can say is that the decision to leave you, my baby, was not easy. I know your Papa will look after you, he loves you so much he would never harm you. But I am terrified that he will harm me. Please forgive me, my baby, remember that I will always love you.

Your devoted Mama xxx

The next envelope was a fourth birthday card dated August 1951. It read:

My dearest baby,

Happy birthday, sweetheart! I am thinking of you today as I write this card. Four already, no longer a baby - but still my baby. You are always in my thoughts, I love and miss you so much. I hope you are happy and that Papa is looking after you. Lilly sends you a kiss for your birthday, and so do I.

Your loving Mama xxx

She was only a quarter of the way through the box, but there were lots of photos, mostly of Lilly, but some of when she was a baby in France. Her birth certificate was also in the box, and she thought to herself on seeing it,

'Now I know where it is - all the trouble I had getting a new one!'

Her mother made her a cup of tea and gave her a fresh handkerchief, as the one she had was now soaking wet from her tears.

"Read the rest another time, let's talk." Lilly returned at that very moment from the tearooms where she had been saying hello to everyone. She was discreetly making herself scarce so her Mama could reconnect to her sisters.

"Before you start talking Mama, I have something for you from Audrey," she quickly ran upstairs and grabbed the scrapbooks before rushing back to the kitchen. "Audrey asked me to give you these and hoped that you would write to her," said Lilly.

Clara opened the first page and soon realized it was a record of her girls' lives. Audrey had done this for her, how could she repay her? It was the most wonderful thing that anyone could have done for her, as she turned the pages it was like being there in that moment of time.

Chantal laughed as she told her the stories behind the photos, and there were pictures that she didn't remember drawing, all kept and placed carefully in the scrapbook. Amongst the very first photos was one of Francine in a pushchair, her arm and leg in a plaster cast smiling into the lens of the camera. Clara looked at Chantal in horror, "What is this? What happened - oh my God, what happened?"

Chantal told her the story from what she could remember, but it was all a bit of a blur. She could only remember the car and then the ambulance, before Audrey taking her home. Clara then noticed a small piece of paper folded to one side of the photo. She gently unfolded it and read the words written by Audrey.

'Frannie was hit by a car. She was waiting for her Papa to come out of the public house one Sunday morning. In the excitement at seeing him, she ran across the road directly into the path of an oncoming car.'

On reading Audrey's words, the guilt that Clara felt was overwhelming, why hadn't she been there to protect her babies?

"Let's not look at anymore," begged Chantal, as they were a little way into the first book. "I want Fran to be here, she needs to see these."

While Lilly and Chantal went off to find Fran, Clara read the letter from Audrey.

My dear Clara,

I hope you are well and happy. Lilly has told me all about your home in America.

Your lovely daughters have over the years become like daughters to me and when realization set in that you were not returning to Jersey, I started keeping a diary and taking photos. I felt sure you would return at some time in the future and then you would have a record of your girls growing up. I then turned all the things I had saved for you into these scrapbooks. I have written an explanation next to some of the items.

Didier has done a good job raising the girls; he gave up drinking shortly after Fran's mishap with a car, and to my knowledge, he has remained sober ever since. He has turned his life around and now has his own successful building firm.

My utmost joy is that Fran and my Michael are to be married, they have been inseparable since babies, so we all felt it was inevitable.

I could write reams about events over the years, but I wanted to give this letter to Lilly to give to you with the scrapbooks.

Lilly is a delight, and so like you.

Please write back.

Best wishes your friend, Audrey xx

As it turned out, it would be a few days later before Clara would sit down with Fran. Clara was disappointed when Lilly and Chantal returned without Fran, trying to explain diplomatically that Fran wasn't quite ready. Clara understood it was a lot to take in, in such a small space of time.

When they did eventually sit down together, as Fran opened her memory box, it was crushing for Clara to hear Fran tell her about her early memories of how she longed for Audrey to be her mummy, of how she was jealous of Mike because he had a mummy and she didn't.

"I even called her Mummy, once," she said, laughing at the memory. "She was very tactful! I remember - I can't remember her exact words, but basically, I was to call her Auntie, not Mummy," said Fran.

They went through the scrapbooks together with Fran telling her what she could recollect, she had no idea that Audrey had kept all this stuff. The photos of her and Michael on their first day at school, of school sports days and school plays in which they both took part.

Clara tried to explain why she did what she did all those years ago, but Fran wasn't really interested. "I just want to move forward; the past is the past. I want to look ahead to the future, I want you to come to my wedding and meet the grown-up Mike. I want you to be 'Mother of the Bride' with Carl and my brothers."

"What about your father, Fran? Will he be okay with me suddenly turning up after all this time?" asked Clara.

"I am sure Papa will understand; he is easy going and it was his idea for us to come here to see you! He even paid the fares, so I am not worried about Papa. He will understand why I would want you there on my big day."

Clara took Fran in her arms and they embraced each other, "Thank you, you don't know what this means to me."

Chantal and Fran discussed their memory boxes at length in the privacy of their bedroom they both admired their mother for what she had done all those years ago. They felt sad that the future relationship with their mother would be a long-distance affair, but at least they had found her and could look forward to their newly found kinship.

Clara was fed up with crying, everything was so emotional she seemed to be crying over every little thing. Her entire body had the sensation that it was under stress, her arms tingled, she had indigestion, her head ached and when she went to bed at night, she felt totally exhausted. She had hoped that once the girls had arrived all the tension and anxiety would disappear, but she was still waiting, thinking to herself that she must go to the doctor, as the painkillers she was taking were no longer working on her constant headaches.

When Clara told Carl about her conversation with Fran in bed that night, he took her in his arms and told that of course she must go, and that Tim must go with her. "But I honestly don't think it is appropriate for me to go. Even if I could get someone to look after the farm, I think only you and the boys should go."

"And while we're talking of going away, I honestly think that you need a holiday Clara, you have been so stressed. All these headaches you have been getting, and the weight you have lost is not good for you, my love. Why don't you go back to England with the girls, go and visit your Mum and Dad; go and see Amélie and your sister," suggested Carl.

"Well yes, that sounds good in principle, but what about the farm? Who is going to look after you and Tim?" questioned Clara.

"I think Tim and I are more than capable of looking after ourselves! Go and have a break, I insist. Go tomorrow and book it," demanded Carl.

"It would be lovely to see Mum and Dad. I think it might do me good to, as you say, have a break and have nothing to worry about. I am just so tired all of the time. Hopefully, a break will make the headaches go away."

Clara fell asleep in the safety of Carl's arms and had the best night's sleep she had had in recent weeks.

Lilly and Tim organized a barbeque for the last weekend before their sisters were due to fly home. They had invited all their friends and their parents' friends, plus all the staff from the tearoom and the live-in workers from the farm. Niamph, James and the twins were the first to arrive; it was a riotous occasion, with lots of dancing, drinking and eating. One of Tim's friends acted as DJ and music blared out of huge speakers set up in the barn.

Everyone was quiet the next morning at breakfast, each nursing a hangover.

All too soon, it was time to leave. Chantal and Fran were delighted that their mother was flying with them to England, they had even managed to incorporate a two-day stay to see their grandparents. Lilly drove them to the station where there were a lot of tears, kisses, and hugs.

CHAPTER 40

Clara had pre-warned her mother of their visit. She hadn't wanted just to turn up as she had done twenty years previously, especially as there three of them this time. Her parents, Jack and Olive, were delighted to see her and even more delighted to meet their two eldest granddaughters. The girls immediately bonded to their grandparents and spoke non-stop that first evening, with Chantal wanting to know all about them. She wanted to know the entire family history, how they had come to be hairdressers and their imminent retirement, so much so that Fran felt sure that Chantal would have gone and vetted the retirement home if she had been allowed!

Fran felt an instant connection to her grandfather; the only grandparent she remembered was her granny, who had died when Fran was quite young. She loved hearing his stories, especially the one when Jeff, her half-brother, had visited them and he had offered him a haircut.

"I have been trying to get him to cut his hair for years, so it would have been a miracle if he had said '*yes*' to you!" said Clara.

Olive told them how she used to tease Jack in the early days of his apprenticeship, as he used to scour fashion magazines and follow the newest trends in hairstyles. "But I told him the only hairstyles he would be giving his clientele would be 'short back and sides'!" These stories even made her mother laugh.

Chantal and Fran's stay was short as they had to get back home; they needed to be back in time to return to work. They made their grandparents promise to come to Jersey for their weddings the following year.

"Try and stop us, we'll be there! Nothing will prevent us, seeing you both married," said Jack.

All too soon the girls were saying goodbye to their new family. Clara didn't want to let go of her daughters, she wanted to stay with them, but knew this was not possible. "We will write, and we will see you next year," said Chantal through a veil of tears. They waved goodbye from the taxi until they could no longer see their mother.

CHAPTER 41

Clara sat down with her father. He wanted to know all about her time during the war in France.

"I thought you would be safe with Clifford in France, but of course no one could have predicted that there would be another war. I remember saying to your mother months before the outbreak of the war, that we should tell you to come home, however, you had other ideas! It was unusual for me to be in the salon at the time when Olga, or Amélie as you know her, turned up earlier this year. I was standing in while Peter, the man who was buying the business from us, went to the bank," explained her father.

"Anyway, she walked up and down the pavement outside several times, looking in the window and then walking away again. I was curious, so I went outside and asked her if she was lost. You can imagine my surprise when she told me she was looking for you. Peter came back at that minute, so I invited her upstairs for a cup of tea as she appeared physically upset. I explained that I was your father, then she told me her story, as I said in my letter," said her father, who was lost in his own thoughts of that day.

Clara went on to tell her father how by pure coincidence she had been recruited by the Maquis, the French resistance organization, during the war years and how she got involved with the rescue of Amélie and her sister Estelle.

She couldn't remember the year from memory of this particular mission. It was such a long time ago, but she estimated that it must have been about 1943, as she did remember that it was the second time that she had met Didier. He had come to the village of Plérin where she was living with her Aunt and Uncle to ask if she would consider helping to rescue two young Jewish sisters from the French side of the border with Belgium. Clara had agreed without any hesitation.

The two little girls spoke a language that neither of them recognized and it was difficult to try and explain to them that their new names would be Amélie and Estelle. These were the names on their new identification papers, and to this day Clara was unsure if they understood. The journey had been fraught with danger but they managed to get the girls from the safe house in Alsace to Nantes, where a British plane dropping off a regiment of American soldiers had agreed to make a landing to airlift the girls to Britain.

Clara's heart had gone out to these two frightened little girls. She couldn't image the horrors they had experienced. At the beginning of the return journey, she had given them each a soft toy, a teddy for Amélie and a fluffy rabbit for Estelle. She had taken the soft toys from an old box of abandoned toys that had once belonged to her cousin, Danielle, which she had found at her Aunt's house before she leaving to undertake the mission.

During the time waiting for the rescue plane to arrive, Clara had written a small note explaining who she was and tucked it into the belly of the teddy bear, through a tiny rip in the bear's arm. She made sure that Amélie was watching her as she put the note in the teddy. Why, she did this she didn't know - perhaps, Clara thought that Amélie might want to know how she came to Britain in the future.

Clara never thought about it again in the years that followed, and it was only when her father wrote to her before Lily's departure for Italy that all the memories had rushed back into her mind. A letter followed shortly after her father's letter, from Amélie herself.

Dear Clara,

I hope you don't mind me writing to you, your father gave me your address. I never thought I would find you with so little information. I travelled to Preston and randomly asked if anyone knew a 'Clara Pape' and a lady suggested the hairdressers, as their surname was Pape. I was so surprised that after very little effort I found your parents!

It is hard to put everything I want to say to you in writing, as a simple 'thank you' seems so meaningless. You helped save our lives. Our parents were taken by the Ustaše and were never heard from again. An uncle helped us escape from the hiding place in our house where our parents had hidden us before their arrest. I have been in contact with all the agencies that help Jewish refugees find their families, but they have been unsuccessful, so we don't know what happened to them.

We were placed with a lovely childless couple in Wales and they eventually adopted us. We had an idyllic childhood growing up on their farm.

I am now married and live in London. My sister, Aneta, returned to our homeland Croatia, formerly Yugoslavia. Her need to return home was stronger than mine. The memories I have are still too raw, but maybe in the future, I might return on a visit.

I would love for you to write to me and if you are ever in England, please contact me, as I would really like to meet with you again.

Yours very truly
Olga Freeman

Clara had arranged to meet Amélie or Olga, in Coventry. Olga would travel up from London by train and Clara would travel down by train, and they would meet at the train station.

It was only after Clara had received the letter confirming their meeting from Olga that she realized that she might not recognize her. However, she worried unnecessarily because as if by instinct, they each recognized each other immediately.

They walked arm in arm to a nearby hotel recommended by the stationmaster, where over lunch Olga told Clara how they had arrived in England. Olga also told Clara how their parents had hidden her and Aneta in a concealed cupboard to escape the Ustaše, and how she remembered seeing her parents being dragged away through a slight crack in the woodwork. It had seemed like hours before their uncle came and rescued them.

Olga explained that she didn't remember much about the journey through France, only that she had been scared and thought she was being taken to meet up with her parents. She did, however, remember the plane.

"We were petrified in that huge plane - well it appeared huge, but looking back it wasn't that big. We had to sit on the floor in the back by ourselves. It was so noisy, Aneta cried all the way. We clung to each other the entire journey and when the plane landed, I thought we were going to die as there was a bump which made us both bounce up and then down again, and then a loud bang. It was a relief when the doors were opened, and two airmen carried us out.

They took us to their base and tried to talk to us, but we didn't understand them. It felt like hours before a lady came and collected us. Then an interpreter arrived and it was such a relief to speak to someone who understood us! I remember asking about our parents, but of course, she didn't know anything.

The lady took us by train to Wales where we stayed with this lovely couple, Hilda and Percy Jacobs. It was so difficult for us initially, going to school and not able to speak English. We were lucky that another boy at the school spoke Croatian and with his help, we eventually learned English.

When the war ended, the authorities tried to trace our parents without success, so Hilda and Percy adopted us." Olga was crying by this time, and Clara tried to comfort her. To give Olga some breathing space before she continued with her story, Clara told all about her life in America and her children. Clara was a bit economical with the truth as it would be too complicated to explain all that had happened to her and the agonizing decisions she had made in the intervening years.

"Tell me about Estelle, or I should say Aneta?" asked Clara.

Olga went on and told her how they had both gone on to university after school, with Aneta choosing to study European History. It was at one of these lectures that she had met her future husband, Saul.

"We hadn't been brought up Jewish, but Aneta more than me, was drawn to the Jewish faith, especially when she met Saul who was a practicing Jew. Aneta, I shouldn't say converted as she had always been Jewish, but she refound and embraced Judaism. When they married shortly after graduating, they made the decision to return to Croatia. They now have three children, two girls and a boy, and their home is definitely in Croatia; I doubt they will ever return to England," explained Olga with a melancholy voice. Clara guessed that she missed her sister.

Olga then reached into her bag that was hanging from the back of the chair, and produced the teddy bear.

"Goodness me!" exclaimed Clara, "I can't believe you still have the teddy!"

"Yes, I have kept it all these years. Your note was almost lost, it was only when Hilda was about to wash him that she discovered the tear under his arm. She was going to stitch it before washing him and found your note. Hilda kept the note safe for me until I was older enough to understand the significance of our journey." Concluded Olga.

Clara went into as much detail as she could remember of the rescue mission, for which Olga was grateful, as it helped her fill in the gaps in her memory.

Olga revealed to Clara that she was pregnant with her third child by her husband Richard, and told her all about their jobs and how they both worked for the same bank in the City of London.

Clara asked her if she was happy, to which she responded, "Yes, but I would be even happier if I could find out what happened to my parents. I have heard people say they want closure in such situations as mine and Aneta's, and that is what I would like - to know they didn't suffer, but I know I would have to face the fact that they probably did suffer terribly."

Clara and Olga walked back to the train station. It was a sad goodbye each promising to write to one another. On the train journey home, Clara reflected on the good times she had with Didier, and how different life would have been had they remained in France. But then she thought to herself, that she wouldn't have met Carl, the love of her life, and wouldn't have had her two gorgeous boys.

Clara arrived back at her parent's house, exhausted. It had been a long, draining day. She could feel a headache coming on and went in search of some aspirin. Her mother seeing her taking the tablets, said, "More tablets Clara? Surely not another headache? I am sure it can't be right that you have so many headaches. Have you seen the doctor?"

"Don't fuss, Mother, it's just a headache!" replied Clara.

The next day Lilly, her sister, arrived together with her youngest daughter, Poppy. It was wonderful seeing her. It had been such a long time. Her little sister was now a middle-aged woman and her daughter a typical teenager, not saying an awful lot and more interested in reading her teen comic.

Although they corresponded on a regular basis, it was wonderful for them both to be able to sit and chat about their families and what they had been doing in their lives. They talked about their children, their husbands and their concerns over their elderly parents. Clara wished that

Lilly could have stayed longer, but she had to get back to her duties as a doctor's wife.

Olive was concerned about Clara, especially when she found her on the floor the next morning. When Olive asked her what had happened, as she helped her get to her feet, Clara replied, "Nothing, I just tripped on the rug!"

But, as Olive said to Jack in bed that night, "She couldn't have tripped. I think she fainted but is not saying, and all those headaches - something is wrong."

"I am sure she can look after herself, don't worry yourself. I'll sound her out in the morning," replied Jack.

Jack did ask Clara the next morning about her fall, but Clara immediately dismissed his concerns "I only tripped Dad, nothing more." What Clara didn't say was that, in fact, she had fainted several times when home in America, and it was only by pure luck that she had not hurt herself when she fell. She had put it down to stress and nothing more.

Saying goodbye to her parents was heartbreaking, although she longed to go home to Carl, she was sad to be leaving them.

"But we will see you next year, Clara, at the weddings! The time will fly by!" stated her mother. She hugged and kissed her parents and thanked them for putting up with her.

"It was lovely having you here, it's still your home!" said a tearful Olive.

The journey home was long and tiring; Clara felt unwell and another headache failed to go away, even with the aspirin.

CHAPTER 42

The journey to Italy was a bit of a blur to Millie, she was so lost in her thoughts of the mother that had given her up for adoption, but she enjoyed the camaraderie with the others in her group at the dig. While digging at least she could concentrate at the job in hand, and she tried very hard to integrate with the group, but it was overshadowed by the anger she felt at not being told the truth by her parents.

The weekend before leaving Italy they all went out to celebrate, and she got very drunk; all she remembered was telling a girl called Lilly, who was part of the group from North Carolina, how she hated her parents and that she didn't want to go home! Lilly appeared sympathetic and said that everyone hated their parents at one point or another.

When one of the group suggested they go and see more of Europe before going home, the idea came to her, she would go in search of her birth mother. She would go to Ireland.

It wasn't easy getting to Ireland from Italy, but with the assistance of a very helpful travel agent, she landed in Dublin. Whilst on the journey, she had made a plan, and written down all the places she had gleaned from the documents she had taken from her father's safe. At Dublin airport, she rented a car and purchased detailed maps to get her started. "A piece of cake!" she thought to herself, thinking that Ireland looked like a small island compared to America, but how wrong she was. Firstly, she had to drive on the left-hand side of the road, whereas she had only ever driven on the right, which was fine until she negotiated the first junction and nearly ended up on the wrong side of the road!

Secondly, it was getting late and she would need to find overnight accommodation. She drove towards Dublin stopping at a garage and asking where the nearest hotel was. Luckily enough, the attendant directed her to one nearby.

The next morning after breakfast, Millie started her journey. Her first stop was going to be the convent where she had been born. She had studied the map the night before, and estimated that the seventy-five-mile drive would take approximately two hours, but what she hadn't factored in was getting lost – twice - and having to negotiate narrow lanes with oncoming vehicles, where she had to reverse into the entrance of muddy fields. She arrived at her destination three and a half hours later, having stopped for refreshments on the way.

The convent of Saint Vincent de Paul was an imposing building on the outskirts of a small town, that she had asked for directions, as the convent wasn't on the map. Millie parked outside the gates and pulled a large cord at the side of the pillars of the gates. After a few minutes, a nun emerged from the building and opened a side gate, "How can I help you, young lady?" she asked.

"Hello, I hope you can help me. My name is Millie; I was born here and I am looking for my mother," replied a flustered Millie.

"You'll need to speak to the Mother Superior, she may be able to help you. Follow me," said the friendly nun. They walked around the building to a side entrance, where they entered through a dark passageway to a large, and not quite so dark, entrance hall.

"Wait here! I will go and tell Mother Superior you are here. Do you know the name of your mother?" asked the nun.

"Yes, it is Niamph Flynn," replied Millie, who could see straight away that the nun recognized the name by the look on her face. "Did you know her?" asked Millie.

"Wait here, I will be back shortly," said the nun.

Millie stood there for a least five minutes before the nun returned. She tried to imagine her mother coming to this place, it was foreboding and smelt musty with religious paintings around the walls, and statues of Jesus and Mary that looked like they needed a good clean. When the nun returned, she asked Millie to follow her.

The nun whispered to her, "Ask to see the gardens when you leave."

"Sorry, what did you say?" The nun put her figure to her lips as if to say 'ssh' as she knocked on the door that had Mother Superior engraved on a brass plaque. She opened the door and inside was a larger than life nun sat behind an imposing desk.

"Thank you, Sister Marie-Joseph, you can go. Now how can I help you, young lady?"

Millie explained who she was and how she had been born at the convent in 1950, her mother was Niamph Flynn and that she was searching for her mother. Millie looked down at the notes and asked the nun if she was Mother Marie-Claire.

"No, my dear Mother Marie-Claire retired some years ago. 1950 you say, I am afraid that we have no records from that time. Unfortunately, we had a flood about ten years ago and the records were severely damaged. So I am extremely sorry, my dear, but I cannot help you," said the not so sorry looking Mother Superior.

Millie was devastated, she didn't know what to say she had not expected this response, she felt a bit faint and asked for a glass of water. The nun who had let her in appeared with a glass of water. "Drink that and Sister Mary Joseph will see you out," said the Mother Superior in a dismissive voice.

"Thank you, Sister, perhaps I could walk through your gardens to get some fresh air before I drive back?" asked Millie.

"Yes, yes, of course! Sister Mary Joseph will show you the gardens," she said, standing by the open door, indicating that it was time to go.

Millie followed the nun out of the same side entrance by which they had entered, turning left instead of right towards the back of the convent. There before her was a beautiful formal garden with two nuns working at the far end.

"I remember your mother," was the first thing that the nun said, and Millie looked at her in surprise.

"Don't look at me, we are certainly being watched! Look at the garden, as though I am telling you all about it," instructed the nun.

"Your mother was here a long time longer than most, that's how I remember her. I knew her as Flynn, as we called all the girls by their surnames. I am sorry I can't be of more help, but I know she came from Co. Westmeath. Perhaps you could go there, she may be still there."

"Thank you, Sister, I have the name of a priest there, so I was going to go there anyway, but thank you," said Millie.

"She was a lovely girl. A teacher as I recall. She was so good with the younger girls, taught some of them to read and write. She was distraught when she had to give you up, I remember that; but then many, many of the girls went through the same trauma. It was so distressing watching all those girls give up their babies," said the nun who appeared to be preoccupied, by perhaps thoughts of the past.

"Good luck, I hope you find her and if you do, please give her my best wishes," she took hold of Millie's hand and kissed it. Millie had driven to the convent full of hope but now she was leaving crushed, praying that this Father Patrick would have some answers for her.

It was a long drive and she stopped several times to take a rest. Millie wanted to get as near as possible to Co. Westmeath, but soon realized she was going in the wrong direction and decided to stop at the next town overnight and start fresh in the morning. She managed to get a room in a public house for the night and after a dinner, provided by the landlady, she fell into bed absolutely shattered.

Over breakfast the next morning, she studied her map in great detail as she didn't want to go the wrong way again. Filling up with petrol at a nearby garage, she set off again full of optimism.

By lunchtime Millie arrived at her destination, the town of Castlewood. It wasn't a very big place, the sort of place where everyone knew everyone else. She stopped at a public house that advertised 'vacancies', thinking to herself that she couldn't face another day of constant driving and secured a room for the night. She could see a church steeple as she parked outside the public house and presumed it would be the church she was looking for.

She asked the landlady if the church she could see was the Church of Our Lady. "It is indeed, why would you be asking?" Millie explained that she wanted to speak to Father Patrick. "You won't find Father Patrick there, he left years ago; it's Father Theodore in charge these days. Now, would you be wanting lunch as the kitchen is just about to close? So, if you want something to eat, you better let me know soon."

Millie was disappointed to hear about Father Patrick but hoped the current priest might be able to help her. While waiting for her lunch to be delivered, the landlady asked her why she wanted to see Father Patrick. Millie wanted to tell her to mind her own business but thought better of it and explained that she was looking for her mother.

"What would your mother's name be?" asked the landlady.

"Niamph Flynn. She lived around here I think, and I presume she was friends with Father Patrick, but I don't know for certain. I'm clutching at straws really," said a downhearted Millie, as hearing Father Patrick had moved on was the last thing she had thought of.

"I don't know her, but I have only been here ten years. I'll ask my husband, he's been here all his life," said the landlady and returned to the kitchen. The husband appeared shortly after with her lunch and laying the plate on the table in front of her and said: "You are asking about Niamph Flynn?"

Millie's heart jumped, "Yes, do you know her?"

"You're American, you've come a long way to find this woman. Anyway, I am not sure, but I had a teacher called Miss Flynn and I think her Christian name was Niamph, but when you are a kid, you don't always know the teacher's full name. How old would she be?" asked the landlord, who introduced himself as Mick.

"I would guess at early forties, but I don't really know."

"That would make her only about six years older than me so too young to be my teacher. I'll ask my mates when they come in for a drink tonight, see if they know her."

"Okay, thank you," said Millie.

It was early afternoon when she arrived at the church. There was nobody around, it was all quiet. Millie walked around the building and saw a workman tending the graveyard, and so went over to ask where she could find the priest.

"You need to go to the parochial house, just go around the corner there. You can't miss it, there's a name on the gate," he said, pointing to her left. Millie found it easily and pressed the doorbell. The door was opened by a lady in an apron.

"Hello, how can I help you?" the lady asked.

"I am looking for Father Patrick, but I understand he is not here any longer, so I was wondering if I could see the new priest? I think his name is Father Theodore," Millie blurted out.

"Father Theodore would be right, but he is on his afternoon rounds and should be back before five. Then he goes directly to the church for evensong, so will be back here at about six o'clock," the lady informed her.

"Thank you, I will come back at six," said a despondent Millie, thinking to herself - another wait, what shall I do now?

Millie decided to take a walk around the town; it was more of a village than a town, but it was referred to as a town on her map. There were shops that you would expect to find, such as a butcher, newsagent, bakery, etc. Strolling up a side road, Millie spotted a small garage and the name of the place was 'Flynn's Repairs'. Intrigued by the name Millie walked to the entrance, there didn't seem to be anyone there, just a few cars and a lot of machinery, so she shouted out "Hello," but there was no answer. She was just about to walk away when a voice shouted back, "Hold on, I will be out in a minute!"

Millie waited at the entrance until a man came out in oil-covered overalls, wiping his hands on an even oilier cloth with oil smears on his face. "Can I help you?"

"Hello, sorry to disturb you, but I was just walking passed and I noticed the name of your garage, Flynn. Are you Mr. Flynn?" asked Millie.

"Yes, that's me," he said as he continued to wipe his hands on the cloth.

"Do you, by any chance, know a Niamph Flynn?" As soon as she said the name, Millie could see by his reaction that he knew Niamph.

"Why, who are you?" he asked

"Sorry, my name is Millie and a woman called Niamph Flynn is my mother; I am looking for her," Millie felt a bit light-headed, 'He knows her, he knows her!' was going around in her head.

"Well, if it is the same woman, then she is my sister, but I haven't seen or heard from her in over twenty years," he replied, "She went to America from what I understand, but that is all I know."

"Did she have a baby in 1950?"

"Yes, I think so. She left home in disgrace; I'm not sure what happened, our mother told us that the baby had died and then we heard that she had gone to America."

"Can I go and see your mother? Where does she live?" Millie pleaded.

"You can go and see her, but you won't get any answers; she's in the graveyard with my father," he answered.

"Oh, I am sorry, do any of your family hear from her, do you know?"

"There is only one of my brothers that lives here, my eldest brother, Shaun. He took over the farm from our father after he died, but I doubt if he has heard anything, as I am sure he would have told me - not that I see him very often. So that makes me your uncle, well, well. That is, if your mother is my sister. Niamph is a common name hereabouts, as is Flynn. Here take my business card and phone me. If you find my sister and she is your mother, it would be great to hear from her," he said turning, around to go back to work and waving his hand to say goodbye.

'What a strange family!' she thought to herself; he didn't seem interested to know he had a niece nor did he ask anything about her. If this was what it was like to meet her uncle, she started to dread meeting her mother - what would her reaction be? As she walked away, Millie wondered what to do next; she had seen the town or at least what there was to see, so she decided to go and see the grave of her grandparents. Why was everything so difficult? What she thought would be straightforward was anything but - perhaps it wasn't to be, perhaps she was never meant to find her mother!

The workman was still busy in the cemetery. On noticing Millie again, he asked "Did you find the place?"

"Yes, thank you, but the priest was out on his rounds." Niamph then asked the man, who she found out was the verger and had been in the town all of his life, where she could find the grave for her grandparents.

He guided her to the far end and showed her the grave; it had a simple stone engraved with:

Seamus Flynn aged 22 years

1930 - 1952

Kathleen Flynn aged 60 years

1898 - 1958

Shaun Flynn aged 65 years

1895 - 1960

R.I.P

"Do you know the family?" Niamph asked the verger.

"Yes," he replied, "I was at school with the Flynn boys; Shaun was older than me and then Colin was younger. There was another one, but I can't remember his name but he was younger as well. They keep very much to themselves; you don't see them often. Well, I see Colin in the pub as he has a garage in the town. There were a lot of them and I think all the girls left. And then Seamus," he said, pointing to the gravestone, "He was a bit 'funny', you know - a mongol!"

Millie looked at him questioningly, "Oh, you mean Down's Syndrome?"

"Yes, sorry, Miss didn't mean to be rude." He replied apologetically.

"I've met Colin, but he's not sure the family I am looking for is his. Where did they live?" Niamph questioned further.

"They still live there Miss, at the farm! About two miles or so out of town," and he proceeded to give her directions.

Niamph thanked him and walked back to the pub. She still had time to kill, so decided to drive up and have a look at the Flynn farm. She found it easily as there were hardly any dwellings on the road leading to the farm. The road turned into a muddy track as she neared the farm, so fearing that she would get the car stuck in the mud, she parked on the verge and walked towards the farm. Her shoes were totally unsuitable for the track; she tried to avoid the mud by walking on the grassy edges and she wished that she had kept the boots that she had bought for the dig, but she had left them behind in Italy. A dog started barking as she approached the farm; there were chickens flying everywhere, and it was really muddy. A woman came out of one of the buildings yelling at the dog to 'Shut up!'. The woman then realizing that the dog was barking at someone, turned around and saw Millie approaching; she shouted out in a thick Irish accent, "What do you want? I am not buying anything and I don't want any of your religious rubbish!"

"I am not selling anything," replied Millie, "Are you Mrs. Flynn?"

"Who wants to know?" the woman asked, apprehensively.

"I am looking for Niamph Flynn!" Millie shouted back, not daring to go any nearer, as the woman was holding the large snarling dog by the collar.

"No one of that name here! Get out of here before I set the dog on you!" replied the woman turning her back on Millie as she walked back into the ramshackle building, dragging the dog with her. The dog continued to bark and Millie decided it was safer to leave, her thoughts going back to what Walt had said about an Irish slum. Perhaps she was better not knowing but she felt compelled to continue with her search - she just hoped the priest would be able to help her. He was her last resort.

At six o'clock exactly, Millie arrived at the parochial house and the same lady as earlier let her in. She led her through a dark entrance hallway and into a small room off the hall. She knocked on the open door and pushed the door further open and Millie could see the priest sitting behind a desk. "This is the young lady I told you about," said the lady. The priest, who Millie guessed to be in his early fifties, was dressed in a smart black suit with a dog collar around his neck, stood up and shook her hand.

"Thank you, Mrs O'Brien," He turned to Millie, "Please come in and sit down. Now how can I help you?" asked the friendly priest.

"I wanted to see Father Patrick, but I understand he has retired and that you replaced him?"

"Yes, that's correct. I am Father Theodore; Father Patrick has been retired sometime now, but perhaps I can help you," replied the priest.

"My name is Millie Henderson and I am trying to find my birth mother," Millie stated Taking out of her bag the note that she had found with her adoption papers, she unfolded it and handed it to the priest. She could immediately sense a change in the priest as he read it. He stood up from his chair and went to the door, "Mrs O'Brien, Mrs O'Brien! Come quick!" he shouted. Mrs O'Brien ran into the room.

"This young lady is Bernadette Flynn!" he exclaimed, handing her the note.

"Bernadette, Bernadette Flynn, I never thought this day would come!" she cried, as she walked to Millie and taking hold of her hand. "My dear, it is so lovely to meet you! We have been waiting for you for such a long time. Father Theodore will explain, now I must get on with dinner! I hope you will stay to have dinner with us, it is the least we can do; you must have come a long way." Millie didn't even have a chance to reply before Mrs O'Brien left the room.

Millie was totally mystified so much so, that it took her a few seconds to compose herself. In the meantime, she watched as the priest went over to a cupboard at the back of the study, opened it and took out a large document box. He carried the box over to the desk and put it in front of Millie. She looked up at the priest, questioningly, "What is this?"

"Look inside! These, my dear, are letters from your mother. She has been writing to you for years! When Father Patrick left, he gave me strict instructions to keep the letters for you, and then after he left, your mother sent the letters to me, to keep for you!" he explained.

Millie lifted the lid of the box and inside there were rows of unopened envelopes all address to her, well to Bernadette. She couldn't believe her eyes - each envelope had a year written on top of it – so she took the earliest date out of the box, tore it open and started to read the letter.

My beautiful baby,

I miss you so much! You will be one year old now, what do you look like my little one? Are your new mummy and daddy good to you? I hope they love you as I love you. Are you crawling around, what words do you say?

I go to America tomorrow to start a new life in New York, my little one, but I think of you every day and will write to you for as long as I live and hope that one day you will read my letters.

My love to you, my baby. Your Mummy xxxx

Millie cried silent tears as she read this first letter trying to imagine her mother writing it all those years ago, 'She's in America,' she thought to herself, so near to her yet so far. Her thoughts were broken by Mrs O'Brien telling them that dinner was on the table.

Over dinner Millie told them about finding out how she was adopted and how she had set out to find her mother. "I should have come here first!" she said, telling them all about her visit to the convent and then the farm.

CHAPTER 43

Lilly found the house was so quiet; her sisters had gone home, her father and brother were working, and her mother was in England. She was preparing to go back to university, she had already loaded her car with all the items she was taking - it was a long drive, so she wanted to leave early the next morning. She wouldn't be back until Christmas. She had thought about coming home for Thanksgiving, but it was too far to travel just for a couple of days. Lilly was looking forward to seeing her friends at university; she had so much to tell them, it had been such an eventful holiday.

The following day she was up at dawn, wanting to make breakfast for her father and Tim before she left.

"Stop fussing over us Lilly, Tim and I will be fine; sit down and eat your breakfast. You need to get on your way, it's a long drive on your own. Don't forget to stop and have a break, I don't want you falling asleep at the wheel," said her father.

"Okay, now it's you who is fussing over me!" joked Lilly.

Lilly attended the University of North Carolina (UNC). She had received her degree in Archaeology and History before leaving for the summer holidays and was now about to start a teaching degree. Her aim was to teach these subjects to high school students. In reality, Lilly loved school and didn't want to leave, so this was one way of never having to leave; she could move seamlessly from student to teacher.

Driving to Uni Lilly suddenly remembered that she had forgotten to show Auntie Niamph the photo of Millie, but the more she considered it the more unlikely she thought it was that this girl would be Niamph's daughter - surely it would be too much of a coincidence! 'I'll show her the photo when I see her next,' she thought to herself.

Lilly soon settled back into university life, catching up with friends and attending lectures. Most of her free time was taken up with assignments and she had little time to think about her summer holidays, which now seemed like a lifetime ago. She spoke with her mother on a weekly basis and had written letters to her sisters and Papa in Jersey.

Unexpectedly, everything changed with a phone call. Lilly's plan to go home for Christmas was abruptly cut short when she received a phone call from her father. As her father rarely spoke to her on the phone, it came as a surprise when she received a summons to go the office of the university's secretary to take the call.

Lilly's blood ran cold as she listened to her father tell her that her mother was in the hospital, explaining that he had found her unconscious the day before on the floor of the kitchen and how she had been rushed to the hospital.

"You need to come home now, Lilly! The hospital ran tests overnight, and the results are not good," he pleaded. Lilly had never seen her father cry, but she could hear the tears in his voice.

"I will leave now! Where are you now, Dad?" she asked.

"Tim and I are at the hospital. I phoned Jeff and he is on his way, but he is in Amsterdam, so it will take some time before he arrives. Drive carefully, Lilly! I don't want you to rush and have an accident - just get here safely."

Lilly had wanted to ask her father more, but he said he would explain everything when she arrived.

The drive home was tense. Lilly wanted to put her foot down on the accelerator to get there quicker, but her father's words resounded in her head so she took it steady. Her heart was pounding all the way. She tried to think what could be wrong with her beloved Mama, so many questions were going through her head.

Lilly arrived at the hospital, parked and ran into the reception. After establishing who she was, they gave her directions to the Intensive Care Unit. Her father and Tim were in the corridor speaking to a doctor when she arrived. She fell straight into the arms of both her father and Tim, and they hugged her tight.

"How is she? Is she okay?"

"The doctor is just giving us an update on her condition. This is Mr Turner and he's the specialist looking after your mother, Lilly." explained her father. The doctor took them into his office. He soon realized that Lilly didn't know what had happened, so explained from the beginning.

"As you know Mr Kennard, your wife, was bought in here yesterday. We initially thought that she could have fainted and bumped her head, thus rendering her unconscious, but as you know she hasn't woken up." Explained the specialist. "As I mentioned this morning the tests, we ran overnight were inconclusive, but I felt that something serious was going on and that is why I asked you to get the family here. We undertook a brain x-ray earlier this morning, and it shows a severe bleed on the brain. You mentioned yesterday that she had been suffering from headaches for some time, so we think she had an aneurysm in one of the blood vessels in the brain, and it has burst. We are monitoring her closely but unfortunately, you must prepare yourselves for the worse. She may not recover, as the machines are currently breathing for her."

The entire room went silent. The family were all in total shock, until Lilly sobbed, "NO! NO! How can that be? She has always been fit and healthy."

Carl held both her and Tim's hands so tight it hurt. He didn't know what to say, but managed, "But she could wake up?"

"Yes, we can't rule that out. As I have said we are monitoring her closely. You can sit with her, talk to her. I will let you know as soon as anything changes," said Mr Turner.

"This can't be happening Dad, I don't understand how it has happened?" asked a distraught Lilly who was crying uncontrollably. Carl held her close to him, attempting to hold back his own tears.

"I don't know either, love, we must be strong Lilly. We must be strong for Mom,"

Tim was totally speechless he took Lilly in his arms and cried, whilst their big strong father hugged them both, and wept with them.

"Have you phoned Grandma and Grandad and told them about Mum?" asked Lilly.

"Yes, I phoned them shortly after I spoke to you and your Grandma told me that your Mom had fainted when she was in England. But apparently, your Mother tried to fob her off by saying she had tripped and fallen. And, Sally said to me this morning that she had found your Mom on the floor one morning, but again your Mother told her that she had tripped and fallen. Sally didn't think any more of it until now," said a distressed Carl.

"Have you told the doctor?" cried Lilly.

"Of course, he said it was another sign of the aneurysm. I just wish she had told me then, I would have made her go to the doctor," said Carl thoughtfully.

Sally had worked for the family for years, helping Clara out in the house. Her husband Joe worked for Carl on the farm, and they were both valued employees and friends of the family.

Throughout the rest of the day and all of that night, they took it in turns to sit with Clara, holding her hand and talking to her. Lilly tried her best not to cry but couldn't help it, the thought of losing her mother was just too unbearable to contemplate. Niamph also came to support them all bringing drinks and food, although none of them felt hungry.

Jeff arrived the following day and their father took him to one side and explained what was happening to his mother. Lilly was at Clara's bedside when he came into the room. She let him take her place beside their mother, he held her hand and kissed it, holding it against his cheek.

Two days later, they were all called into Mr Turner's office. "I am so sorry to have to tell you, but we think the chances of recovery are very slim. The machines are keeping her alive. With your permission, we would like to switch the machine off to see if she can breathe for herself. If not, then you need to think very carefully about letting her go - in other words, we would not switch the machine back on. I know this is a difficult decision for you all to make, please take your time and come and see me if you need to ask any more questions. I will see you in the morning," explained a solemn Mr Turner.

The family sat in the hospital chapel and discussed the option that Mr Turner had given them. None of them wanted to make the decision. They were already traumatized at seeing Clara wired up to all the machines that were keeping her alive, it all felt so surreal.

"Perhaps we should all go home, have a goodnight's sleep and decide in the morning?" suggested Carl.

"No, I can't leave her Dad, she would be all alone." said Lilly, this statement was echoed by Tim and Jeff.

"I know, I don't want to leave either, but we will have to make the decision. I have no magical answer, I wish someone would make the decision for us but they can't! It's up to us to decide."

It was Niamph who helped make the decision for them as she explained what the nurse had said that there was a possibility of brain damage due to the amount of time on the machine. "Isn't it better to remember her how she was, full of life and always there for you all? You wouldn't want her to be stuck, perhaps in a wheelchair or in bed, unable to do anything for herself. She would hate that."

Lilly phoned her sisters in Jersey to explain the situation. It was a heartbreaking call, one she didn't want to make but knew that she had to.

The machine was switched off at six that evening. The family and Niamph sat with Clara, with their father holding her hand as she slowly passed away; it was all very peaceful. Lilly was praying hard for her mother to breath by herself, but it wasn't to be. Carl had lost his wife, the children had lost their mother, and Niamph had lost her best friend.

CHAPTER 44

Lilly couldn't bring herself to go back to university after the funeral. All she could think about was her mother in that box in the ground. As they lowered the coffin she wanted to scream "Stop, stop!", she wanted to check to make sure her mother wasn't still alive.

She could hear her father at night going downstairs after they had all gone to bed. She would find him in the morning asleep on the settee with her mother's dressing gown held tightly in his arms. He was finding it hard to sleep in their bed without her; he missed her so much that it physically hurt. When he eventually went back to work it was like he was on autopilot. Tim was dealing with Clara's death better than his father and he was the one organizing the running of the farm, even though he was suffering as much as the rest of the family.

Jeff had reluctantly left the week after the funeral, he had commitments to keep and couldn't let down his bandmates. So, Lilly decided to put her teaching course on hold, explaining to the university that she needed to be at home to help her father. Plus, she wasn't feeling too good. It started with being sick each morning and feeling tired. Initially, she had put it down to the amount of work she was doing to keep the house running for her father. It was a constant round of cooking, washing up and cleaning; she didn't know how her mother had kept up, even with Sally there to help her.

It was Niamph that made her go to the doctor, asking, "You aren't pregnant, are you?"

"No, don't be silly! Of course not," she had replied. However, once that thought was in her head, she couldn't get it out. She racked her brain, but she couldn't remember when she had had her last period. Then with a sinking feeling in her stomach, she remembered the day after the dance in Jersey, and it all started to fall into place. Being drunk, not remembering getting home, and being sore the next morning. 'Oh my God! No please, oh God no!' she thought, 'Bernie raped me!'

Lilly had lived in Holly Springs almost all her life and the family doctor had looked after her for as long as she could remember, so she felt extremely embarrassed sitting in front of him a few days later, attempting to explain the reason for her visit. He didn't appear to judge her and only asked her a few basic questions, before telling her to provide a urine sample to the receptionist for testing and to sit in the waiting room while he saw his next patient.

It seemed like an age waiting for the results. Lilly tried to read a magazine but couldn't concentrate on the words. She made her way back to the doctor's consulting room when her name was called and he confirmed to her what she already suspected, estimating that she was at least ten weeks into her pregnancy. He gave her a prescription for iron tablets and told her to come back in one month. 'Is that it?' she thought, 'How will I explain this to Dad?'

Raleigh had grown over the past two decades from a small town to nearly double its size, and where once there had been a small convenience store there was now a large supermarket; the town had spread out beyond its original boundary, with tiny villages that had once stood apart from the town were now seamlessly incorporated. A variety of new stores now formed part of the town centre.

Niamph lived a short walk from the doctor's surgery and Lilly made her way there; she needed someone to confide in, and her first thought was Auntie Niamph - although she rarely called her Auntie nowadays.

She entered the stationery shop owned by Niamph and Uncle James. The shop formed part of their home where they lived with their twin boys. The bell over the front door tinkled as she opened it. Niamph employed a lady to help run the shop and recognizing Lilly as she entered, she broke off from serving a customer and merely said, "She's in the back."

"Thank you," replied Lilly, making her way to Niamph's kitchen. Niamph had transformed James' former family home into her own. The once dark dingy kitchen was now bright and airy with bi-folding doors leading out into a small garden.

"Lilly, how lovely to see you! Is everything okay? It's not often you come here." Questioned Niamph, "Are you coping okay? You need to get extra help so you can go back to your studies."

"I'm fine, Niamph - well just about. And I'm not going back to university!" Lilly announced.

"Why not? Your dad wouldn't expect you to give up your course just to look after him and Tim. You could easily get someone to help Sally; I can ask James to put an advert in the paper," suggested Niamph.

"No, it's not that – Niamph, I don't know how to tell you," she said, sitting down on the nearest chair. "I'm pregnant! Oh God! I don't know what to do! What will Dad say? What shall I do, Niamph? What shall I do?"

A surprised Niamph sat down next to her and took her hand, "It's not the end of the world, Lilly. What about the father? Have you told him?"

"I have only just found out myself! And the father? Well, how do I explain Auntie? It happened in Jersey!" and she went on, trying to explain and put into words what happened.

"Oh, Lilly, that is awful! You should write to your sisters and tell them. He needs to be made responsible for his actions - I could kill him! Lucky for him that he is so far away otherwise...!" Niamph was angry, not with Lilly but with the boy.

"First let's have a cup of tea, and then we will see what to do," suggested Niamph. They discussed at great length the options available, but in reality, there were only two - keep the baby or give it away. Niamph wanted to shout at Lilly 'Please, please don't give it away!', thinking to herself that she would do all she could to help Lilly, even if it meant looking after the baby herself.

"I have to go, Auntie. I need to help Sally to get the lunch ready. They will all be sitting around the table banging their knives and forks demanding food!" joked Lilly.

"Try not to worry Lilly," said Niamph. "I'll come around in the morning and we can tell your father together."

CHAPTER 45

Millie arrived back in Boston a few days after her meeting with Father Theodore, and told her mom all about her trip to find her birth mother. Although she felt as though she had betrayed her mom and dad, she tried to explain the overwhelming urge she felt to find the woman who gave birth to her.

"Your father and I have given you everything Millie - a lovely home and education, and you have never wanted for anything. In a way I understand, but on the other hand I do feel hurt, Millie. And what can this woman give you? after all, she did give you away! Have you thought of that Millie?" stated a distressed Grace.

Millie had thought of that. She had read the first five or six letters over and over, and she still had a box full to read. She decided to take a break and delay contacting Niamph, as she needed time to think. Instead, she would go and look at her Uncle Ethan's galleries to see which one she would like to work in.

There were quite a number of galleries to visit and over the next few weeks Millie travelled from one to the other, spending a couple of days at each before making her decision.

When she returned home, she continued through the box of letters, with each letter changing as the years went by; going from baby talk to school days, and then teenage years. Niamph would ask about her first day at school and then her school subjects, what were her hobbies? In turn, Niamph told her about her move from New York to North Carolina, then news and photos of the birth of her twin brothers. This information was the turning point for Millie - she wanted to meet her brothers, no matter what her mom said.

Grace was worried for her daughter as she didn't want to see her let down. Yes, there was a great number of letters from this woman, but in none of them did she actually say she wanted to meet Millie, or Bernadette, as she called her. When she pointed this out to Millie, the response she got was 'Then, why did she write all those letters?' to which, she thought to herself was 'A good point!'. Grace realized that she would have to respect her decision and let Millie go and find her birth mother, even though it hurt terribly.

Millie had thought about just turning up on her birth mother's doorstep but instead decided to write her a letter. If Niamph didn't want to see her, then Millie thought a letter would be better than being told face to face. It was a difficult letter to write and she wrote quite a few before perfecting the wording of the final version.

Dear Niamph,

My name is Millicent Henderson, but you know me as Bernadette and I understand that you are my mother. I traced you through Father Theodore in Ireland, who kindly gave me the letters and cards you had written to me since giving me away shortly after my birth.

I would very much like to meet you. If you should wish to meet me, please write to the address below.

Best Regards

Millie

Millie mailed the letter the same day and waited.

CHAPTER 46

Lilly waited anxiously for Niamph to arrive the following day. She had hardly slept all night, trying to decide what to do about the baby. If only her mother were here; she would know what to do. She would be there to guide her and support her; she missed her so much.

If Lilly kept the baby, then her entire life would change. She would have to give up her ambition of being a teacher and she would be tied to the farm. Not 'tied' she thought to herself, she loved the farm and she wouldn't be lonely, as there was always lots of people around.

Niamph had phoned earlier that morning, to say she would come just after lunch. "Ask your dad not to go straight back to work; just make some excuse. I am sure you can think of something," suggested Niamph.

It was simple as it happened, as her father said to Tim at the lunch table that he had some telephone calls to make after they had eaten, and told him to go back to work without him. "I'll be along in about twenty minutes." He stated.

As soon as Tim had gone, Lilly said that she would like to have a word with him before he went back to work.

"Okay, I suppose you want to get back to Uni! Let me just make these calls," replied Carl. Lilly knew her father was still trying to come to terms with her mother's death and he put on a brave face, but they all missed her terribly.

Niamph arrived as promised and sat at the table waiting for Carl to finish his calls. Lilly sensed that Niamph was happy about something; she was clutching an envelope in her hand, and she kept looking at it and smiling.

"What's in the envelope? You look like you have won the first prize in a competition," asked Lilly.

"Better than that, I will tell you after we have spoken to your dad," said Niamph.

"Speak to me about what?" asked Carl taking a seat at the table.

"Dad…", began Lilly.

"Yes, what's the matter? Are you okay? Tell me you are okay." Carl, now concerned with what his daughter was going to say especially as Niamph was there, suddenly felt sick with concern.

Niamph took his hand, "It's okay," she said.

"Dad, I am so sorry, but I am pregnant!" Lilly blurted out, with tears beginning to fall gently down her face.

"Oh, thank goodness for that! I thought you were going to tell me something much worse," he said with a sense of relief, then suddenly realized what she had said. "How did that happen? I didn't know you even had a boyfriend. Why haven't we met him?"

"Hold on, Carl," said Niamph and turning to Lilly, "You need to tell your dad the entire story, or do you want me to?"

"No, I will," replied Lilly bravely.

Lilly slowly told her father the entire story. Carl was furious, "I'll bloody well knock that little bastard's block off!"

"Carl, that's not very helpful. Lilly needs to make some decisions and we need to help her," said Niamph.

"What decisions? She's having a baby! Oh, you mean giving up university?" realized Carl.

"Carl, she is having a baby with no husband! Does she keep the baby and give up all hope of a career, or does she give it away and carry on with her studies as planned, next year?" explained Niamph.

"Oh, I see. Why can't she do both? Surely, we can sort something out, it's only a baby," he said. "Anyway, you are not giving it away! No grandson of mine is being *given away* even if it means employing someone to look after him!"

"It's not your decision, Carl. What do you want to do?" Niamph asked Lilly.

Lilly had thought of nothing else since she had found out she was expecting. She had seen the effect of giving a baby away on Niamph, but on the other hand, how could she keep it and continue to study?

"I want to keep it!" she announced suddenly, wondering to herself when had she made that decision.

"Good, we will get through this together! Now I must get back to work," Carl said, kissing his daughter and then Niamph before leaving.

"Men!" said Niamph, "They think everything is so straight forward! But seriously Lilly, I will help you all I can and I'm relieved that you have decided to keep the baby. I know what it is like to give one away. And on that note..." Niamph waved her letter in the air with a big beaming smile on her face. "You will never guess what I received this morning?"

Lilly had already guessed, but she didn't want to spoil Niamph's moment, she wanted to share the enjoyment. Niamph didn't wait for Lilly's response. She was just so excited to tell someone. She had tried to phone James, but he was out on an assignment.

"It's a letter from Bernadette! I can hardly believe it," then burst into tears she was so happy.

Lilly read the letter, 'So coincidences do happen!' she thought. She was over the moon for Niamph.

"Hold on a minute! I have something to show you," said Lilly, running upstairs to get her photos. She hurriedly shuffled through her photos to find the one she wanted to show Niamph.

Showing the photo to Niamph and explaining about meeting Millie in Italy, "I kept meaning to show you this, but kept forgetting! I didn't know then that Millie was your Bernadette, but she looks so uncannily like you. How spooky is that? That I should meet your daughter," said Lilly, hugging Niamph, "I am so overjoyed for you. So, tell me, when are you going to meet her?"

They sat chatting for over an hour, Lilly telling Niamph all she knew about Millie, but leaving out what she and Jenny had thought about her being a spoilt brat; Niamph wouldn't want to hear that.

After Niamph had left and while she was washing up the lunch dishes, Lilly started to plan her future. She started by writing down everything she would have to do, so that she could sit down properly with her father and discuss how the future would pan-out. There were so many things to sort out; she could easily run the farmhouse, she had helped her mother numerous times and she had taught her how to cook, plus Sally was always there to help. During the summer months, her mother had initially employed Sally to help so that she could concentrate on the Tea Room, but Sally now had a family of her own to look after. Latterly, her mother had employed seasonal labour, but that would have to change. Luckily the Tea Room was closed for the winter, but by the time it opened again in the spring, she would be heavily pregnant. She needed help now.

Lilly also needed to write to her sisters. She had worked out that sadly she wouldn't be able to go to their weddings; she would be too heavily pregnant to travel for Fran's wedding and then would have a small baby for Chantal's. She was so disappointed, hoping to herself that Tim and Jeff would go.

Lilly had already decided not to tell her sisters about Bernie. She felt they might blame themselves for not looking after her, despite the fact that she was partly responsible for getting so drunk.

As it turned out, her father had thought of all the same problems and had already phoned Niamph and asked her to advertise for some full-time help, even asking her to interview and choose the most appropriate person. "With Lilly's help, of course, as she is the one that will have to get along with them after all," he said to Niamph.

Carl told Tim of the forthcoming baby to avoid Lilly any embarrassment. Tim was unsure how to react. On one hand, he was thrilled that he was to be an uncle, but on the other hand he felt sad for Lilly as she didn't have a husband to support her.

By the time Jeff found out she didn't have to actually tell him. He had arrived home unexpectedly to surprise the family and had looked from her developing bump to her face stating, "What the hell? Why didn't anybody tell me?"

"Like when were we meant to tell you? We hardly hear from you from one month to the next," replied Tim, grabbing hold of his brother in man hug. "Good to see you mate."

Lilly's sisters had written lengthy letters, stating how sorry they were that she was not going to be at their weddings, but delighted to hear that they were to be aunties, "Papa is not happy; he says he is too young to be a granddad!" Letters from her Papa were infrequent, so instead she relied on Fran and Chantal to provide her with all their news, using the excuse that he was not very good at writing in English.

CHAPTER 47

Niamph was deep in thought. She was worried about Lilly having only just lost her mother, and now finding she was pregnant. How would she cope with a baby on her own? Niamph vowed that she would be there for her no matter what; she would do what Clara would have wanted her to do. But first, she had promised to go and be with her while she broke the news to her father, Carl.

Niamph was putting on her coat and as she grabbed her car keys, she heard the shop doorbell tinkle; it was the postman. Jo-Jo, her assistant in the shop, handed her the mail. She quickly glanced through and was just about to put the unopened mail on the table, when she noticed a handwritten envelope with a Boston postmark on it. 'Who do we know in Boston?' she thought to herself. She didn't want to be late for Lilly so she quickly ripped open the envelope, stopping in her tracks as she opened the single sheet of paper and read the first line, 'My name is Millicent Henderson, but you know me as Bernadette'.

Niamph's heart almost stopped beating. She slumped into the nearest chair and read the rest of the short letter. She didn't know whether to laugh or cry. She immediately attempted to phone James, but he wasn't in his office - just when she needed to tell someone, especially her husband. She placed the letter in her handbag and hurried to Clara's house, except Clara wasn't there anymore. Niamph still thought of it as Clara's and she supposed she always would. She so wanted to show her best friend the letter but it wasn't to be, running to her car as she didn't want to be late for Lilly.

Niamph was full of nervous energy waiting for James to come home from work that evening. As soon as he walked in the door Niamph was telling him about the letter, talking so quickly he had to stop her, "Hey, hey slow down! Hello sweetie!" he said kissing her cheek.

"Sorry, hello! Look! Look I've got a letter…from Bernadette," she said again quickly, waving the letter in front of him.

"Really!" he said with surprise, "Let me look," he said, taking the letter from Niamph. James sat down and read it, looking up at Niamph, then read it again. He stood up and hugged his wife, both now crying tears of joy.

"What's the matter Mommy?" asked Bradley and Scott, in unison looking worried at seeing both their mother and father crying.

"It's your sister, she has sent me a letter!" The twins didn't really know what was going on, of course. They knew about their sister, but she was a name not a real person, so they didn't quite understand.

Niamph told James that evening when the boys were in bed, about Lilly's news and how Lilly had met Millie and showed him the photo that Lilly had taken.

"My god she looks just like you - in fact, it could be you! I can't quite take it in that Lilly has met her! It's a surreal coincidence, don't you think? If someone wrote that in my newspaper, nobody would believe it!" he said. "How did Carl take the news, by the way? Imagine - him a grandpapa?"

"He appeared to take it well. I'm not sure he actually took it in, but I will try and speak to him on his own. I told him I would be there to help, so we will have to wait and see," explained Niamph. "I've written a letter back to Bernadette, or I should say Millie. It's going to be difficult calling her Millie, what do you think?" she said, handing the letter to James to read.

“Sounds good, not over the top. How many versions did you write? I can imagine you saying ‘Come now! Come now!’ - even that wouldn’t be soon enough!” he joked, handing the letter back to her.

“Only three. I hope she telephones, you can’t correspondent by letter very well - I have so many questions! Anyway, I will mail it in the morning. Hopefully, I can catch the early post. Imagine, she is only in Boston!”

Three days later at three o’clock in the afternoon, Niamph answered her telephone, “Hello, this is Millie.”

CHAPTER 48

The lady employed by Lilly, with the help of Niamph, was Fay. She was a fifty-year-old mother of two grown children, both of whom had left home, one was living and working in Washington and the other in San Francisco. Fay lived in nearby Garner and was recently widowed. She explained to Lilly that her eldest son had wanted her to go and live with him in Washington, but she had lived in North Carolina all her life and didn't want to move. "All my family and friends are here. I don't want to go to a big city where I wouldn't know anyone."

Fay fitted in with the family perfectly. Lilly would have liked her to live in but she didn't want to leave her home. As she lived only a twenty-minute drive away, it wasn't much of a problem.

Fay treated Lilly like a daughter and as her pregnancy progressed, Fay would make her rest and put her feet up. She taught her to knit and Lilly could be found sitting in her Gamy's old rocking chair on the verandah knitting baby items. Everyone fussed over her, Tim called her 'Tubby' and the baby 'Bubby', and he loved asking 'How are Tubby and Bubby today?' He thought he was funny, but their father didn't approve of the joke.

Tim, Jeff and their grandparents, travelled to Jersey for Fran and Mike's wedding. It was the first journey Tim had taken outside of America and it was an eye-opener for him, giving him the travel bug. They returned with loads of photos so that Lilly felt as though she had been there herself. Amongst one of the group photos was Bernie. She didn't feel angry with him any longer and kept the photo to show her son or daughter someday in the future.

Lilly's baby daughter was born on a warm June morning after eleven hours of labour, with Niamph at her side. She weighed a healthy seven pounds eight ounces. She was beautifully perfect with a light covering of dark downy hair. Lilly named her Eliza Clara, for her beloved Mama.

CHAPTER 49

Millie arrived in Raleigh two weeks after first making contact with her mother, Niamph. It was an emotional reunion for them both, but especially so for her mother. She couldn't bring herself to call Niamph 'Mom', as it felt disrespectful to Grace. It was Niamph that came up with Máth, which was the shortened version Máthair, the Irish for mother.

Millie felt at home with Niamph and her stepfather James, and she adored her two little brothers. She shared something special with these two little boys that she never had with her two elder brothers, although she remained very close to Larry and Izzy.

Niamph sat with Millie for long periods of time explaining what had led to her being put up for adoption, and how she had made her way to America. In turn, Millie told Niamph all about her life with her mother Grace and her father Sam, plus her two brothers, explaining that they had all been adopted from Ireland.

Millie now split her time between Boston and Raleigh. The difference between the two homes was indescribable; the Boston home was a showhouse, whereas Raleigh was a home.

Millie and Lilly became friends and would often spend time together while Millie was visiting Niamph. She enjoyed taking the twins to the farm where they could run riot without doing any harm, taking them back to their mother exhausted, something which Niamph didn't always appreciate, as they would come back filthy dirty. It was an unlikely friendship, as their backgrounds were totally different. What turned out more unlikely was the friendship that developed between Jeff and Millie.

Jeff was a rock star travelling the world with his band and was two years younger than Millie. He was also not the sort of boyfriend Grace wanted for her debutante daughter. To say that Grace was dismayed on meeting Jeff for the first time was an understatement, but the more that Grace objected, the more Millie attached herself to Jeff. Whereas Niamph knew that realistically the relationship would run its course, it was just a matter of waiting.

For the first time in her life, Niamph was truly happy. She had all her family around her; a husband she loved unequivocally and three beautiful children. And then there was Lilly, her best friend's daughter, with her daughter and Niamph's goddaughter, Eliza. What more could she want?

THE END

Printed in Great Britain
by Amazon